Praise

BLOGGER GIR

"What a fun book. The characters were incredibly well-written. I felt like I understood everyone's personalities and quirks, almost as if I knew them personally myself. Meredith Schorr is a talented author and I'm glad she has other books out for me to read!"

— Becky Monson, Bestselling Author of the Spinster Series

"Sassy, sexy, endlessly entertaining, and full of laughs (as well as some heart-wrenching moments), *Blogger Girl* is one of those books that keeps you up at night because you can't wait to see what happens next."

— Tracie Banister, Author of *Mixing It Up*

"America finally has its own version of Britain's Bridget Jones!"

— *Books in the Burbs*

NOVELISTA GIRL (Blogger Girl Series #2)

"A strong and confident heroine, a sexy boyfriend you can crush on, supportive friends, and plenty of conflict leading to comical results, culminating in a very satisfying ending...Once you start this book, you won't be able to put it down."

— Erin Brady, Bestselling Author of *The Shopping Swap*

"A perfect mix of romance, conflict, and humor, *Novelista Girl* solidifies Schorr's place among best-sellers Sophie Kinsella and Emily Giffin."

— Carolyn Ridder Aspenson, Bestselling Author of *Unbinding Love*

"Absolutely brilliant chick lit, I couldn't put it down, and I highly, highly recommend."

— *Chick Lit Plus*

JUST FRIENDS WITH BENEFITS

"Meredith writes with wit, candor, humor and vulnerability that illuminates the struggles of dating and relationships."
— Nancy Slotnick, Author of *Turn Your Cablight On*

"The perfect vacation read. The dialogue flows like beer at a beach party."
– K.C. Wilder, Author of *Fifty Ways to Leave Your Husband*

A STATE OF JANE

"I laughed my way through this novel. A must-read."
– *Chick Lit Plus*

"A witty true-to-life story that will not disappoint you, it is chick lit at it's very best!"
– *Jersey Girl Book Reviews*

"I am a huge fan of chick lit, but this book was so much more. It has become one of my favorite reads!"
– *The Little Black Book Blog*

HOW DO YOU KNOW?

"Meredith Schorr is an author to watch."
– Tracy Kaler, Founder and Editor of *Tracy's New York Life*

"You won't forget this delightful cast of characters or Schorr's sharp, candid insights about the plight of the modern woman."
– Diana Spechler, Author of *Who by Fire* and *Skinny*

"I think every woman will relate to Maggie and her friends, no matter her age or relationship status."
– *Chick Lit Club*

How Do You Know?

Books by Meredith Schorr

JUST FRIENDS WITH BENEFITS
A STATE OF JANE
HOW DO YOU KNOW?

The Blogger Girl Series

BLOGGER GIRL (#1)
NOVELISTA GIRL (#2)

How Do You Know?

Meredith Schorr

HENERY PRESS

HOW DO YOU KNOW?
Part of the Henery Press Chick Lit Collection

Second Edition | February 2017

Henery Press, LLC
www.henerypress.com

Trade Paperback ISBN-13: 978-1-63511-157-6
Digital epub ISBN-13: 978-1-63511-158-3
Kindle ISBN-13: 978-1-63511-159-0
Hardcover Paperback ISBN-13: 978-1-63511-160-6

Printed in the United States of America

In Memory of Alan Blum

ACKNOWLEDGMENTS

Thank you to Abbe Kalnick, Hilda Black, Ronni Candlen, Jenny Kabalen, Shanna Eisenberg, Jennifer Baum, Jennifer Levin, Marisa Glasser, Hilary Grossman, and Elke Marks—you helped inspire this novel by being fabulous, sassy, intelligent women on the far side of forty who demonstrate daily that age really is just a number.

My deepest gratitude goes out to my brilliant beta readers: Natalie Aaron, Anna Garner, and Samantha Stroh Bailey. This novel wouldn't be nearly as good without your honest and thorough feedback. I am so grateful to have such amazing authors in my corner. More importantly, I'm so proud to consider you all my friends. Special thanks to Ally Bishop for your developmental assistance with the original version of this book.

Thank you to my fabulous publisher, Henery Press, especially my ace editor, Erin George. Being in the Hen House is a dream come true.

I offer heartfelt and undying appreciation to my sister, Marjorie Bollard. Without your lifelong unconditional love and support, I would never have the guts to put stories out there for the world to read. Heck, I might not have the courage to leave my apartment. You are my rock, my conscience, and my hero, and I love you so very much. Thanks for being my first beta reader too!

Thank you to my mommy, Susan Goodman, for your overwhelming enthusiasm for my writing, including my blogs (although I know you read them hoping for scoop on my love life). You're the best mom in the whole wide world and I love you to infinity.

I will be forever grateful to my fellow Chick Lit Goddesses for providing an outlet to exchange advice and ideas, and offer encouragement on writing, publishing, marketing, and a whole lot more. Special thanks to the "beach babes"—Francine LaSala, Eileen Goudge, Jen Tucker, Julie Valerie, Josie Brown, and the aforementioned Samantha Stroh Bailey.

Thank you to book bloggers everywhere for being awesome and helping spread the word about my books: Melissa Amster, Kaley Stewart, Mary Smith, Samantha Janning, Ashley Williams, Isabella Anderson, Marlene Engel, Aimee Brown, Bethany Clarke, Uma Kayla, and Kelly Perotti among others.

Thank you to Deborah Shapiro for being my sounding board and a constant shoulder to cry on when I need it. You are the second best boss in the world, and I know you'll understand why I can't assign you the number one position.

Finally, thank you to Alan Blum, to whom this book is dedicated. When you died, you took a piece of my heart with you. There are not enough words to express what your love and friendship meant to me, and I miss you each and every day.

July

"A toast to the birthday girl!" Melanie says, raising her watermelon martini.

Jodie and Amanda lift their glasses and repeat Melanie's sentiment.

Despite my friends' insistence on taking me out, I'm not entirely convinced turning thirty-nine is worth celebrating. Just the same, I lift my drink as high as I can without spilling it all over the table and lightly clink my glass against theirs. "I appreciate you ladies coming out for a mid-week celebration."

"It's about time you joined me in the dreaded countdown to the big four-oh," Jodie says. She's only seven months older than me, but when we were roommates in college, she gloated when she turned twenty-one first. She's not gloating anymore. "And besides, your swan-like fall before was well worth the cost of a babysitter. You'd think by the ripe old age of thirty-nine you would have learned how to walk properly. But, nope equally as klutzy now as you were at nineteen. And completely sober, to boot."

I blink my blue eyes hard hoping to erase from my brain the memory of tripping over an invisible crack in the sidewalk, falling on the pavement, and exposing my leopard-print G-string thong to passing pedestrians. "Is it bad that the sole thought in my head mid-plummet was 'Thank God I waxed'?"

Melanie snorts. "The thought would never have crossed my mind, which I think is worse, especially for Barry's sake. But between the lawyer gig during the day and chasing after the boys at night, my husband is just lucky I remember to shave my armpits."

"But you made time for your favorite colleague," I say. Melanie is an attorney at the New York City law firm where I work as the marketing manager.

"You bet. I'm on a one-drink maximum, though, since I have an early morning training run tomorrow."

"I'm so impressed with your running ethic, Melanie." Amanda sips her drink, then wipes the sugar from her upper lip and frowns. "I'm happy to celebrate with you, Maggie...but didn't you want to celebrate with Doug?"

"Having a boyfriend doesn't mean I can't ring in my birthday with my girls. And you know Doug. He's not the 'let's get drunk during the week' type of guy." Doug and I have been dating for almost three years and share an apartment, but I'm very proud that I've never let my relationship with him get in the way of time with my girlfriends. "I couldn't possibly tackle another birthday without a drink. Anyway, he's taking me out for dinner on Saturday night, and Sunday we're celebrating with an all-day Joss Whedon television festival—back-to-back episodes of *Buffy the Vampire Slayer*, *Angel*, *Firefly*, and *Dollhouse*. Doug even dug out the old-fashioned popcorn maker from the back of the closet."

Melanie pushes her fiery-red, fringe-style bangs away from her green eyes and smiles at me. "Fun. You guys turn watching television into an art form."

"Where is he taking you on Saturday?" Amanda asks.

"No idea. He's surprising me. But it's not like it's a landmark birthday. Thank God," I say, muttering the last part. There is a rolling in my stomach at the thought of turning forty in three hundred and sixty-five days. I take an extra big gulp from my drink to speed up the intoxication process so I'll feel better, at least temporarily, about this impending milestone.

"You still have an entire year, Mags. I only have five months. And nine days," Jodie says, faking a shiver.

"But at least you've been married. And have kids. I'm certain turning forty wouldn't bother me as much if I felt like my life had changed more since turning thirty, aside from me sprouting a few more wrinkles around my eyes."

"As of last month, I'm officially divorced. And I thought you were iffy about the whole kids thing," Jodie says.

Amanda looks at me with raised brows. "You are?"

"I'm undecided." I remove the elastic band from my wrist and pull my dirty blond hair into a long ponytail. Even with the keratin smoothing treatment I splurged on to keep my naturally wavy hair from getting out of control, it's too humid to feel my hair on my back.

Amanda runs a finger along the sugar rim of her glass, then licks the skin clean. "Don't you think you should figure that out?"

"What is there to figure out? If it happens, it happens. If it doesn't, it wasn't meant to be." The truth is, I don't know if I want to be a mother, but I hate the stigma associated with being forty and childless. I also loathe knowing if I wait too much longer, my "mature" eggs will make the choice for me.

"What does Doug say about it?" Melanie runs her hand across her bangs again. Since she chopped her ginger locks from long layers to a sleek, shoulder-length bob, she's constantly playing with it, almost as if checking to make sure it's still there.

"Whether or not to have kids is not a popular discussion in our home. Most couples plan a marriage before they plan a family, right?" From where we are sitting outside on the patio, I peer inside the dimly-lit lounge, noting how much more crowded it's become since we arrived. At least as the birthday girl, I won't be expected to go up to the bar. Birthdays are good for some things.

"Speaking of which, I think Doug should shit or get off the pot. It's been almost three years," Amanda says matter-of-factly.

"Who said I want to get married?" Amanda has been single since we met four years earlier and I sometimes wonder if her propensity to see everything in black and white is one of the reasons.

Amanda gapes at me, her already large hazel eyes wide as saucers. "You don't?"

"I don't know," I say, looking down.

"That's a popular answer this evening." Jodie finishes off her martini in a single swig. "Did any of you watch *The Bachelor* last night? What is up with all of the crying? Kleenex should definitely get some advertising spots."

"Train wreck central," Melanie agrees.

"It was the most dramatic rose ceremony yet," Amanda says, laughing.

I glance at Jodie with my heart full of love and gratitude for her successful change of the subject. She is one of the few people who know I struggle with being certain Doug is the one. Though I'm in love with him and care for him deeply, I sometimes lack the butterflies and that "can't live without you" feeling I always thought meant true love. If it does, and Doug isn't the one, am I wasting time that should be spent on finding the man who is? And, at almost forty, has that window already closed? Is passionate love only available to the young?

I know I will have to work through my feelings eventually, but it's not something I want to do on my birthday. The truth is, I know I want to get married. I'm just not certain I want to marry Doug.

But my heart also aches at the thought of losing him.

*   *   *

Several hours later, I stumble into my apartment and change out of my clothes as quietly as possible to avoid waking a sleeping Doug. Hungry, I open my refrigerator and survey the contents. Considering I went food shopping on Sunday, I'm disappointed with the choices. The problem with food shopping sober is that nothing I buy is the slightest bit appealing when I'm tipsy. I open the refrigerator to remove the bag of frozen edamame when a pair of arms embraces me from behind. I feel Doug's warm breath on my neck as he whispers, "Happy Birthday, babe" in my ear.

I turn around and see him smiling down at me, the dimple in his left cheek pronounced. "Thank you, sweetie." At five foot eleven, Doug is five inches taller than me. I reach up and wrap my arms around his neck. I kiss him softly on his full lips before giving him a squeeze. When we pull away, I lean my back against the refrigerator. "I'm hungry."

Doug moves closer to me. With a glint in his green eyes, he says, "What are you hungry for?"

I bite my lip and give him a guilty look. "Food?"

Doug cocks his head and grins. "Too many cocktails, huh?" He knows when I've had too much to drink, I'm more interested in spooning than sex.

I shake my head, but then confess, "Yes. In the morning. I promise." I almost always wake up in the mood.

Doug kisses my forehead. "That's okay. I can tell when you've over-imbibed by the color of your eyes—red, white, and blue like the American flag. Your less than delicate movements down the hall are also a giveaway. You sound more like a sumo wrestler wearing clunky shoes than a one hundred and something pound woman in bare feet."

"I thought I was quiet," I say, dropping my chin.

"You weren't." He yawns as he runs a hand through his unruly blond hair. I do love that he still has a full head of thick locks. Then again, he's only thirty-six.

I poke him in his trim belly. "Wanna make me something to eat?"

Doug nods. "Least I can do for the birthday girl if she's not in the mood to get laid." Gesturing toward our breakfast bar, he says, "Have a seat." Then he sticks his head in the refrigerator. With his back to me, he calls out, "Frozen pizza, eggs, or pancakes?"

I sit down on one of our red leather bar stools and place my elbows on the yellow counter. Along with the frosted glass wall that separates our bedroom from the living room, the bright and colorful kitchen is my favorite part of our apartment. "Something less fattening, maybe? I'm turning forty, and my metabolism is slowing down."

Doug turns around and raises an eyebrow. "Have you been lying about your age? I thought you turned thirty-nine, not forty."

"Same thing," I mutter.

"Not the same thing. Besides, you don't look your age. You certainly don't act like it either."

"What are you getting at, lover boy?" I tease. I definitely party more than Doug, but it's not like I'm going to raves or doing keg stands with the college kids.

Doug sits down next to me and plants a kiss on my chin. "It means you're fun and full of energy. More than me, and I'm supposed to be the younger one." He smiles. "Peanut butter and jelly?"

I smile back. "Perfect. Wanna split the sandwich with me?"

"You only want half? I promise you won't get fat from eating the entire sandwich, and you'd still have a hot body if you did. I'd still ravage you." As he says this, he runs two fingers up and down my arm and then rubs the constellation of freckles around my wrist—he calls it my "freckles bracelet."

I let out an involuntary giggle—my wrists are very ticklish—and squirm from his touch. "It's not about the calories. I'm in a generous mood is all."

Walking back to the refrigerator, he says, "Aren't you sweet?"

He prepares my sandwich, carefully spreading the crunchy peanut butter on both sides, just the way I like it, without getting any peanut butter or jelly on the counter. I woke the poor guy out of bed with my drunken loud footsteps, and rather than complain, he's making me a snack. I adore this man and am acutely aware of how lucky I am to have him in my life. I want more than anything to accept him as the one for me. I walk over to him and stand on my toes to kiss the back of his neck. "I love you," I whisper.

Doug turns around and smiles. "I love you too." Handing me my half of the sandwich, he raises his own half in the air. "*Bon appetit.*"

I take a bite of my sandwich. "How was your day?"

I am charmed by Doug's boyish love of chocolate milk and observe him beguilingly as he downs an entire glass without taking a breath. "Like any other day, except better since it was my girl's birthday."

"I like being your 'girl.' It makes me feel nice and young."

"I prefer 'lady.' You're my lady. Has a nice ring to it." He winks. "Except it makes me want to break into song. *You're my lady. Of the Morning.*"

Laughing at his off-key rendition of the Styx song, I say, "I thought you were going to say, 'except you're no lady.'"

"I'm hoping you won't be much of a lady come morning, if you know what I mean." He waggles his eyebrows suggestively.

I roll my eyes. "You're so corny."

"But you love me."

"That I do."

As I lay in bed later, wrapped in Doug's arms, I try to push aside the stubborn streak of doubt that lingers in my gut. I remember the day I met Doug almost three years earlier on the subway. I was meeting Amanda to watch post-season baseball at a bar uptown when I instinctively touched my left ear and noticed the absence of the diamond stud I wore almost daily. My mom bought me the pair for my thirty-fifth birthday, and I couldn't bear the thought of losing them. I got up from my seat and paced the train car, praying I had lost it while confined in that small space. Doug, ever the gallant guy, asked me why I was so troubled, and when I told him, he solved the mystery of the missing earring almost immediately. It was actually still on my body, dangling miraculously from the collar of my trench coat. It was the first of many times Doug helped me find lost items. If Doug isn't the one, where do I go from here? Forty is like a train approaching me at warp speed while my shoelace is caught in the track.

*   *   *

I wake the next morning to a dull headache from too much vodka and Doug's erection against my back. Despite my mild hangover, I'm feeling amorous, and I flip over to face him and plant a kiss on his collarbone. He gives me a lazy grin as if he's still half-asleep. "How's the birthday girl feeling this morning?"

"No complaints." I scooch closer to him and wrap one leg over his. "How are you?"

Doug adjusts his body so he's hovering on top of me. "I'm good, too." He slides down the length of my body, taking my panties down with him. "What's this?" he asks, tapping the Spider-Man bandage on my knee with his thumb.

"It's nothing. I fell last night."

Doug looks up at me. "You fell last night? Why didn't you tell me?"

"Because it was nothing."

"Seriously? Aren't you a bit old to be falling down drunk?"

His assumption irritates me and I sit up. "I wasn't drunk."

Doug raises an eyebrow. "Pardon me. I meant 'buzzed.'"

Pushing him off of me, I vault out of bed and face him, hands on my hips. "I'll have you know, Mr. High and Mighty, I fell before I even had one drink. I tripped on the street. And I assure you, it was not a result of inebriation. Apparently klutziness is not an attribute I'm apt to grow out of in my advanced age." It's true most of my nights out include indulging in alcoholic beverages, but Doug knows I rarely drink enough to catch more than a light buzz.

Doug doesn't respond as he releases a heavy sigh and drops his gaze to the floor. Casting it back on me, he says, "I'm sorry. I shouldn't have assumed."

I grab the blanket we had thrown on the floor last night and toss it back on the bed. "No, you shouldn't have."

Doug pats the bed next to him. "Have a seat."

I sit and let my feet dangle over the edge of our bed. I can't look at him. I'm too bothered he jumped to conclusions, and I'm hurt he suggested birthday drinks should be reserved for the younger crowd. As if there's an age limit for having fun on your birthday.

Rubbing my thigh in a circular motion, Doug whispers, "I didn't mean to upset you."

Finally, I turn to him. "And if I *had* fallen down because I was drunk? Would it have been the worst thing in the world?"

Doug slowly shakes his head. "No. Of course not. I just worry about you."

I stand up. "I'm a grown woman. You're supposed to be my boyfriend, not my dad." As the words come out of my mouth, I'm fully aware I tend to fall for men who want to take care of me. Maybe because my own father did the bare minimum. Mitch, the guy I dated before Doug, was ten years older than me. At over six feet tall, he would always lean down and lovingly button my jacket when we went out, while I beamed up at him, inhaling his spicy aftershave. I often wondered if I saw him as a lover or a doting father figure. We broke up amicably after about nine months when his job relocated him to London. I might be attracted to men who watch out for me, but judging my social drinking habits at my "advanced age" is not the same as removing crumbs from my hair or fixing my remote control.

Doug stands up and places his hands on my shoulders. When I refuse to meet his gaze, he lifts my chin, forcing eye contact. "I know. Let me make it up to you." He motions toward the bed.

I have completely lost the mood by then and am grateful to see it's already eight thirty. I shake my head in regret. "Gotta get ready for work. Rain check?"

"Of course." Doug regards me with sad eyes. I know he's sincerely sorry for upsetting me. I kiss him on the cheek and head to the bathroom.

As I walk to work later that morning, I keep thinking, "I'm thirty-nine. One more year in my thirties. One more year until I can no longer call myself a "thirty-something." One more year until I'll need an annual mammogram and will be considered a cougar for dating a younger man. I approach the revolving door of my office building and exhale loudly, resulting in a funny look from another woman walking inside. I give her an apologetic smile and bite my lip. I wonder how old she is, and if she'd think I was a complete freak if she knew what I was thinking.

* * *

"It was good, Mom." I put my office phone on speaker after my neck cramps from cradling it.

"Who all went?" my mom asks.

"Me, Jodie, Melanie, and Amanda." I try to multi-task by reading through the list of potential taglines for my law firm's rebranding efforts, but I can't concentrate.

"I'm glad you had fun. We'll see you guys on Sunday night, right? I bought lamb chops. Helen and Cheryl are coming as well. With the kids."

"We'll be there," I chirp happily. My mom always makes my favorite meal for my birthday, and I'm excited to see my Aunt Helen, my cousin Cheryl, and "the twerps." After my dad left my mom and fled to the other side of the country when I was six, my mom and I moved in with Aunt Helen (my mom's older sister) and her now-deceased husband, Walter. We lived as one big family until I left for college and my mother purchased her own small house. Only two years older than me, Cheryl is the closest thing I have to a sister. At the sound of knocking, I turn my attention to Philip, one of the firm's partners, who is standing at my door. "Mom, I have to go. Love you." I wait for her to say bye before hanging up. In a bright voice, I say, "Hey, Philip."

Philip runs a hand through his thick dark hair and gives me a sheepish grin. "You didn't have to hang up on your mom for me."

"Not a problem. We were finished anyway. She wanted to know how my birthday was." I gesture to my guest chair. "Have a seat." As the partner in charge of the rebranding committee, Philip weighs in on the legalities of using certain taglines and logos—for instance, if they're too similar to phrases used by other companies. "I was going through the short list of available taglines before my mom called."

"We'll get to that later. Happy birthday." He smiles, revealing a straight, slightly crowded row of top teeth, and slight laugh lines appear at the corners of his warm brown eyes. With long eyelashes completely wasted on him, he could pass for Anne Hathaway's older brother. Or maybe her dad. How old is Anne Hathaway these days?

"Thanks. It was yesterday." I wonder if he knows how old I am. Most people peg me for early thirties. According to his firm bio, Philip graduated law school in 1997, placing him at approximately forty-five, but I still hope he won't ask my age. A gentleman never would.

"Well, happy *belated* birthday."

"Thanks aga—"

Interrupting, Philip says, "We'll have to celebrate. Drinks after work?"

I eyeball Philip in surprise. I glance at his left hand, and the wedding band on the finger he is currently tapping along my desk. Does he mean just the two of us? I clear my throat. "Sure."

"So, which taglines survived the search?"

I slide the list to Philip. As he studies it, I stare at the top of his head, noting the hints of gray in his hair. How come gray hair on handsome men makes them distinguished and sexy, while gray hair on a pretty woman means she's getting old and should head to the stylist for a two-hundred-dollar touch up?

Philip looks up at me. Either not noticing I was staring at him or pretending not to, he scratches his jaw. "I don't like any of these. I want something catchy. 'Large law firm capabilities. Small law firm rates'? Not so much," he says. I typically prefer clean-shaven men and don't like when Doug lets more than a day's scruff accumulate, but Philip carries his closely-trimmed beard well—less *Rolling Stone* and more *GQ*.

"I agree with you. That sucks." We had asked the employees to suggest ideas, offering a five-hundred-dollar American Express gift card to the winner. So far all of the suggestions had been losers, and the taglines I'd personally thrown into the mix were already used by someone else.

Philip chuckles. "Back to the drawing board."

"I'll keep thinking over the next few days and touch base with you after the weekend. There must be something both original and not already taken. Should I send another firm-wide email asking for more suggestions?"

Standing up from his chair, Philip says, "I'd like to see what you come up with first. You could save us five hundred dollars."

"I guess since it's part of my job description to be creative, it would be unprofessional of me to accept the gift card if the winning tagline is one of mine?" In a display of exaggerated disappointment, I push my lips into a pout.

Philip hovers over the desk and locks eyes with me, then whispers, "I won't tell if you don't."

I feel a blush creep across my cheeks. "I can live with that."

"Happy birthday again. I owe you a drink." Philip winks at me and walks out.

After he leaves, I open a new document and start brainstorming. *Midsize Law Firm, Huge Results.* I shake my head. Another loser. My heart beats rapidly, and I close my eyes as I think about Philip's drink invitation. I wonder if he means it. Then I wonder why I care so much. After all, he's married, and I have a boyfriend.

* * *

As I stroll up and down the aisles at the grocery store, absently throwing items in my shopping bag, I decide I will absolutely not have drinks with Philip unless it's a group thing. Although our banter has never crossed the line, it borders on flirtation. At least on my end.

My body's reaction to him is not simply that of an employee to her supervisor. Being alone with him under the influence of alcohol is asking for trouble, and I won't risk it. I would never cheat on Doug, and I'm definitely not a homewrecker. At the same time, having the feelings in the first place is disturbing. I don't believe being in a relationship with one person means I'll never be attracted to someone else, but I wonder why being in Philip's company evokes bodily responses that are not always present with Doug, whom I love with all my heart.

* * *

I take a final peek in the mirror and pretend to pick something up off the ground to confirm I can bend down in my dark blue, low-cut skinny jeans without showing the crack of my ass. It's Saturday night, and Doug is taking me out for my birthday dinner.

"Ready, babe?" Doug calls out from our living room.

I brush a layer of rust-colored shadow across my eyelids to make my blue eyes pop. "Five more minutes. Five more minutes for you to finish watching last night's episode of *The Late Show with Stephen Colbert*." Doug loves the show—one of the only ones we don't watch together—so I figure it will buy me the extra time I need to get ready.

"I finished already."

I turn around to find Doug standing in the doorway of the makeshift frosted glass wall we built in our large studio to turn it into a one bedroom. He's wearing his nicer jeans, i.e. the ones that fit him snugly in the butt and don't have frays on the bottom, and a green and white gingham shirt that brings out the color of his eyes. He's shaking his head at me in what I know from our years together is mock annoyance. I quickly transfer my necessities (comb, license, credit card, lipstick, and keys) from my larger handbag to my smaller evening bag. Grinning, I say, "Then what are we waiting for? Let's get outta here."

An eight-minute cab ride later, we are sitting across from each other at a small table at Alta, a Mediterranean/Spanish tapas restaurant we have wanted to try for a while. The one time we attempted to get in with Melanie and her husband, we hadn't made a reservation and were told we'd have to wait until eleven p.m. to eat. We weren't cool enough to dine so late and opted to go elsewhere. This time Doug made a nine p.m. reservation, and surprisingly we are seated immediately. I order a glass of Cava, a sparkling wine from Spain, while Doug orders a Hennessy and tonic, and we drink quietly while perusing the menu. When Doug reaches across the table and squeezes my hand, my first impulse is to pull it back. I try to cover by scratching my arm as if I have an itch. I smile at him. "Thanks for making the reservation."

"I'm glad they weren't booked months in advance. I want to make you happy on your birthday."

"You always make me happy, Doug."

I look at him fondly. It's true. He always makes me happy. But...I'm scared something is missing. I shake my head.

Noticing the gesture, Doug asks, "You all right there, camper?"

I nod, thankful when the waitress comes over to take our order before I have to answer. I stifle a giggle as she blatantly leans her chest into Doug's face when answering one of his questions about the menu options. I'd be annoyed if he wasn't so clueless when other women flirted with him. While Doug orders the bacon-wrapped dates, fried goat cheese, crispy Brussel sprouts, braised short ribs, and lamb meatballs for us to share, I try to steady my nerves by taking small sips of Cava. It's my birthday dinner, and I want to live in the moment. I know Doug and I will have a great time, and although forty feels like a deadline by which I need to come to terms with my doubts, I still have almost three hundred and sixty days to go. Practically an entire year. I don't want to waste it worrying. Everything will unfold naturally. I bring my glass to my mouth, already feeling much better.

"It might be an odd time to bring this up, but are we okay?"

Choking on my Cava, I cover my mouth with my hand. I swallow hard. "Why would you ask that?"

Doug does a half shrug. "I don't know, Mags. You seem restless lately."

I chew on my bottom lip, feeling sick to my stomach and not at all excited for the feast the waitress will soon deliver to our table. I don't want to discuss this now, but I'm a horrible liar. When I was nine years old, I accidentally broke the leg off one of Cheryl's Barbie dolls. I had been playing with a classmate of mine while Cheryl was at a Little League softball game. I left the Barbie doll in the room we shared, praying she wouldn't notice since she claimed to be too old to play with Barbies. My prayers were not answered, and she confronted me later that day. Too slow on my feet to come up with a good excuse, I blamed it on my friend, and then immediately confessed it was not, in fact, my friend who was the guilty culprit, but me. I suck.

"Maybe I have been. I've been thinking too much."

Doug smirks. "You? Think too much? No."

"Ha ha."

Doug reaches across the table and squeezes my hand again. This time I don't let go. He studies me. "What have you been thinking about?"

I bite the inside of my cheek, contemplating how to say it. I finally blurt out, "Turning forty, us, turning forty, my life, turning forty." I avoid eye contact. I hate that I'm so single-minded on turning forty and know Doug hates it too.

Doug removes his hand from mine. "Okay. I get the 'turning forty' part, but the 'us' part concerns me."

I take a deep breath in and let it out slowly. "I love you, Doug. I really do. But...aren't you ever uncertain about, well, the future?"

His face despondent, Doug frowns and slowly shakes his head. "No. I can't say I am. But I guess you are?"

The waitress has placed a few of our dishes on the table, and I absently shove a stuffed date in my mouth. It might as well be dirt. Knowing it's too late to seamlessly change the subject, I dip my chin downward. "I think I'm feeling stressed about getting older and wondering if I should be more settled by now." I face Doug again. "I always thought I'd be married and finished having kids at this stage of my life. Forty seemed so old when I was younger, and here it is— looming."

Doug takes a long sip of his drink. "Do you want to get married, Mags? You drop the subject whenever I bring it up."

"I *do* want to get married. And that's what concerns me. Why do I keep changing the subject? Why is it I'm living with such an amazing man who loves me so much, and yet I don't have a secret stash of *Bride Magazine* under our bed like most girls who've been living with their boyfriends for two years?"

"You mean you don't?" Doug jokes.

I appreciate his attempt to lighten the mood, but I know this won't end well. "I worry if this..." I point at him, and then at me. "If you and me are right, I shouldn't have these doubts." I see the sadness in Doug's eyes and fight the urge to stab myself with a fork for hurting him.

He scratches his head. "What do you want to do about it? Do you want to break up?"

I sit up straight in my chair. "No."

"Well, I'm not sure how to respond to this, Maggie."

"I don't want to break up," I say as an alternative solution percolates in my mind. "But a time-out might not be a bad idea. Maybe I should take the next year to figure out what I want so I can have all of my ducks in a row by the time I turn forty. That way, I'll be sure." I wonder why I didn't think of this earlier. It's a fabulous idea.

When Doug jerks his head back at my suggestion, I have a feeling it means he doesn't think it's fabulous at all. Keeping his stare on me, he says, "Let me get this straight. You want to take a year hiatus to decide what *you* want to do about us. And I'm supposed to wait to see what you decide?"

It seemed like a good idea in my head, but when he puts it that way, it sounds really one-sided. "If I take time now to confirm my wavering is simply me being stupid and not based on something solid, we can move forward free of doubts."

"What about what I want?" Doug asks.

"What do you want?" I whisper.

"I want you to be sure about us now. I want to pretend this conversation never happened."

I nod. "Let's do that." I raise my glass and clink it against his. "Cheers." I smile even as I feel tears brimming in my eyes. There is no way we can erase this conversation from our memories, unless he is Jim Carrey and I am Kate Winslet in *Eternal Sunshine of the Spotless Mind*, and we both know it.

Doug shakes his head. "If only it was that easy."

"What do we do now?"

Doug stands up, and for a second, I think he is going to walk out on me. "I need to use the bathroom."

I watch his back as he walks away. When I can't see him anymore, I reach into my bag and pull out the two Excedrin I always keep in my purse in case of a headache. I swallow the pills down with my Cava and grimace as the fizz from the drink burns my throat. Afterwards, I stare at the uneaten plates of food on the table. What a waste. When I look up, Doug is walking toward me with watery eyes. He sits down without saying anything. I am about to break the silence with some stupid joke when he says, "I love you, Maggie."

"I love you too," I say, meaning it.

"But you're not *in love* with me." He doesn't ask it as much as state it as fact.

"I am *in love* with you, Doug. I just—"

"You just what?" he interrupts, sounding angry.

I whisper, "I worry it's not enough." My voice sounds like it's coming from someone else's mouth.

"I think we should break up, Maggie."

My body involuntarily jerks at his words, and I grip the table for support. "You mean permanently or a temporary break?"

"It's been three years, Maggie. If you're not sure I'm the one by now, chances are I'm not. I don't want to waste more of your time." He pauses. "Or mine. I'll hunt for a new apartment."

I swallow back my tears. This is not how I imagined the night would unfold. "Are you sure you want to do this?"

Doug gives a slight shake of his head. "I'm sure I don't want to do this. But I'm also sure I have to. I'll stay with Connor tonight and pack up some of my stuff while you're at your mom's tomorrow night."

I try to imagine my family's reaction to hearing Doug and I

broke up, and that he moved out to live with his older brother. I can't. I'm pretty certain my own reaction will be delayed since I currently feel like this is happening to someone else.

Doug continues speaking. "I'll take care of the bill. You should get out of here."

"I can't let you pay for all of this." I point at the uneaten food. "I ruined my birthday, and now you're going to pay for it?"

Doug drops his credit card on the table. "Your birthday was Tuesday so, no, you didn't ruin it. But you did break my heart."

"Doug..."

Not meeting my gaze, he says, "Just go, Maggie."

I stand up but linger. I don't want it to end this way.

"Please, Maggie. Go."

And so I leave.

I barely feel my feet touch the ground as I weave my way through the crowded bar. When I reach the exit, I turn around and contemplate running back to Doug to tell him it was all a big mistake. A tear drops onto my cheek, and I wipe it away as I momentarily observe the happy people drinking at the bar. There are several groups of female friends gabbing amongst themselves while stealing surreptitious glances towards the handful of guys at the bar. Unfortunately for them, most of the men appear to be on dates. I wonder if any of them will break up before the night is over, like Doug and me. Since I have no idea what I would say to Doug if I went back to the table, or if I even want to say anything at all, I turn around and walk out onto 10th Street. A cab immediately stops in front of the restaurant, almost like Doug personally phoned in the request to get me as far away from him as possible, as soon as possible. I step into the cab, say, "Twenty-seventh and third," and shut the door. Then I lean my head against the seat and close my eyes.

Later that night, after I go through the motions of getting ready for bed—change out of my clothes, wash my face and brush my teeth—as if the night is no different than any other, I slip between the crisp eight-hundred thread count sheets Doug and I splurged on at Bed Bath & Beyond and bring the upper sheet to my chin despite it being eighty-five degrees outside. I take a deep inhale expecting to smell Doug, but since I put on clean sheets that morning, his scent has been completely washed away.

When my eyes open the next morning, my body feels cold despite it being the height of summer. I flip over and move closer to Doug, whose skin is always warm. But I'm alone in the bed. As the events of the night before come back to me, I bury myself under my covers and weep until the alert of a text message entices me to come out from hiding. My heart beats rapidly, wondering if it's Doug saying he's changed his mind.

It's Cheryl. She's asking when I'm planning to arrive at my mom's house for dinner. She's hoping to get there around five and wants to make sure she won't have to wait around without me there. I completely forgot about the dinner. Funny how only a few days prior, I was so excited for lamb chops and an evening with my family, and now I'd almost prefer to go to the gynecologist. *Almost.* I would definitely prefer to go to the dentist, though, and that says something.

I'm going to have to explain Doug's absence, and I'm not sure they'll understand. I debate making up some excuse as to why Doug can't make it, but my family is well aware of my lack of talent in the lying department. I text back to Cheryl that I will try to be there as close to five as possible. We love our mothers, but their endless questions about our personal lives are easier to take when we team up, and the distraction of Cheryl's children is never enough. They are completely capable of asking how Cheryl's husband's business is doing, and if the recession has affected the garment district while painting little Cady's toenails. And they have no problem asking when Doug is going to pop the question while helping three-year-old Michael create a plane with Legos. I am positive they've already discussed the possibility of Doug proposing on my birthday as they had the year before and even the year before that, and they're hoping for the big announcement tonight. They will get a big announcement, all right, but it won't be the one they expect.

I make myself a cup of coffee with the Keurig Doug had insisted we buy instead of spending money getting my daily coffee at Starbucks. As I bring the hot cup to my mouth and inhale the hazelnut aroma, I recall with fondness the many times over the years Doug did the leg work to save us money because I was too comfortable with the status quo or just too lazy to switch cable and internet providers or apply for credit cards that give rewards for spending. But I was the one who planned our vacations, scoped out new restaurants, and was his personal director of recreation. We made a good team and with one confession of doubt, we are over. It doesn't feel real.

I let my head rest on the table for a few moments while breathing in and out through my nose. Finally, I sit up with renewed determination. I told Doug I needed time to think and he's given it to me. Despite his refusal to make it a temporary break, I know we'll find our way back to each other if it's meant to be. For now, the time I desperately need to get my ducks in a row is upon me, and I'm not going to waste it.

* * *

I step off the train in Peekskill, a suburb about forty-five minutes outside of the city—where I grew up and where my mom still lives—and walk up the hill to the house my mom purchased after I went away to college.

I'm cautiously optimistic my break with Doug is for the best, but I'm also not deluded regarding the persuasive powers of my family to make me doubt every single decision I make. My mother's support is important to me, but in this instance, I'm craving Cheryl's reassurance I did the right thing by being honest with Doug about my concerns. I know she loves Doug and would be ecstatic if the two of us tied the knot and started a family, but even more than that, I know she loves me and wants me to be happy. If my happiness doesn't coincide with letting things play out with Doug, she will support our break (or breakup) wholeheartedly. I want to get her alone and in my corner before I spill my guts to my mom and Aunt Helen, but I know the likelihood of getting Cheryl into the bathroom for a pow-wow before my mom asks Doug's whereabouts is pretty much impossible. I'm going to be on my own.

I knock on the door, my heart slamming against my chest. Even the inviting smell of potato soufflé with cooked onions wafting onto the front porch does nothing to wipe away my apprehension over facing my family as a single, thirty-nine-year-old woman.

The door opens, and my mom's smiling face beams at me across the threshold. She opens her arms and brings me into her fold. "Happy birthday, sweetheart." She kisses me on the cheek, no doubt leaving a hot pink stain in the shape of her lips.

I squeeze her back and hold tight. "Thanks, Mom," I say into her strawberry-scented hair before stepping into the house. I wave at Aunt Helen as she stuffs a cracker with chopped liver into her mouth.

My mom peeks over my shoulder. "Where's Doug?"

Totally prepared to tell my mother I will explain later, I blurt out, "He's not feeling well. He wanted me to send his apologies and begged me to bring home a doggie platter." Without taking a breath, I continue with my lies. "Don't blame him. I insisted he rest and avoid the germs he'd face on the train." I simper. "We might have partied a bit too hard last night for my birthday." I push past my mom and walk farther into the house, willing my pulse to stop racing. I don't recognize the lying alien who has taken control of my body. As I make my way to Aunt Helen, I announce, "More food for us."

While hugging Aunt Helen, I browse the room, noting the box of Legos and Dr. Seuss books. Cheryl had obviously been there at some point, but there is no sign of her now. Aunt Helen, who bears a strong resemblance to my mother with short hair colored ash-blond straight from a bottle of Clairol, light blue eyes matching mine, and a stocky body, gives me a kiss before releasing me. "Happy Birthday, honey. How does it feel to have only one year left of your thirties?"

I offer a fake smile. I hate when people say things that are obviously of a sensitive nature in the guise of being funny or helpful—something my aunt is famous for. Experience has taught me not to complain about it, get defensive, or even acknowledge being offended because it will only encourage more of the same. "Feels fine, thanks. Where are Cheryl and the kids?"

At that, the front door opens, and Cady and Michael race toward me with Cheryl following behind with a bag of groceries. Cheryl's shoulder-length, dark-chocolate hair shows no trace of gray, her subtle makeup application is flawless—emphasizing her almond-shaped brown eyes—and her black skinny pants and zebra-printed cashmere sweater fit her slender figure perfectly. She could easily pass for a wealthy housewife of New York whose children are raised by a nanny while she lunches with the Junior League. In reality, she works a full-time job as a certified medical assistant on top of caring for a husband and two young children. Unlike me, she didn't go through an awkward phase in middle school complete with braces and zits on her chin. Her natural beauty is one of the many reasons I idolized her growing up.

"Hi Aunt Maggie," Cady says, throwing her chubby arms around my legs. Michael stands back and waves shyly. "Hi Aunt Maggie," he says.

I'm technically their cousin, but when Cheryl and I were teenagers, we decided our children would refer to us as Aunt Maggie or Aunt Cheryl respectively. Only time will tell if anyone will call Cheryl "Aunt," since that is dependent on whether anyone will call me "Mommy." I lean down and kiss Cady's hair. Like my mother's, her hair smells like strawberries. I walk over to Michael with Cady still attached to my leg and ruffle his hair. "Hi there, buddy boy. Been discovered by Hollywood yet?"

Blushing, Michael shakes his body from side to side. "No," he says shyly. I peep over his head at Cheryl and give her a knowing smile. With his doe eyes, olive complexion, and thick head of chestnut hair, Michael is the spitting image of Cheryl and breathtakingly gorgeous. Cady, on the other hand, looks freakishly similar to her aunt Maggie with strawberry blond hair, blue eyes, and freckles. Cady's delivery took twenty-nine hours and, according to Cheryl, it was the most horrifyingly painful experience of her life. When people comment on Cady's likeness to me, Cheryl often jokes, "She's definitely mine, and if she's not, I want those twenty-nine hours back."

I give Cheryl a kiss on the cheek and a light hug. "Hey," I say and follow her into the kitchen where she drops the groceries on the counter.

"Happy Birthday, Magpie. Where's Doug?"

"Sick." I lift the layer of aluminum foil off a platter and take a peek at my mom's noodle casserole. "Where's Jim?"

"Working. I'm starving. Dinner almost ready?"

I stifle a giggle. Cheryl and I are all about the food.

My mother walks into the kitchen and lights the stove. "Hold your horses. I'm heating up the soup now."

I wonder if other families regularly eat soup for dinner in the summer. Not gazpacho, vichyssoise, or cold cucumber soups as seen on many New York City restaurant week menus, but my mother's specialty, hot matzo ball soup. It doesn't matter if it's one hundred and six degrees outside, the air conditioner is blasting, and the guests are wearing next to nothing, if my mother is making dinner, matzo ball soup will be on the menu, especially if we're celebrating a birthday.

Hoping to avoid an extended one-on-one conversation with Cheryl within earshot of my mother and Aunt Helen, I waste some time finding an available outlet to charge my phone and then go to the bathroom. A few minutes later, I'm sitting at the dinner table, all of us in our usual spots: my niece and nephew on either side of me, and Cheryl directly across.

"Did your father call to wish you a happy birthday?" my mom asks.

"Yes."

"I'm surprised that deadbeat even remembers your birthday," Aunt Helen mutters into her soup.

"He sent me a card too," I say loudly. Aunt Helen helped nurse my mother's broken heart after the divorce, and her hatred of my father does not appear to have waned at all in the last thirty years. I'm not prone to defend my father, whose role in my life has been one step above that of an anonymous sperm donor, but I don't like when Aunt Helen disparages him in front of me. He's still my dad. Therapy in my twenties enabled me to overcome my daddy issues and accept his paternal limitations. Mostly.

My mom smiles at me across the table. "How is he?" Unlike her sister, my mother encourages me to nourish the limited relationship I have with my father despite their past.

"Same old. He mentioned something about a possible business trip to New York later this year." I use air quotes when I say "business trip," because the details on how my father makes a living are sketchy. My gut tells me I'm better off not knowing.

"When was the last time you saw him?" Cheryl asks.

I shrug, staring down at my bowl of soup. "Five or six years ago." My gaze meets hers briefly, and I see the pity in her chocolate eyes. Growing up, Cheryl was right there with me each time my father cancelled plans or stood me up. I wasted hours staring out the window waiting for his car to pull up the driveway, and it was Cheryl's shoulder I cried on when I didn't want to burden my mother with my grief.

"I say a change of topic is in order," my mom says. "Where did you eat last night?"

I take a spoonful of hot soup and blow on it before answering. "Alta. It's a tapas restaurant."

Gawking at me with widened eyes, Aunt Helen blurts out, "You went to a topless restaurant?"

I chuckle. "Tapas. Not topless, Aunt Helen."

"It's small plates, Mom," Cheryl says. "You order a bunch of different smaller dishes and share them."

Aunt Helen makes a sour face. "I hope there was enough food."

"There was." I frown, picturing our table from the night before full of uneaten dishes.

"You okay, Mags?" Cheryl asks.

Before I can answer, my mom says, "Maybe something Doug ate made him sick."

"Maybe." I glance over at Cady, who has noodles all over her hands and has managed to get more soup on the table than in her mouth. "You enjoying your soup, sweetie?"

Cady looks up at me with a piece of carrot on her upper lip. "Yes!"

"It seems Cady shares more with her Aunt Maggie than freckles," I say, referring to her messy eating habits.

Aunt Helen interjects, "Your mother and I thought maybe Doug would pop the question this year. You've been dating four years, right?"

I clear my throat. "Less than three actually."

"Why buy the cow when you can drink the milk for free?" Aunt Helen mumbles it just loud enough for me to hear.

I drop my spoon into my now empty bowl, and the metal against the ceramic causes everyone to eyeball me in surprise. "Sorry," I mutter.

"Come with me," Cheryl says.

"Now?"

"I want to give you your birthday present."

"Why can't it wait until after dinner?" My mom looks baffled.

Standing up, Cheryl says, "Because it can't. We'll be right back."

I shrug helplessly at my mom and follow Cheryl into the living room.

Cheryl sits down on the upholstered loveseat with a flower motif and pats the spot next to her. Then she angles her body toward mine. "Spill."

The timing of the conversation is not ideal, but since I'm itching to open up to Cheryl, I embrace it. "I lied about Doug being sick."

"No shit. Where is he?"

I take a deep breath and consciously exhale to the count of

three. It's a meditation technique I found online and usually practice in my own company, but I need to calm down. "He broke up with me."

Her eyes bug out. "He *what*?"

"Well, he didn't want to, but when I asked if we could take a break, he thought a permanent breakup was the best thing for both of us. He's moving out as we speak," I say as my lips tremble involuntarily. I can't let myself cry with my mother and aunt in the next room. I replay my conversation at the restaurant with Doug to Cheryl.

Cheryl reaches out and squeezes my hand. "Wow. I didn't see this coming, Magpie. I'm so sorry."

Over the years, I confided my concerns to Cheryl that maybe someone else out there could make me even happier than Doug. She told me time and time again that no relationship was perfect, and the crazy passionate, heart-thumping stage did not last forever, but in the right relationship, it would come and go and never disappear completely. From her definition of a good relationship, I was in one with Doug.

"Why did you tell our moms Doug was sick?" Cheryl asks.

I shake my head. "I didn't plan to lie. It just came out."

"You're gonna get busted eventually. Why not come clean now before you dig yourself deeper?"

Narrowing my eyes at her, I say, "And listen to my mother rant about how special Doug is? And how lucky I am to even find a younger guy who is willing to be with me even though having babies might be challenging? And if I start all over now, by the time I meet a guy, get engaged, and then married, I'll be at least forty-two before we're ready for children." I add the numbers in my head. "And that's assuming I even meet a guy by the time I'm forty. I know it, and she knows it." I bite my lower lip. "I don't think I can bear to see the fearful expression on her face. Especially during my birthday dinner."

Cheryl pats me on the back. "I think you're projecting your own worries onto your mother. I seriously doubt any of that would even cross Aunt Doris's mind. In any event, she definitely wouldn't voice her unease." Letting out a long, low sigh, she adds, "I can't say the same about my own mom."

I chuckle in agreement.

"We all love you and want you to be happy, you know?"

I look down at the beige carpet and nod. My mother always tells me I'm the most important person in her world, and the quality of my life is the driving force behind her own happiness. I don't want to cause her undue stress. I know she'll promise to support my decisions no matter what, but her eyes will give away her concern over my choices. I'm not ready to face it.

Cheryl continues. "I adore Doug, Mags. He feels like family and always has. But if he's not the right guy for you, then he's not the right guy for you. You've never been completely certain, so maybe it's for the best. And remember, I might have married younger than you, but I didn't have the kids until later in my thirties. You have time."

All I wanted was Cheryl's blessing and she's given it to me, along with reassurance I'm not five minutes away from menopause. "Thank you. The lingering doubts suck, though. I wasn't sure he was the one when we were together, and now that we're not together, I'm not sure he's *not* the one. I wish I could see into the future." I run a hand through my hair and let out a loud sigh.

"Sorry, Magpie. No crystal ball here. There are no guarantees in life. Even the most passionate relationships can fizzle. And sometimes the couples who seem perfect to the outside observer are not what they appear. Life is all about risk. You take a leap of faith and hope for the best."

My stomach sinks. "Are you saying I should have taken that leap with Doug?"

Cheryl stands up. "This goes beyond you and Doug. There's no such thing as a 'perfect couple.' It takes a lot of patience and compromise to maintain a happy relationship for the long haul even under the best of circumstances."

I'm about to ask if she's speaking from experience when she

says, "Let's go back before they eat all the lamb chops," at the same time my mother yells, "Girls!"

Cheryl and I make eyes at each other and laugh. "They're going to ask what you got me for my birthday."

Cheryl frowns, reaches into her pocketbook and hands me a white envelope. "Happy birthday."

I open it to find two open-ended tickets to Six Flags Great Adventure.

"I know how much you and Doug love amusement parks," she says sheepishly.

I miraculously make it through the rest of the dinner without getting caught in my lie. I admittedly shove even more food down my throat than normal, including a third lamb chop, a double helping of soufflé, and a piece and a half of birthday cake to keep my mouth busy. I'll wait until a later date when we're alone to tell my mom. No need to get Aunt Helen and the kids involved. At least that's what I tell myself to justify being chicken shit. At the rate I'm going, I'll gain ten pounds before the truth comes out. I won't be skipping spin class this week, that's for sure.

Hugging me goodbye, my mom squeezes me tight for a moment and then pulls away and hands me a shopping bag. "There's enough soup in there for you and Doug to have dinner one night."

With as much authenticity as I can muster, I say, "Thanks, Mom. I'm sure Doug will be thrilled."

August

"Earth to Maggie."

I look over at Melanie. We're eating lunch on a blanket in Bryant Park, a public park near our office and a popular hot spot for nine-to-fivers on their lunch hours. "Sorry. What were you saying?"

"I was telling you about the two mini cakes we ordered for Lloyd's birthday. One with a picture of The Hulk and the other with Iron Man since all the kids love *The Avengers*." Melanie takes a bite of her sandwich and points to a group of guys sitting in the shade about fifty feet away from us. "But you were too distracted by the summer associates over there to hear a word I said. I know you're on the prowl for fresh meat, but don't you think they're a bit young for you?"

I snort. "I already did the cougar thing, remember?" It's been almost a month since Doug and I broke up. I'm coming to terms with it, and I'm more confident each day it was the right thing to do given my uncertainty. But the apartment is so quiet, and I miss his running commentary while we watched television. I also miss accidentally brushing up against his feet at night with my restless tossing and turning. And, of course, the sex.

"A three-year age difference hardly makes your relationship with Doug a May-December romance," Melanie says knowingly.

Still focused on the group of summer associates, I smile at Philip when he catches my eye and waves. I figure he volunteered to join the young law school students as the token partner. Or maybe someone on the Management Committee enlisted him. Friendly and charismatic, he is a good choice.

"Or maybe someone a bit older has caught your eye," Melanie suggests.

I turn to face Melanie, who contemplates me, then Philip, and then me again with her eyebrows raised. Fiddling with the buckle of my sandal, I say, "Yes, I think he's sexy. But he's married. I might be a heartbreaker, but I'm not a husband stealer."

"Philip is separated."

My mouth falls open. "He is?"

Melanie's lips curve up. "You didn't know?"

I shake my head. "No. Our conversations have generally been related to the firm's rebranding efforts. I obviously don't spend as much time at the water cooler as I should."

"I don't think it's fodder for the water cooler necessarily, but he showed up at the lawyer's summer retreat solo. Since he's one of the more attractive partners, word of his impending divorce spread like lice in a first grade classroom." Melanie raises an eyebrow again. "You interested?"

My eyes follow Philip—looking fit in a pair of gray suit pants and a light blue button-down shirt—as he dumps the remains of his lunch in a trash can and walks back to the associates. The younger guys appear to be fully engaged in what Philip is saying to them. As if sensing someone's eyes on him, he turns his head and meets my gaze. I quickly dart my head back to Melanie. I can feel myself blushing as I remember Philip mentioning birthday drinks. It's been a month, but my initial reluctance to accept his invitation has changed to eagerness for him to ask me again. Suddenly he's available, and I'm too bashful to even make eye contact. The butterflies dancing around my stomach feel unfamiliar yet wonderful.

"Mags?"

I smile at Melanie. "Yes?"

Melanie tilts her head to the side. "Why are you looking at me like that?"

I narrow my eyes at her. "Like what?"

"Like you're withholding information from me. If I have lettuce in my teeth, tell me now. Is it my hair? I still can't get used to it." As she says this, Melanie pats down her bangs.

"You don't have anything in your teeth, and I've told you a million times I love your hair. The bangs direct attention to your gorgeous green eyes." I give Philip a quick once-over and turn back to Melanie. "When's the next Associate's Night Out?" Once a month, the firm foots the bill for the associates to go to happy hour after work. Partners are encouraged to go as well. Something to do with building morale and camaraderie.

"It's this Thursday. Why?"

"Can I come as your guest?"

Melanie beams at me. "Of course. But I thought you didn't want to go because it would be crashing a lawyers-only event." Melanie is a senior associate in the litigation department, but is closer friends with me than she is to any of the attorneys at the firm. Since the firm's marketing department is a party of one, I'm a bit of a loner at work. Melanie has asked me to join her at the Associate's Night Out almost every month, but I've always declined.

"It *would* be crashing a lawyers-only event, but..."

"But what?"

My eyes twinkling, I say, "It's different now."

Melanie narrows her gaze at me. "Different how?"

"I'm single, and Philip is getting divorced."

* * *

I'm proofreading the press release I've prepared regarding the firm's hiring of a high-profile partner for the bankruptcy department, which is as boring as it sounds, when my work phone rings. I glance at it and see M. Cantor on the caller ID. "Hey Melanie."

"This is your fifteen-minute warning if you want to make yourself pretty before we head over to the bar."

"Are you implying I'm not already pretty?" I joke.

"Nope. I'm stating in plain English that I've gone out with you enough times to know you need fifteen minutes to brush your teeth and refresh your makeup before leaving the office."

It's comforting to have friends who are so familiar with my habits. Although our respective positions don't require us to spend much time together at work, we met at the annual Christmas party my first year at the firm three years earlier. I was waiting for my turn at the bar behind John Sullivan, the firm's Director of Finance. John was deep in conversation with Neil Black, the firm's Managing Partner, and was oblivious to the line forming behind him. When the bartender looked over John's shoulder to take my order, John turned around in surprise and accidentally threw his drink—a generously-poured glass of red wine—across my body. I remained riveted to the spot in shock and horror, but Melanie took notice of my attire—a light blue linen camisole under a winter white pantsuit. She grabbed me by the elbow and led me to the bathroom where she attempted to minimize the damage with the Tide Stain Stick she always carried in her purse after one too many spills at the hands of her two boys. Unfortunately, it worked better on removing juice stains and SpaghettiOs from cotton than it did Bordeaux from winter white. It was the first and last time I wore that outfit. When I opened the envelope containing my bonus check the following week, there was an extra five-hundred-dollar gift certificate for Bloomingdales from John. I considered myself lucky—not only because the suit only cost me three hundred dollars, but also because Melanie and I were fast friends from that night on.

"I'll head over to your office in twenty minutes and we can leave from there. Since I'm crashing, I definitely need to walk into the bar with an associate."

"Fifteen minutes, not twenty," Melanie corrects. "And I can only stay about an hour. I've either worked late or trained with my runner's group the past few nights and feel shitty about the lack of time I've spent with Barry and the kids. I probably would have skipped it this month if it wasn't for your crush on Philip."

Hit with a pang of guilt, I say, "Please don't feel obligated. It's not like I won't have plenty of opportunities to see him outside of tonight."

"It's fine. Besides, I am dying to see how you work it. I've never known you single."

I'm not sure I even know how to work it. I was a decent flirt back in the day, but I'm out of practice. I guess I'll find out soon. Standing up, I grab my toothbrush and toothpaste from the bottom drawer of my desk while still holding the phone. "Off to the bathroom. See you in a few."

* * *

I eye my almost-empty glass of Prohibition Punch. My face is likely as red as the cushy chairs in The Campbell Apartment, the classic cocktail lounge in Grand Central Station where the Associate's Night Out is taking place.

My rosy complexion is not only a direct result of drinking, but because of my close proximity to Philip. We are technically sitting next to each other, but he's at one table and I'm at another. The venue is so crowded that the tables we had reserved are within touching distance of each other. Philip faces some attorneys at his table, and I have been chatting with Melanie and a few other associates at mine. Aside from a quick nod acknowledging my attendance, we haven't said a word to each other yet. But I am indubitably aware of his presence.

"I need to head out," Melanie says, standing up.

I take one last desperate sip of my drink. I wonder if it's my cue to leave since I'm only there pursuant to her invitation. Since I haven't accomplished what I came to do, I'd prefer to stick around. I figure Melanie is unimpressed with how I worked it, and so am I. I give her a questioning glance and shift in my seat as if I am going to stand up as well.

She whispers, "Stay." Gesturing in Philip's direction, she winks at me.

I sit back in my chair and mouth, "Thanks."

"See you tomorrow." After another knowing glance in Philip's direction, Melanie weaves her way through the crowded bar and up the narrow stairs into Grand Central Terminal where she'll catch her train home.

While inwardly strategizing a good opening line to use on Philip when I finally garner the nerve to turn around, I focus on the trio of associates sharing my table and discussing plans for the upcoming Labor Day weekend. I'm about to ask if any of them have ever done a tour of the wineries in Long Island when Philip gently nudges me with his arm. I take a deep breath and turn my body around enough to face him.

"Nice to see you here, Ms. Piper," Philip says with an easy grin.

"Nice to be here," I say, returning his smile as my heart pounds against my chest. While I hope the conversation will eventually extend beyond pleasantries, the way we are currently positioned is not conducive to extended banter, and I try not to fidget.

Philip points to an empty chair across from him. "Why don't you move here?" Jutting his head toward the associates at my table, he says, "Unless I'm interrupting something."

The attorneys, all in their late twenties, are talking amongst themselves about a friend's crazy shore house in Belmar, New Jersey. They are oblivious to my participation or lack thereof in their conversation, and since the only reason I'm in the bar in the first place is to talk to Philip, I grab my purse from the floor and join him at his table.

Eyeing my empty glass, Philip says, "Someone needs a refill." He waves over the waitress, and after ordering another Prohibition Punch, I absently tuck my hair behind my ears and brace myself to work it.

"Never seen you at one of these before," he says.

"I've never been to one before. I figured it was time to accept Melanie's invitation before she stopped asking."

Philip rubs his thumb along his beard and studies me. "You

don't need an invitation from Melanie. Consider yourself an honorary attorney and come anytime you want."

"Consider me honored," I say with a grin. I remove my cardigan sweater and place it on the back of my chair. The air conditioning is blasting in the bar, but suddenly I'm warm. The strapless navy and white polka dot sundress I'm wearing shows off my décolletage and my abundance of freckles. I hope Philip has a thing for freckles like Doug, who liked to play connect the dots with them during foreplay. I push Doug out of my mind, focus on Philip who is looking fixedly at me, and take a sip of my drink. I hope he'll say something flirtatious.

"I was thinking about what you suggested at the last business development meeting."

I've been watching his slight Adam's apple bob up and down as he talked but am jerked back to attention by his last words. "What suggestion was that?"

"About getting a Twitter account for the firm."

"Oh, yeah. What do you think?"

I take another sip of my drink, dreading the inevitable hangover it will cause and knowing it will probably all be for nothing if my conversation with Philip is limited to marketing strategies.

Philip grins. "I think it's a terrific idea. The firm might be over a hundred years old, but it doesn't mean we shouldn't keep up with social media. But you were right. We'd need to pinpoint the kind of message we want to send."

I nod. "Absolutely. I think the account should be administered by one person to ensure our tweets have a consistent voice. We could have a general email address set up for attorneys to forward noteworthy events, articles, and the like, but only one person should do the tweeting."

"And that person should definitely be you. But we should talk more about it to nail down the types of people and organizations we want to connect with. It's time to take this old-school firm into the twenty-first century."

Even though my work plate is already overflowing, I'm flattered Philip thinks I'm the person to put in charge of this new account. I love that he has confidence in my skills, since many of the older partners dismiss me as being too young and too female to take seriously. My crush seems one-sided, which is disappointing, but my career is important to me. Besides, combining business and pleasure is a bad idea, and it's too soon after breaking up with Doug. For a second, I think ahead to my next birthday, and I swallow hard.

Philip stands up. "I should get out of here. But join us again next month. You're a nice change from the stuffy lawyer set." He winks at me.

Before I can stop myself, I blurt out, "You're not the slightest bit stuffy." I instantly feel my face flush and stare stupidly down at my drink. Considering he spent the entire time talking about work, I'm not sure I believe my own statement. When I summon the balls to face him, I find him staring at me with a look in his cocoa-colored eyes I can't quite gauge.

Philip's cheeks dimple and he sits back down. "Well, I think that might be the biggest compliment anyone at the firm has ever given me."

"Seriously? I find that hard to believe," I say honestly.

A twinkle in his puppy dog eyes, he says, "What kind of accolades do you think I receive from my esteemed colleagues?"

I scratch my chin, pretending to ponder the question. "I would imagine people have commented positively on your skills as an attorney."

Dismissing me with a wave of his hand, Philip says, "Good attorneys are a dime a dozen in this place. Or at least I hope so."

"Okay. What about that you're approachable and friendly?"

Philip gives me a closed-mouth smile and nods. "I suppose I've heard that before, but it's not exactly a blush-worthy compliment now, is it?"

I cock my head to the side. "I wasn't aware you were hoping for a compliment which would make you blush." As Philip remains riveted in place, seemingly eager for my next words, it dawns on me this is my chance to "work it."

Philip rubs the back of his neck. "Oh, now I'm fishing. I'm being silly. Let's forget I brought it—"

Interrupting him, I say, "How about you have the most beautiful brown eyes I've ever seen on a man?"

In the mere seconds it takes him to respond, I feel like I've aged several years, and as I wonder whether what I'd said could be construed as sexual harassment in the work place, I think I might throw up.

His hand still stroking his neck, he mumbles, "Well, Maggie Piper, I'll be damned. You did it."

"Did what?" I ask in a low voice. Got myself fired?

"You managed to give me a blush-worthy compliment. Thank you."

Figuring I'd know if I offended him by now, but still in a state of shock that I blatantly hit on a partner, my pulse slows down marginally. "You're welcome." Faking coolness, I add, "Should I be insulted you doubted my compliment-giving skills?"

"I don't doubt any of your skills, Ms. Piper," he says with a wink.

My body flushes with warmth as my mind goes straight into the gutter.

"Speaking of your skills..." he says, leaning back in his chair.

I lean forward in mine.

"Has the firm ever sent you to the annual Legal Marketing Association conference?"

It isn't what I expect to hear, although admittedly nothing about the preceding conversation has been predictable. I shake my head. "Nope." I gave up asking. The firm professes to want to up its standing amongst other similar-sized law offices, but evidently doesn't think investing in the continuing education of its marketing manager is worthwhile.

Philip's eyes lock onto mine. "Would you like to?"

I nod while holding his gaze.

"The conference is next month in Orlando. I'm going," he says, never severing eye contact. "And I think you should too." He glances at his watch and then stands up. Grabbing his suitcase, he says, "This has been a pleasure. Truly. But if I don't go now, I'll miss my train." Then he gently squeezes my shoulder. "Enjoy the rest of your night, Maggie. I'll be in touch about the conference."

I can't help but wonder how his strong hands would feel on other parts of my body. Paranoid he can read my mind, I choke out, "Thanks. You too," and watch him say his goodbyes to the others before walking out of the bar.

*   *   *

I keep my eyes closed and try to focus on something, *anything*, to keep my mind off of the hot sun beaming down on me. I remember spending hours upon hours playing with Cheryl on the beaches of the Jersey Shore when we were children—building castles and taking turns burying each other in the sand. And I recall numerous vacations when I was in my twenties and early thirties with my friends drinking beers on the beach from morning until happy hour. Now I can barely sit in the sun for twenty minutes without getting restless. It's no use, so I open up my eyes, sit up, and spray SPF 50 across my arms and legs. Covering my eyes with one hand, I wave the bottle across my face.

From the beach chair next to me, Amanda giggles. "You're so funny with the sunblock, Mags."

I point my finger down the length of Amanda's golden-brown body and up to her face. "Only someone with your naturally-tanned complexion would think I was funny." I doubt Amanda has ever experienced blisters from forgetting to reapply sunblock after extended time in the water. And I can still recall the nights I woke up screaming from the burns I got from sunbathing with Cheryl. She would use baby oil as suntan lotion when we used to sunbathe as kids, so it was only natural I would do the same. Only Cheryl has a complexion like a Greek goddess. I, on the other hand, have slightly more pigment than an albino and had to keep a container of cold aloe on my nightstand to slather on my skin every few hours. I have finally learned how to obtain a nice tan (for me), but it only took me about thirty-five years to get the process down to a science.

Regina, one of Amanda's colleagues, leaves her towel to grab a bag of green grapes from the cooler. Holding the bag out to me, she says, "How's your boyfriend? Doug, right?"

I glance at Amanda in time to see her shaking her head at Regina. "Um, we—"

Interrupting me, Amanda says, "Nice, Reg. They broke up. I thought I told you."

Regina runs a comb through her wet raven hair and frowns at me. "I'm so sorry." Then she glares at Amanda. "You didn't tell me." Pushing the grapes at me, she says, "Please take one."

As if eating a grape will make the moment less awkward, I pop one in my mouth. "It's okay. It's been over a month now."

Regina sits back down on her towel. "Do you mind if I ask what happened? You guys were dating for a long time, right?"

Before I can answer, Amanda's other friends return from the public bathroom and sit down next to Regina on their beach towels.

"What did we miss?" One asks.

"Maggie was about to tell us why she and her boyfriend broke up after five years," Regina says.

"Three years," I quickly correct, and immediately feel stupid. I eyeball Amanda, desperate for an escape, but she's focused on the sand. It looks like she is trying to dig a hole to China, but I know it's a ploy to avoid laying eyes on me. She practically begged me to tag along to Point Pleasant for the holiday weekend and promised me her friends would not be annoying. Promises Schmomises.

I know there is no way I am getting out of New Jersey without spilling the details of my breakup. I do the best I can to explain it to them so they'll approve of my decision but not blame it on any shortcoming in Doug as a boyfriend.

"And so there you have it. I had doubts and didn't want to invest in a future I wasn't certain of," I say assuredly. I'm not sure why I care what they think, but I yearn for their validation—just not at the expense of their opinion of Doug.

"Wow," Regina says. "You told him you wanted a break, and he broke up with you. Harsh."

"That's not how it happened." My scalp is burning, and I pull my beach hat out of my bag and place it securely on my head.

"Maggie's right. Doug wasn't harsh at all," Amanda says.

I flash her a grateful smile for finally joining the conversation and taking my side.

"He was heartbroken," she exclaims.

Or not.

"For what it's worth, I'm impressed. Breaking up with Doug was very brave," Regina says.

"What do you mean it was brave?" I think going the distance with Doug despite my pesky apprehension would have been the valiant choice.

Regina regards me with kind eyes. "I doubt many women in our age group would be able to walk away from a man who wanted to marry them, especially a man they cared about and who was good to them. But you knew something was off and refused to settle." She beams at me. "That, my friend, is brave."

I look at the other girls who nod in agreement.

"Thanks, Regina. I hadn't thought about it that way. But to clarify, nothing was off with Doug. It was more like..." I hesitate while trying to explain what I've never been able to put into words. "I loved him, but worried something was missing."

Amanda nods. "I'm sure you'll meet the guy who completes you in no time," she says confidently.

Regina takes a gulp of her water bottle, making a loud suction noise in the process. "Good luck with that. We're all still single, and the biological clock is tick-tocking away."

Amanda says, "Maggie isn't sure she wants kids."

Wishing she quit after "he was heartbroken," I glare at Amanda, but she's abandoned her hole to China in favor of building a sand castle.

"How old are you again?" Regina asks.

"Thirty-nine." *Less than eleven months away from turning forty.*

"Wow, I had you pegged for thirty-two-ish. You've got great skin," she says.

"Thank y—"

"It's great you don't want kids, though. You can afford to be brave," she says.

As I view the four attractive, intelligent, and single women before me, all nearing or on the dark side of thirty-five, I don't feel brave—slightly light-headed from the heat and seriously freaked out over my recent relationship choices, but not at all brave.

*   *   *

"Oh my. What do we have here," exclaims Regina, a huge grin spreading across her pretty face.

I take a sip of the frozen Rum Runner I waited in line over twenty minutes for and turn towards the bar crowd. "What *do* we have here?" *Besides a fire hazard.* I'm not at all surprised by the quantity of people at Martell's Tiki Bar on the Saturday night of Labor Day Weekend, and while I usually prefer more elbow room and less wait time at the bar, I'm pleased to see how well the famous beach bar has bounced back after Hurricane Sandy. I'm also happy I opted to order *The Yard* for an extra shot of rum. Each drink is going to have to do double duty unless we become very friendly with one of the bartenders.

"Hottie McHotties in the house," Regina says.

My eyes sweep the beach. Almost every guy sports a shaved head, a goatee, and tattoos. They're definitely not my type, but I understand the appeal.

"I think you might have to inch your skirt a little higher up your thigh to compete with the ladies," I say, pointing at our competition, who are practically naked. I push out my chest, trying to get as much mileage out of my 32Bs as possible. I survey my own outfit. I'm wearing a knee-length baby blue sundress with spaghetti straps and silver wedges. I don't fit in with this crowd, but neither do my friends, especially Amanda, who is wearing a Lilly Pulitzer flower skirt, a pink camisole and a white cardigan. She is definitely more Hamptons than Jersey Shore. Thankfully, Regina's suggestion we go to Jenkinsons, the indoor club next door, was shot down by the rest of our votes to enjoy the warm weather and drink on a patio.

Focused on a group of guys about twenty feet away, Regina says, "I see someone I like. Catch you guys later."

I give Amanda a questioning glance. She raises an eyebrow. "You're gonna go over there just like that?" I ask.

Regina nods. Taking my advice and pulling her form-fitting skirt farther up her thighs, she says, "Gotta be in it to win it. Ciao bellas." Then she tucks her hair behind her ears, revealing gold hoops. "You guys coming?"

Since this is her gig and her friends, I defer to Amanda. If I know her at all, she'll want to stay behind. I have no preference in either direction, though I'd be willing to bet my next paycheck I won't meet my match at the Jersey Shore on Labor Day Weekend.

Amanda cocks her head and gives the group of guys a once-over. "I think I'll pass," she says, taking a sip of her strawberry daiquiri.

"We'll catch you later. Text us if you meet any cute guys," Regina says.

We watch her walk away, then we turn to each other and laugh. "Is Regina always so aggressive when it comes to meeting men?" I ask.

Amanda nods. "Kind of, yeah."

"Good for her." I envy girls who can take the reins when it comes to flirting. I usually wait for them to approach me. I have my share of exceptions, usually facilitated by alcohol, but Regina took about two sips of her drink before joining the cast of Jersey Shore look-a-likes like she was Snooki.

Frowning, Amanda says, "I worry about her, to be honest."

"Why's that?" Regina is a grown woman in her late thirties. I assume she can take care of herself.

"She floats from one unsuitable or unavailable guy to another."

I strain my eyes to spot Regina standing with the group of guys. "Really? Like who?"

"Well, first there was her on and off again friend with benefits who she thought would eventually want more than just sex. She was right. Only he didn't want it with her. He's been with his girlfriend for a year now. Then there was the twenty-five-year-old writer who still lived in his parents' basement." Amanda shakes her head. "I think she's basically given up."

I narrow my eyes at her. "Given up on what?" It seems to me Regina is totally in the game.

Amanda bites her lip and looks at the ground. "Getting married, having a family. Settling down. So she figures she might as well have casual fun."

I jerk my head back. "That's nuts. She's only thirty-eight."

"Being single in New York City after a certain age is a tough gig," Amanda says. "And good luck dating in the work place. The chances of finding a single, cute, straight, age-appropriate male teacher at the grammar-school level is slimmer than Taylor Swift writing a song not inspired by an ex-boyfriend."

I tug at my straw with my teeth and take a long sip of my drink, shivering from the strength of the extra shot of rum at the bottom of my cup. I want to ask Amanda about her own experiences, since I can't remember the last time she tried meeting someone despite men eyeballing her all the time, but decide against it. I need to steer the conversation away from dating. I had an earful at the beach earlier. I lift my empty cup. "Time for a refill. My treat."

My phone vibrates, and while we wait to get the bartender's attention, I check my messages. A text from an unknown number causes my heart to stop for a beat.

"Maggie, it's Phil. I hope you're having a great holiday weekend and staying out of trouble. We're all set for the Legal

Marketing Conference next month. Lila will arrange for flight and hotel rooms for both of us. We'll talk more next week, but I wanted to give you the good news. I'm really looking forward to it."

I take a sharp intake of breath and feel my face flush. Philip could have emailed to my work account or even waited until after the weekend to tell me about the conference in person, but instead he searched for my personal phone number and sent me a text message on a Saturday night. Amanda is saying something to me, but I can't hear her. I will be attending the Legal Marketing Conference with Philip. *Phil.* We'll be attending it together, and his secretary will be arranging flight and hotel reservations for both of us. Which means we'll fly out together. As the bartender finally takes my drink order, I wonder what else Philip and I will do together. I try to keep my wits about me and focus on the professional aspect of the conference, but I can't stop the jolts of excitement running through me at the thought of spending so much time with my work crush—my newly single work crush—outside of the office. I pay the bartender, tipping generously, and grab our cups. After handing one to Amanda, I clink mine against hers and flash her a broad smile. "Cheers."

September

"I'm not thrilled this conference is being held on Yom Kippur," my mom says to me over the phone. I am lying in bed with my computer propped on my knees while I multi-task a work assignment with a marathon of *Criminal Minds* on A&E. Before I met Doug, I bypassed any television show with stories "ripped from the headlines." A few months of cohabitating with Doug turned my avoidance of violent-themed entertainment into an all-out addiction to any crime-related show, including *Criminal Minds*, *The Following*, and *Law & Order: SVU*. Initially, it was because I was at the mercy of Doug to program the DVR, but before long, I was the one planning our Sunday afternoons of watching back-to-back episodes in bed. We turned off our phones, closed the shades, and were transferred to a world of unconscionable crimes. I often have to watch with one hand covering my eyes, but I love them.

"Yom Kippur will be over by the time the convention starts." Considering my family's religious practices are limited to eating enormous amounts of food on the holidays, I don't know why my mother is so bothered.

"I'm disappointed you and Doug won't be breaking the fast with the family."

I bite my nails until I remember how much money I spend on gel manicures. "We're disappointed too," I lie. In truth, I am thrilled with the timing of the convention, because it is a built-in excuse not to bring Doug over to my mom's for dinner. The week before, to avoid telling her that Doug and I had broken up, I said the reason Doug missed Rosh Hashanah dinner was because he was working late. He's a copywriter for a local radio network and works long hours from time to time. For all I know, he *did* work late on Rosh Hashanah, but it feels like someone is digging a hole in my tummy each time I lie to my mom. Even though I shared a house with Aunt Helen, Uncle Walter, and Cheryl growing up, I developed a "mom and me against the world" mentality. Kind of like Lorelai and Rory on *Gilmore Girls*, except my mother didn't have me at sixteen years old. Even when I was younger, when most kids kept silent about what went on at teenage parties, I confided to my mother about getting to first base while playing Seven Minutes in Heaven and Spin the Bottle. I never kept my boyfriends from my mother. Not confessing to breaking up with Doug is eating away at my insides, but each time I open my mouth to tell the truth, another lie escapes instead. Cheryl was right when she said I would dig myself in deep. I'm buried so far under my lies, I don't know how to claw my way out.

"Doug is still welcome to come without you, you know."

"He's not Jewish, Mom, and won't be fasting." I roll my eyes.

"I know. But he likes bagels, right?"

"Right," I mumble.

"And he always compliments my egg salad."

I smile despite myself. Doug always knew how to charm my mother, and she does make a tasty egg salad. "You can make it for him another time." Looking over at the muted episode of *Criminal Minds* on my television monitor, I wonder what the profilers would say about me. *The "unsub" is a compulsive liar with a chronic need to avoid disappointing her mother.*

"Fine. Tell me more about this symposium."

I breathe a sigh of relief for the change of subject. "It's a conference for law firms and in-house legal departments to talk about how changes in society have affected branding and marketing practices in the legal arena. Basically, it should help me learn how to do my job better. Good networking opportunities as well." I'm excited about the conference and not only because I'm attending it with Philip. But mostly because I'm attending it with Philip.

"Well, have a great time. And we'll make plans for dinner when you get back. Or maybe we'll come into the city for a show. Helen wants to see the new Nathan Lane play."

"Sounds good." I hope I won't need to find another excuse for Doug's absence, but as difficult as it was to end a relationship after close to three years, telling my mother about it is proving to be even harder.

* * *

Watching the seemingly never-ending line of other passengers make their way to the economy section of the plane, I sit back in my own first class seat barely able to contain my joy. I take a small sip of my complimentary Sky Breeze and marvel at how much leg space I have.

"You comfortable?"

I turn to Philip sitting next to me by the window and nod. "Absolutely. Like the saying goes, once you go first class, you never go back."

Chuckling, Philip says, "I'm pretty sure that's not how the saying goes."

Feeling the vodka go to my head already, I urge him on. "And how *does* the saying go?"

Philip clears his throat and shakes his head. "As a straight, white male who has no desire to do the research required to confirm or deny the accuracy of that particular saying, you won't be hearing it from these lips." As he says this, he taps a finger along his full lower lip.

Before I have a chance to embarrass myself by listing the many things...naughty things...I would like to hear from those lips—as well as the places on my body I want to *feel* those lips—the flight attendant blessedly removes my drink in preparation for take-off. Thankfully, I'm not so far gone to forget I need to keep my wits about me. This is a business trip, after all.

As if reading my mind, Philip asks, "Did you get a chance to check out the list of breakout sessions?"

"Yes." As the plane takes off, I reach into my carry-on bag and pull out the pages I printed off of the conference website. Leafing through the papers, I say, "I already signed up for 'Integrated Approaches to Law Firm Marketing and Public Relations in the 21st Century.' I thought I should run the rest of them by you before planning my itinerary since there's a lot of overlap."

Philip nods. "How about over dinner later? Some of the restaurants in the vicinity of the hotel seem pretty neat."

I'm charmed by his use of "neat." Not an adjective I would expect a forty-something man to use, but Philip makes it sound hip and, well, neat.

"Are you a foodie?"

Unblinking, Philip says, "If I say yes, will you think I'm a snob?"

"Absolutely not. We live in New York City. We have access to some of the best restaurants in the country, maybe the world. Would be a shame to spend your evenings eating fast food."

"Yeah, but the health benefits are substantial," he deadpans. "What about you?"

"It's a toss-up."

Philip leans in closer to me. "Between?"

"Any Tom Colicchio restaurant and...wait for it...Ray's Famous Pizza." I try to keep a straight face but moments later, I chuckle. "Just kidding, obviously. Although my ex never met a slice of pizza he didn't like."

Frowning, Philip says, "Yeah, I heard about the ex."

My head shoots back. "What did you hear? That he loved pizza?"

Locking eyes with me, he says, "No. That you broke up."

I feel my cheeks flush. I had no idea Philip even knew I had a boyfriend. Trying to recover, I say, "Yeah, we ended things a couple of months ago." I bite my lip. "I didn't realize my relationship status was being discussed."

Philip smiles softly. "It wasn't. I met with Melanie the other day, and she let it slip that you'd been burying yourself in work since your breakup and were excited for the conference as a change of pace." His eyes scan the length of my face until, once again, they meet mine. "I promised her I'd show you a good time. Please don't be mad at her."

I stare back at Philip and whisper, "I'm not angry."

Grinning wider than a five-year-old boy on Christmas morning, Philip says, "Great," and high-fives me.

When I exclaim, "Fantastic," in return, we both laugh. We continue our witty repartee until the pilot eventually announces our descent into Orlando and directs us to prepare for landing.

Returning my seat to the upright and locked position, I think about my promise to Philip not to be mad at Melanie. I snicker to myself. Mad at her? I'll be sure to thank her later.

*   *   *

Philip tosses another empty oyster shell in the bucket and points at the cold seafood platter we're sharing at The Oceanaire Seafood Room. "You take the last shrimp."

"Are you sure?" I really want it.

Eyeing the jumbo shrimp longingly, Philip shakes his head. "I was secretly wishing you would say you were too full, but, yeah, I'm sure." His lips twitch in amusement. "Seriously. Go for it. I think I ate twice as many oysters as you did." He looks at my almost empty pint glass. "And let's order another round of beers."

Taking one last swig of my beer, I say, "You didn't eat twice as many oysters as me. But you did eat a couple more." Two more to be exact, and, yes, I am counting. I love seafood platters. Especially ones piled high with my favorite assortment of shellfish—shrimp, oysters, crab legs, and lobster. Doug and I used to feast on platters like the one Philip and I are sharing a couple of times a year, but this platter is particularly fresh and delicious. Maybe it's the Florida ocean water or maybe I'm feeling fresh because Philip looks particularly delicious. With a pair of faded jeans, he is sporting a white button-down shirt with the sleeves rolled up to his elbows to reveal tan arms. The top two buttons of his shirt are open, making him appear nice and relaxed. Between the casual dress, jovial banter, and the round of beers we've shared, it's hard not to forget we're in Florida for a business meeting.

He regards me with amusement. "Did you seriously count how many oysters I ate?"

"I'm very territorial about my seafood."

Philip studies me. "Evidently. Do you want me to order more?"

"No, thanks. I'm full." Picking up the last piece of shrimp and dipping it into my container of cocktail sauce, I say, "Well, I *will* be full as soon as I eat this." I swallow it and then wipe my mouth with my napkin. "Delicious."

"I agree. You glad we opted for this and the appetizers rather than main courses?"

"Absolutely."

"What are you hoping to get out of this conference?" He pushes his plate out of the way and places his elbows on the table.

I hesitate. There is much I hope to accomplish at this conference, but I'm only comfortable sharing about half of it with Philip. I take a brief pause to clear my head of the beer, which might be affecting my ability to answer questions like this sensibly. "I want to make sure I have all of the tools at my disposal to do my job well. I would hate for Kellian & Hall to lose out on business due to archaic marketing strategies. I've asked to attend this conference before, but gave up after years of being shut down. Thank you for going to bat for me. It means a lot."

Philip runs a hand through his graying dark hair and sighs. "It blows my mind you haven't been sent before." He leans forward. "Between you and me, one of the biggest weaknesses of K&H is functioning like we have shallow pockets. We worry so much about every dime, and we don't always allocate our funds wisely. Any money spent sending you to this conference will be earned back if you take the knowledge offered to you and run with it."

I nod. "And I plan to."

Philip takes a sip of his beer and smiles at me. "I've no doubt."

I smile back, suddenly feeling shy.

Running his thumb over his lower lip, Philip asks, "What else?"

As I watch his finger caress his mouth, a zip of electricity travels through my center, and heat rises to my neck and face. "Can I tell you after the conference is over? I would hate to announce my list of goals and then fail miserably."

Philip nods. "That would be acceptable."

"What about you?"

He cocks his head to the side. "What about me?"

"What do you hope to get out of this conference?"

"Can I tell you later too?"

I laugh. "Sure."

He gives me a sheepish grin. "This is all new to me as well."

"What's new to you? The marketing side of a law practice?" It's true he was only recently assigned to the committee when another partner left the firm.

Philip raises an eyebrow. "Yeah. The marketing side of a law practice. That's exactly what I meant." Then, his lips curled up slightly, making me wonder if he was referring to something else entirely.

After dinner, we take a cab back to the Hilton Bonnet Creek where the convention is taking place and where all of the attendees are staying. Waves of anxiety crash in my belly as I stand in the elevator with Philip on the way to our respective rooms. The night has the air of a date, but it isn't a date. That's what I keep telling myself. But the tone of the night is very date-like—the way Philip angled his body toward mine at the table, how he maintained eye contact when we spoke, and how I dread saying goodnight and hope it's not awkward.

There are jitters in my tummy as the elevator approaches my floor, and I stare straight ahead, watching the lights change as we ascend from the lobby to the first, second, and third floors, and finally to where my room is on the fourth. When the door opens, I take a deep breath and turn to Philip with a smile I hope comes across as natural. "Thanks so much for dinner. It was fun." I hold my hand out to keep the door from closing.

Philip takes a step forward. "I had fun too, Maggie."

"I'll talk to you tomorrow then?" I have my hand in the open space between the elevator and the floor and push hard on the door as it comes at me again.

Noticing me struggling, Philip snickers and holds the door open button. Feeling my face get hot, I bend my head down and mumble, "Yeah. That would have been smart."

Philip leans closer and lightly tousles my hair. "You're funny, Maggie."

I raise my head to meet his eyes. "I'll be here all week."

Philip keeps his stare on me. "Good to know." He winks.

I walk out of the elevator, turn around, and give him a wave. "See you tomorrow. Sweet dreams." I instantly wish I could take back the last two words.

As the door closes, I hear Philip say, "Sweet dreams to you too."

When I arrive in my "deluxe room," which is surprisingly spacious for a basic hotel room, I sit on the edge of the queen-sized bed and take a deep breath, contemplating the awkwardness of my and Philip's goodbye. I hope it wasn't as bad as I think it was, and that we will act completely normal in the morning when we meet for Opening Remarks and the Keynote Address for the conference.

I walk into the bathroom and inspect my face with the magnifying mirror. Despite the stale airplane air from earlier, my skin looks fresh and dewy, and a smile confirms I don't have any embarrassing particles of food in my teeth. Things with Philip are still platonic, but at least I'm pleased with my appearance. I wash the makeup off my face and remove my phone from my bag to charge it overnight. I debate calling Melanie, but it's way too late to disturb a working mother of two young boys. And there isn't much to tell her anyway. As I search the room for an outlet, my phone pings the delivery of a text message. My heart stops when I see it's from Philip. He wrote, "Is it me or was that awkward?"

With shaky hands, I write back, "Was what awkward?" even though I know exactly to what he is referring.

A few seconds later, my phone pings again. "I felt like a gawky pubescent teenage boy saying goodbye to you in the elevator, and I have no idea why."

I smile and type back: "So did I, except make mine a teenage girl. WTF?" I second guess the acronym but decide to go for it.

"LOL. Are you decent?"

I scrutinize my current attire. I'm still wearing my outfit from dinner—white capris and a blue and white gingham halter top. I write back, "I'm dressed if that's what you mean."

"Do you mind if I come by? Just to talk?"

Swallowing hard, I type, "Sure. I'm in room 409."

"Okay. Be there in a few."

I race back into the bathroom and run a brush over my teeth to remove the taste of beer and salty oysters. Then I apply a light dusting of blush and translucent lip gloss. Enough makeup to give off the appearance of not wearing any. I sit on the edge of the bed and will myself to be cool even though I'm not. I have a feeling something big is about to happen, and I'm not sure I'm ready for it. But I'm glad I only finished half of my second beer so I'm neither sleepy nor drunk.

There is a knock at the door. Ready or not, Philip is outside my room. *Just to talk.*

I smooth out my hair and walk to the door as calmly as possible. After a deep inhale, I open it to find him standing there with a sheepish grin on his face. He's still wearing his white button-down shirt from dinner but has changed out of his jeans into a pair of khaki shorts which come down to his knees and show off his muscular legs.

I give him a shy smile while giving his body a once-over as nonchalantly as possible. "Come on in," I say, moving aside to let him pass me. Then I follow him into the main area. Asking him to sit on the bed might be presumptuous, so I motion to the armchair in the corner. "Have a seat." Then I sit down at the swivel chair by the desk. "Can I get you anything?"

"Maybe a beer, but only if you join me."

I grab a can of Becks from the minibar for him and a tiny bottle of rosé for me. After handing him his beer and pouring my wine into a plastic cup from the bathroom, I sit back down, raise my cup, and say, "L'chaim."

Philip lifts his can. "Cheers."

We take a sip of our drinks while checking each other out in uncomfortable silence.

The quiet in the room is unnerving, and I'm relieved when Philip finally breaks it. Clearing his throat, he says, "Okay, here's the thing."

I hold my breath.

"I really like you, Maggie. You're a breath of fresh air."

"I like you too, Philip," I say as my belly flips.

Philip's lips curl up. "I'm glad you like me too." Staring at the blue and brown-checkered carpet, he continues. "But I'm not sure what we're doing here. We work together. You technically work *for* me. Not to mention, I've only been separated a few months and this..." He points to me and then to him, "feels like more than merely colleague relations." He lifts his head and meets my gaze.

I can't argue with that. Softly, I say, "All true." I bite the inside of my cheek.

"How do you feel about this?"

"I, uh, I like you. It's weird. It's difficult to think of you as my boss." I rub the back of my neck. "I don't mean to be disrespectful. You're so down-to-earth. It's easy to think of you as a colleague, not a superior."

"I'm not 'superior' to you in any way," he says with a chuckle.

"You know what I mean."

"So you think of me as a colleague?" He frowns.

I can't help but smile. "A colleague who is very easy on the eyes."

Philip stands up. "You're not so bad yourself. Those freckles are unbelievably sexy."

I stand up too. "I'm glad you think so, since not liking freckles is kind of a deal-breaker with me." I run a hand up my bare arm. "There are many more freckles where these come from."

Philip cocks his head to the side. "How many freckles do you think you have?"

I have no idea. Doug tried to count once, but I distracted him before he could finish. I brush the thought of Doug out of my mind and answer, "Hundreds."

By then, Philip is standing right in front of me, with barely room to pass a pepper shaker between us. "Hundreds? I'm guessing thousands." When he runs his fingertips slowly up my arm, my lips part, as if anticipating his next move.

"Maybe millions," I say in a quiet voice.

"Trillions," he whispers before softly brushing his mouth against mine.

I close my eyes as I kiss him back. The embrace leaves me weak in the knees. As I grip his arms for support, I'm very pleased at the size of his biceps and hope it matches the size of his...other parts. Never removing his mouth from mine, he leads us to the bed.

Hovering on top of me, he asks, "You sure you want to do this?"

Arching my back as he trails kisses along my neck, I whisper, "Positive."

*   *   *

"Did you get what you wanted out of this conference, Ms. Piper?" It is the final night of the convention, and after putting in a brief appearance at the cocktail party, Philip and I snuck back to my hotel room. Lying on our sides facing each other, we are in my bed, completely spent after a sweaty lovemaking session.

I shift closer to him and wrap one of my legs around his. "I did indeed. Did you?" It has been a perfect trip. Besides consummating my relationship with Philip, I picked up countless tips I know will help me in the workplace. It's a wonder I was able to concentrate during the breakout sessions, since I mostly wanted to play back my time with Philip over and over again. At first, it was strange being intimate with someone new after three years. His body fits mine differently than Doug's, but discovering what Philip enjoys is fun. Almost as fun as being on the receiving end as Philip figures out what I like.

"I did. I can't believe we have to go home tomorrow." He brings his hand to my face. Softly caressing my cheek, he says, "I don't think you need more Florida sun."

Fearful my face resembles the inside of a pomegranate, I ask, "Is it bad?"

He kisses my forehead. "Not bad at all."

"Good. So we have all day tomorrow. Flight doesn't leave until almost nine p.m., right?"

"Correct. I have a final breakfast meeting in the morning, but let's do something after. Any thoughts?"

According to the clock on the nightstand display, it's already close to two in the morning. I sadly conclude that by the time I wake up, Philip will be long gone for his meeting. But his wanting to spend an entire day with me somewhere neither boardroom nor bedroom related is encouraging. "How about Disney World? We can ride Space Mountain."

Philip makes a sour face. "I hate rollercoasters. I was thrilled when my kids finally lost interest in amusement parks."

I suck in my breath at the mention of kids. I assume he has photos of them in his office, but I never had a reason to ask before. "How old are they?"

"Thirteen and fifteen. They'd rather text friends nonstop on the weekends than spend quality time with their dad." Giving me a wry smile, he says, "It makes me sad, but I don't miss the amusement parks."

A product of a broken home myself, I'm certain his children are happy he's a constant presence in their lives, even if they pretend to think he's an annoying parental figure. "How about Epcot? We can go to Germany and drink lots of beer so we can pass out on the flight home."

"I was thinking about the Orlando Museum of Art or maybe the Science Center. If we have time, we can stop by the Mall at Millenia. Ever been?"

I shake my head. "Never done anything in Orlando besides theme parks." I'm disappointed by the idea of being in Orlando without going to an amusement park, but I don't press.

"You're adorable."

The truth is I hate shopping on vacation and would rather spend my last day in Orlando screaming at the top of my lungs on a thrill ride than accruing more useless information at a museum. But as Philip trails kisses down my body, I question how much any of that matters.

October

"My mom asked if something was going on between you and Doug. Presumably because your mother is concerned," Cheryl says.

"What did you tell her?" I hold my breath and remove the phone from the receiver. I'm at work with my office door open. Speakerphone is fine for discussing what costumes Cady and Michael are going to wear for Halloween, but not for my relationship drama.

"I told her I had no idea what she was talking about and I hadn't seen you guys in a while." Cheryl exhales deeply into the phone. "Keeping your secret is getting old, Mags."

Since there are no major holidays between Yom Kippur and Thanksgiving, there weren't built-in excuses to get my family together for dinner, so I have successfully avoided telling my mom about Doug. I twirl a hair around my finger. "I promise I'll tell her soon."

"Please do. I'm not sure what you're waiting for anymore. If you're worried she'll have nightmares about you turning into an old maid with twenty cats, tell her about Philip." As if she thinks she might still be on speakerphone, Cheryl lowers her voice and asks, "Things still going well with you guys?"

I get a warm and fuzzy feeling at the sound of his name. "Yes, things are going well. He's amazing. And he can't keep his hands off of me."

"Well, I'm glad you're happy. Don't forget the 'can't keep your hands off each other' stage doesn't last forever."

The wistfulness in her voice isn't lost on me. "Things okay with you and Jim?"

"Things are fine," she says flatly. Then, in a much more animated voice, "Someone wants to talk to her Aunt Maggie." In the background, I hear Cady say, "I do. I do!" and then in a breathy voice from holding the phone too close to her mouth, Cady says, "Hi, Aunt Maggie."

"Hi sweetie. What's new in Cady Land?"

"Mommy bought us candy for Halloween!"

"What kind did you get?" I remember how our mothers used to embarrass us by giving out loose change and hope Cheryl has broken that tradition.

"Weeces Pieces. But Mommy won't let me eat any yet."

I stifle a giggle at Cady's mispronunciation. Cheryl is concerned she'll start school still unable to say the letter "r," but I think it's adorable. "Yum. I love those. Did you get your Halloween costume yet?"

"Yes!"

Besides an inability to pronounce the letter "r," Cady can never anticipate my next question. "And what is it?"

"A pwincess."

"I'm sure you'll be the prettiest pwincess...um, princess ever. What about Michael?"

"Spidowman. What aw you gonna be?"

"I'm not sure yet, but you'll be the first to know when I figure it out." I follow the sound of throat clearing to find Philip leaning against my office door. He smiles at me, and I immediately feel a pulsing between my legs. Maybe the "can't keep your hands off each other" stage won't last forever, but we are certainly in it now. At least I am. Philip whispers, "We're late for a meeting." I hold up two fingers. "Honey, Aunt Maggie has to go back to work now, but can you tell your mommy I'll talk to her later?"

"Okay. Hold on a second." I hear her say, "What?" Talking to me again, Cady says, "Mommy says you bettow tell Aunt Dawis about Uncle Doug soon. Tell haw what?"

My face gets warm as if Philip can hear both sides of the conversation. "Um, nothing. Tell your mommy I said okay. Love you, sweetie."

"Love you too."

I hang up the phone and say to Philip, "Meeting? What meeting?"

"Business development. It's starting..." He glances at his watch. "Now."

I jerk my head back. "First I heard of it." I grab a legal pad and stand up.

Philip rolls his eyes. "Why am I not surprised?"

I follow Philip to the conference room where we sit side by side at the long table. I'm responsible for putting together the firm's quarterly newsletter, so during the meeting, I jot down notes regarding newsworthy cases the firm has recently picked up to include in the next edition. When Philip's foot rubs against my calf, my butt lifts off my chair in surprise. From the corner of my eye, I glimpse him writing vigorously on his own notepad, but I also notice him barely suppressing a smile.

I give a subtle shake of my head and take a sip of water. I am determined to remain focused on the meeting, but Philip rubs his foot harder against my calf. I grit my teeth and press my lips tightly together, all the while keeping my gaze fixed on Neil Black, the firm's Managing Partner, as he announces the intellectual property department has assumed representation of a major television network. It's big news, and as Philip squeezes my thigh, I try not to squirm. I write "Big News" on my notepad and circle it. Philip snickers loud enough for me to hear, and I glance at him while gently removing his hand and kicking his foot away. I mutter, "You're killing me." His mouth twitches as he writes "Big News" on his notepad and circles it. I kick him again and mutter, "Stop" while trying not to lose it.

When Neil asks if anyone has anything else to add, Philip raises his hand. For a second, I think he's going to broadcast our covert game of footsy to the room, but, of course, he doesn't.

Completely composed, he gives a detailed account of the connections he made at the Legal Marketing Conference, only leaving out the naughty bits. Not nearly as quick to recover, I stare at my notepad the entire time he speaks, trying to remember the nature of the "Big News."

* * *

I point my chopsticks at Philip. "You need to control yourself in the workplace." It's later that night, and we're at my place eating sushi after working up an appetite in the bedroom.

Although we haven't told anyone in the office we're dating—aside from Melanie—we decided it isn't necessary to keep it completely classified either. The firm doesn't have a policy against inter-firm relations, and since I'm not even on the legal staff, and Philip is commencing divorce proceedings with his wife, he says he can handle any repercussions if we're found out. I'm not nearly as confident, but my excitement over being with him way overpowers any paranoia I have about ethics in the workplace. In all honesty, the mostly-secretive nature of our relationship is a turn-on and fuels my attraction to him. Nevertheless, there is a lot of white space between hiding our relationship and practically fornicating in the conference room.

Philip swirls more wasabi into his dish of soy sauce and grins. "I couldn't resist. You're so easily flustered."

"Not true. It actually takes a lot to ruffle my feathers." Still chewing a piece of salmon avocado roll, I cover my mouth. "But since my skin is virtually translucent, any change in color from the slightest blush is very noticeable."

Phillip nods, his lips pursed. "Very solid point, Magster."

I laugh at his nickname. Leaning back in my chair, I say, "The new season of *Grimm* starts tonight. I'm stoked."

"I've never seen the show."

I wink. "Tonight's your lucky night."

Shaking his head, Philip says. "I'll pass. I'm not much of a television person. I only bought one for my new apartment because of the kids. They're with me every other weekend, and the fifty-inch flat screen is how I bribe them to spend time with me."

My mouth gapes open. "You seriously don't like television?"

He chuckles. "Aside from CNN, no."

"That's crazy." Philip's aversion to watching television is disconcerting. Curling up on the couch in front of the small screen is one of my favorite pastimes. Doug and I are even supporting members of The Paley Center for Media, previously the Museum of Television and Radio. I paid the whopping two-hundred-and-fifty-dollar membership fee for each of us as a combination birthday/anniversary present after we had been dating a year. Last year, our membership came with access to a weekend-long screening of all the new fall television shows before they aired. We had a blast, and I hoped Philip would share my enthusiasm for the telly. I suppose reducing my viewing time—after I watch the season premiere of *Grimm*—could be a healthy change.

"To each his own," Philip says. "Anyway, you watch. You mind if I call my kids?"

Philip is the first guy I ever dated who has children or has even been married before. After a certain age, I know it is to be expected, and I assume if things progress he'll introduce me to them. He told them he was dating someone, which means they're probably plotting my death already.

"Of course not," I say. I would prefer his warm body to snuggle against during such a creepy show, but if I get freaked out by a particularly gruesome scene, at least he'll still be close enough to protect me.

Philip grabs his cell phone from the table and stands up, but then he hesitates. "You never wanted kids, Mags?"

Narrowing my eyes, I say, "What do you mean?"

Philip shrugs. "You've never been married, so I wondered if you'd ever wanted kids."

I swallow hard, the sushi I had devoured lodged in the pit of my stomach. "Why do you say that in the past tense?"

Philip sits back down and cocks his head to the side. "I don't follow you."

"You asked if I ever wanted kids as if it's too late. Just because I haven't been married, doesn't mean I don't want to get married. Nor does it mean I *won't* get married. And I can still have children. Many women have children in their early to mid-forties, and I'm not even forty." *Yet.*

Philip's face turns red, and he extends his hand across the table to cover mine. "I'm so sorry, Maggie. I didn't mean to suggest you didn't have more time." He scratches his head with his other hand. "Can we pretend this conversation never happened?"

"Not everyone gets married and has children in their early thirties like you did," I say.

Philip nods silently.

I can tell he feels horrible, but I want him to understand. "Not everyone reaches traditional milestones at the same age." I stand up. I'm shaking and don't want him to see it.

As I stand with my back to him, his arms encircle my waist. He whispers in my ear, "You're right. I'm wrong and I'm sorry. Go watch *Grimm,* and I'll join you after I say goodnight to Skylar and Pete. It will probably be a brief phone call, since grunting one-syllable answers to one-sided questions is their idea of a conversation these days."

The rest of the night goes by without incident, and when Philip leaves, he kisses me goodbye and mentions he has his kids until Sunday morning. But he asks if I want to go with him to the James Turrell exhibition at the Guggenheim Museum on Sunday afternoon. I agree, despite having never heard of the artist.

I go to sleep embarrassed by my outburst even though it seems to be forgotten. I barely know Philip and am already showing weakness and desperation over my aging eggs. For a future baby I'm not even sure I want. I assumed dating an older guy would ease my anxiety, but so far it hasn't. I remember when Doug and I discovered I was three years older than him. I asked if it concerned him, and he said no. I said most men preferred younger women, and he tapped me on the nose and said he was not like most men, and I was definitely not like most women, "in the best way possible." My age, his age, our age difference, was never an issue, but I wonder if things would have changed had we stayed together. As I hug my pillow and summon the sleep fairy, my heart aches for the sense of security I always took for granted.

*   *   *

Amanda and I walk carefully down the steps to the food court at Grand Central Station, trying not to get trampled by the hordes of twenty-somethings dressed up for Halloween. "Do you smell what I smell?" I ask.

Amanda closes her eyes and sniffs through her nose. "Shack Burger."

The Shake Shack used to be a single-location, outdoor burger stand located downtown in the middle of Madison Square Park, but capitalizing on its success, additional locations were opened on the Upper East Side, the Upper West Side, Times Square, Citi Field (home of the New York Mets baseball team), and now inside the food court at Grand Central Station. Carnivorous city dwellers and tourists wait in long lines to sink their teeth into the "Shack Burger," what many burger connoisseurs, including myself, consider the best burger in Manhattan. Since eighty percent of the people in Grand Central tonight are early twenty-somethings squeezed into tight Halloween costumes like sexy cowgirls and naughty nurses, the wait for the Shake Shack is reasonable. I'm guessing the partygoers are afraid eating a burger and fries will result in busting out of their miniscule getups.

I cock my head toward the line. "Should we?"

Amanda scrunches her forehead. "And deal with the wrath of Jodie when we're not hungry for her lobster truffle macaroni and cheese? No way." Jodie asked us to keep her company while her kids went trick-or-treating with their father, hence the reason we are in Grand Central Station on a Saturday evening taking a train to her house in the suburbs of Westchester. Had I known so many people would be taking the train outside of the city for Halloween festivities, I would have suggested leaving earlier in the day. "You're right." Looking at Amanda hopefully, I say, "How about we split one?"

"No." She chews her lip. "But the train isn't on the track yet, and the smell is torturous. I think we should wait upstairs."

Both disappointed and relieved that Amanda has enough willpower for both of us to resist the call of the Shack Burger, I say, "Agreed. Browse the Apple Store?"

We head up two flights of stairs until we reach the spacious Apple retail store.

"Do you need anything?" Amanda asks.

I take stock of the crowd, a mixture of tourists and local hipsters, and contemplate which display table to check out first. "No. Do you?"

Amanda removes her iPhone from her bag and holds it in the palm of her hand. "I'm due for an upgrade, but really don't want to spend money on a new phone until I have to."

"What operating system are they up to now? The 72S?" I joke.

Rolling her eyes, Amanda says, "You're asking me? I was still using a flip phone when you got your first iPhone."

"Only because Doug was always on top of..." Before I can finish my sentence, I spot a tall guy across the room wearing a khaki windbreaker over a pair of baggy blue jeans. He is leaning over one of the displays and has his back to me, but I can see wisps of dirty blond hair sticking out of a blue baseball cap. I clamp my mouth shut and swallow hard. Then he turns halfway around, and I recognize the button nose.

"Doug was always on top of what? You? No wonder you broke up with him. Variety is the spice of life."

"We need to leave," I say, still staring straight ahead.

"What the—"

"Now." I jog back down the stairs, across the Main Concourse, and back up the stairs on the other side of the terminal. I hear

Amanda calling from behind me, but I don't slow down until I reach the cramped bar at Michael Jordan's Steakhouse.

Catching my breath, I say, "I'm sorry. I couldn't stay there." I wipe sweat from my brow.

Also breathing heavily, Amanda says, "Jeez, Mags. You need a beer that badly?"

"Doug was there."

Amanda's eyes bug out. "Your Doug?"

I nod.

"He was in the Apple Store?"

I nod again.

"Did he see you?"

"No." Considering the maniacal way in which I ran out of the store, I certainly hope he didn't see me.

"Why didn't you want to say hi?" Amanda asks.

I press two fingers against the bridge of my nose. "I don't know. Not ready yet." I haven't seen him since the night we broke up. He came to the apartment a few times to gather his belongings, but he always made sure I wouldn't be home.

Amanda purses her lips together and studies me. I'm expecting a lecture, but she glances at her watch and says, "We need to get on the train now anyway. Are you okay to go back downstairs?"

Staring into space, I absently nod. "Doug's still in the store, so we should be safe for now." He can spend hours window-shopping gadgets. "But we should hurry. He has a nasty sweet tooth. Wouldn't surprise me one bit if he craves a black and white shake from the Shake Shack." Unlike Amanda, he is completely devoid of willpower.

Amanda pats my shoulder sympathetically. "Let's do it."

A few minutes later, we're safely tucked away on the train and out of eyeshot from Doug. I lean back against my seat and close my eyes. When I open them a moment later, Amanda is studying me with a crease in her forehead.

I cock my head to the side. "What?"

"Can I say something?"

A question like that from Amanda is usually rhetorical, so I say, "Go for it."

"I don't understand why you were so freaked out over seeing Doug. Was he with a girl?"

"No!" *Was he?* "I didn't see who he was with and assumed he was by himself."

"You're gonna have to face him at some point, you know."

"I know. I was caught off guard. What if he asked how I was? Or if I was dating someone?" I chew on a fingernail.

Amanda raises an eyebrow. "I doubt he would bring that up while standing in the middle of the Apple Store. But would you tell him about Philip if he did?"

I remove my finger from my mouth. "Tell him I'm already dating someone else? We practically just broke up."

"He moved out over three months ago."

I'm grateful Amanda wouldn't let me eat a burger. I might have needed a barf bag. "I can't do it."

"Maybe he's dating someone else too." Amanda opens her hazel eyes wide and innocent as if Doug dating another girl is a good thing.

I close my eyes and exhale deeply. "Not ready to hear that either."

"I see."

I open my eyes. "What do you mean, 'I see'?"

"I think if you were truly happy with Philip, you would want Doug to find someone else too."

I take a deep breath and hold it in. How can Amanda possibly put herself in my shoes? She hasn't had a single boyfriend the entire time I've known her. I can't even remember her crushing on anyone. "Don't you think you're simplifying things, Amanda? Emotions are not that black and white. I *am* happy with Philip, but it doesn't mean I don't still have feelings for Doug. And as much as I wish I could say I would be happy for Doug if he fell in love with someone else..." I shake my head. "I guess I'm not that great of a person. And what if Doug is still in love with me? The last thing I want to do is rub another man in his face. A man I work with and knew before we even broke up. Oh, God, if Doug knew about Philip, he might think I cheated on him." I bury my head in my hands. "It's too soon."

"Time doesn't heal all wounds," Amanda says softly.

I swallow down my growing annoyance and face her. "Amanda, I know you mean well, but please don't tell me how I'm supposed to feel about Doug."

"I wasn't talking about you," Amanda says before staring out the window.

This is not what I expected her to say. "Who are you talking about then?"

Amanda continues to stare out the window. I tap her on the arm. "Amanda?" When she turns around with tears spilling out of her eyes, I nearly piss my pants. "What's wrong? I didn't mean to yell at you. I'm so sorry." I know she is emotional, but I obviously underestimated the extent of her sensitivity.

"It's okay." She shakes her head and waves me away. "Never mind."

"Never mind? You're obviously upset. Please talk to me," I plead.

Amanda takes a deep breath and wipes the corners of her eyes. "You don't know about my first boyfriend. Noah."

"You've never mentioned him." Or any guy for that matter.

"We grew up together. We dated through most of high school and college and for three years after. We were talking marriage."

"What happened?" I hold my breath as I await her answer. Jodie introduced me to Amanda when they met in a book club years four years earlier. Though our initial acquaintance-like relationship eventually morphed into a close friendship, we never got around to swapping our dating histories.

Amanda shuts her eyes. Meanwhile, I pray it isn't something like he died in a car accident or dumped her for a supermodel or a man. All would be equally traumatizing. After an extended pause,

Amanda finally opens her eyes. "I was twenty-five. All of my friends were single, going out every weekend, and hooking up with new guys. Online dating was at the height of popularity, and I felt like I was missing something. Noah and I were amazing together, but I began to resent that he was the only guy I'd ever slept with." She buries her head in her hands and mumbles, "I was such a fool."

"What did you do?"

Amanda lifts her head and meets my gaze with wet, dull eyes. "I broke up with him. I said I thought we were too young to settle down. I was so positive I would enjoy playing the field, and then when I was ready, either someone even better than Noah would come along or we'd find our way back to each other. Because, seriously, who meets the love of her life in high school?"

I open my mouth to respond but before I get the chance, she raises her voice and says, "You know who met the love of her life in high school? Me."

In a softer voice, I say, "What happened after you broke up?"

"I got a shore house with my friends in the Hamptons, messed around with a lot of guys, and fooled myself into thinking I was having fun. The truth was I missed Noah each and every moment. I tried to move on, but then I realized all of my friends who were serial dating were searching for exactly what I already had and gave up. I went crawling back to Noah, but it was too late."

"He wouldn't take you back?"

Amanda blinks back more tears and slowly shakes her head. "He'd met someone else."

"Oh, Amanda, I'm sorry." I stroke her back. "But what about after they broke up? Did you try again?"

"They didn't break up. They got married. I almost moved back to Canada when I found out."

"Why would you consider that? You haven't lived in Canada since you were seven."

"I still have some cousins in Alberta. The point is, I wanted to run away."

I let her words sink in. I definitely have a better understanding as to why Amanda can be such a know-it-all about men—she doesn't want us to make the same mistakes she did. But it doesn't explain why she won't date now. "Amanda?"

"Yeah?"

I try to find the appropriate words. "I can only imagine how heartbreaking that was for you, and I'm so sorry things didn't work out with Noah. But surely you don't believe he's the only man you can ever love." When she doesn't respond, I question, "Do you?"

"I had my one great love, and I blew it. End of story."

I shake my head in vehement disagreement. "You can have your pick of men. They check you out all the time." Case in point, there is a guy across the aisle clearly eavesdropping on our conversation and stealing glances at Amanda.

"They never approach me. I think Noah was the one. The only one."

"I bet the reason guys don't ask you out is because they can see the invisible 'not interested' sign on your forehead. You were only twenty-five. Are you even sure Noah was the one? I know you hold yourself responsible, but surely you're romanticizing the relationship. If you had gotten back together, it might not have worked out anyway."

As I watch a film of pink travel from Amanda's neck up to her forehead, I know I have overstepped. I brace myself for her wrath, but she calmly says, "I don't think so, Maggie."

I feel like I dodged a bullet since she didn't yell at me, so I don't argue. Instead, I whisper, "Okay." I close my eyes for the rest of the trip and try not to think about Doug and whether he's dating someone. My rational side insists he has every right to move on, but my emotional side isn't ready to let him go.

*   *   *

I wait until I hear the familiar snore cut loose from Amanda's mouth. She's sleeping in the twin bed next to me in the pink and purple bedroom shared by Jodie's daughters. I carefully lift myself out of my own bed. Closing the bedroom door behind me, I tiptoe into the living room where Jodie is already waiting for me with a generously poured glass of cabernet.

"That didn't take long," Jodie chirps happily.

I put a finger to my lips. "She'll be so hurt if she knows we're talking without her."

Jodie pouts. "I know, but I never get you all to myself anymore."

I sit down next to her on the couch and kiss her cheek. "I miss you too."

Jodie stretches herself across the length of the couch with her legs extended over my lap, and drapes an afghan over her knees. "My life is utterly boring, Mags. I take the kids to school in the morning, go to work, pick the kids up, make dinner, put the kids to sleep, chug a glass of wine, go to bed. End of story." She yawns for emphasis.

I pat her legs. "It can't be that bad."

"It's pretty mundane." She sits upright, pushing the blanket onto the wood floor. "But you'll get a kick out of this story."

"Oh, do tell." Jodie always had the best stories in college.

"Picture this: Jodie..." Pointing to herself, she says, "That would be me."

I nod. "I figured as much."

"Jodie had a long and dull day. Went exactly as stated a few moments ago: I woke the kids up, made the kids breakfast, took the kids to school, *yada, yada, yada*. The children were particularly rowdy that night—my fault for letting them eat Oreos so close to bedtime. I figured it was my turn for some fun, so I grabbed my vibrator from the top of my closet—"

"Oh, no. I have a feeling I know where this is going."

Jodie laughs, covering her cheeks with her hands and shaking her head. When she shows her face again, her skin color matches mine after a long day out in the sun. "Wait for it. So I'm at it for maybe two minutes and start to feel that practically forgotten pressure build up and, *oh*, it feels so good—"

I put my hand up. "TMI."

Glaring at me, she says, "Prude. Anyway, without any warning, Chloe storms into my room and jumps on my bed. Without thinking, I release the vibrator from—you know—and toss it down the length of the bed without turning it off."

"And then what happened?" I ask even though I'm afraid of the answer.

"I tried to ignore the noise, hoping if I don't mention it, Chloe might not notice. I mean, she has little ears, maybe she can't hear the sound, right?"

I nod. "Unlikely, but I'll go with it."

Jodie rolls her eyes. "Of course, she heard it. She says, 'Mommy. What's that buzzing sound?' and shoves her little body under the sheets to find the source of the sound."

I try to picture little Chloe chasing the sound of a vibrator. "Oh my God."

Stifling her laughter, Jodie puts a finger to her lips and points in the direction of her daughters' bedroom where Amanda is still sleeping. "Shhh."

I take a gulp of wine. "What did you do?"

Jodie gives me a solemn expression. "I did what all good parents would do. I followed her under the covers, grabbed the vibrator out of her curious little hands, and told her it was a mini vacuum cleaner and I was cleaning the lint from my sheets."

"You didn't."

"What else was I supposed to say? 'Chloe, your mommy is in desperate need of an orgasm'?"

I chuckle. "That would have opened up a whole new line of questioning."

"Exactly," Jodie says, taking a sip of wine. "And I figure she won't be having sex until she's at least ten so I have time."

I sit up. "Ten?"

"I'm kidding, but they do start real young these days."

"Yikes." I was seventeen and still among the first of my friends to lose her virginity.

"That was my excitement for the month. How about you? Things going well with your new man?"

"So far so good. I have to restrain myself from initiating sex during office hours. He's got mad skills." I bite my lip. "I don't mean to rub it in."

"At least one of us can get off without battery-operated machinery."

"I'm surprised you invited us tonight. With the kids away, you could have finished what you started before Chloe so rudely interrupted you last time."

"Who said I won't once you go back to sleep?"

Throwing a decorative pillow at her, I say, "You're so gross."

Jodie laughs, but then her face turns businesslike. "Seriously, though. This Philip dude makes you happy?"

"Yeah, I think I'm happy." I bring my wine glass to my lips and let it linger a moment before drinking. "It's different, though."

"Different from what?"

I shrug. "Just different. He's so...grown up."

Jodie snorts. "I hate to break it to you, Mags, but so are you."

"Don't remind me."

"Still younger than me, kiddo. And you don't show your age like I do," Jodie says, pointing at the faint lines around her blue eyes which have deepened over the last couple of years. "And if I don't color this hair soon, I might be mistaken for a Brillo Pad."

Jodie does have more wrinkles than I do, but she's as adorable now as she was in college. She's not classically beautiful, but her warm and expressive face is indicative of her bubbly personality. "You'd be the hottest Brillo Pad on the block."

Jodie snorts. "Have you seen my neighbors? Not much of a compliment."

Rolling my eyes, I say, "I know I'm not much younger than Philip, but he's already been married. He has partial custody of two teenagers and a high-powered job. I, on the other hand, consider canned chicken noodle soup and a bag of chips to be a good dinner. It's nuts. When I was with Doug, I worried he would dump me for a younger chick, and dating Philip, I fear he's going to discover I'm still a child in a woman's body."

"I hate to break it to you, but your lanky body and teeny titties aren't very womanly."

"Screw you."

One eyebrow cocked, she asks, "Did you seriously worry Doug would dump you for a younger chick?"

"No," I confess.

Jodie shakes her head. "I didn't think so. Was it weird seeing him today?"

I bite my lip as I recall how caught off guard I was by seeing him in the Apple Store. I wasn't going to mention it, but Amanda blurted it out over macaroni and cheese. Probably sensing my discomfort, Jodie didn't question me about it at the time, but I should have known she was waiting until we were alone. I down the rest of my wine. "I wasn't expecting it."

"The first time you run into an ex is always the toughest. At least he wasn't with a girl."

"Amanda thinks I should *want* Doug to meet someone else." I glance down the hallway and whisper, "Did you know about Amanda and her first boyfriend?" Her *only* boyfriend. I'm still floored by her confession.

Jodie stands up and removes our empty wine glasses from the coffee table. "Amanda needs therapy." I follow her into the kitchen where she rinses the glasses with water and places them gently in her dishwasher.

"Enough about me and Amanda. What about you?" I say, leaning against her refrigerator.

Tying her curly locks into a bun on the top of her head, Jodie says, "What? My adventures in vacuuming aren't exciting enough for you?"

With probing eye contact, I say, "Maybe if you dated, you could allow your vacuum to charge for a change."

"Can we stop speaking in metaphors?" Jodie says, crossing her arms against her chest.

"Have you thought about dating?"

"Of course I have. But I've only been divorced for four months."

"You were legally separated for several years before that."

"True, but my life is so hectic right now."

I raise my hand in protest. "Objection. You complained only a few minutes ago your life was utterly mundane. A man could certainly shake things up."

Pushing my hand away playfully, Jodie says, "Overruled. Hectic and mundane are not mutually exclusive. Don't worry your freckled face over me, Magpie. I'll get back in the game at some point. I promise." She sighs and then draws me into a hug. When she pulls away, she says, "I hate to be a party pooper, but I'm beat."

My lips curling, I say, "Is 'beat' code for something else? If I barge into your bedroom in thirty minutes, will I catch you 'vacuuming' your bed?"

Jodie smiles and taps me on the nose. "You think you're so cute, don't you?"

"Yes, ma'am."

November

My mom places half a ruby red grapefruit on a plate in front of where I'm sitting at her kitchen table and kisses the top of my head. "I'm sorry I don't have soup for you tonight. I was too tired," she says.

I spoon a chunk of juicy grapefruit into my mouth. "No need to apologize," I say and follow her with my eyes as she walks back into her kitchen. "Will you please sit down with me?" My mom's most recent guilt trip was epic, so I took the train straight from work to join her for dinner.

"Eat your grapefruit. I'll be right there." She bends over the stove to check on the roast beef. She removes it from the oven rack, places it on a large dish, and brings it over to the table. I stand up and help her with the side dishes—sautéed string beans and Fettuccini Alfredo.

It takes three more trips into the kitchen, but once we're both sitting at the table with a full plate of food and tall glasses of Diet Coke in front of us, we catch up on each other's weeks. I tell my mom about my latest project at work and she brags about winning two dollars and seventy-five cents in her latest mahjong game. Conversation momentarily halts as we dig into our meal until my mom breaks the silence. "What's going on with you? How's Doug?"

Swallowing a string bean, I say, "I assume he's okay. I almost bumped into him in Grand..."

At this, my mother puts down her fork and knife and stares at me. My cheeks burn and, afraid to meet her gaze, I study the blue flowers which are etched into my dinner plate while wishing I could jump back in time ten seconds to before I shoved my foot into my piehole.

"Am I missing something?" she asks.

My hands begin to shake. Back in high school, my mom got me a job working for a woman who owned a catering business out of her home. After nine months, my boss, Mrs. Brind, gave me an ultimatum—either show more passion for the job or don't come back. Since I felt absolutely no passion for being stuck in her windowless basement every afternoon for two hours with zero human contact while I reviewed inventory, I took the latter option. When I broke the news to my mom, I worried she would be disappointed in my choice, but she gave me a hug and said Mrs. Brind needed a regular dose of mouthwash and a lip wax (both true). Today, I am crippled with fear she will think less of me as a result of breaking things off with Doug, thereby solidifying my fate as a single, forty-year-old woman. And Doug is a much more appealing adversary than Mrs. Brind and does not suffer from halitosis.

I pinch my lips with my thumb and index finger and slowly make eye contact. "There's something I need to tell you, Mom."

"I knew something was wrong. What is it?" There is a touch of impatience in her voice, but her forehead is crinkled with concern.

As fast as I can, I blurt out, "Doug and I broke up." I swallow hard and avert eye contact as my heart beats rapidly. I observe her reaction. She doesn't say anything, and I wonder if I should provide more information or wait for her to ask.

Finally, she leans against her chair and blows out her cheeks. "What happened?"

I open my mouth hoping for a seamless delivery of the information, but before any sound comes out, my mom cuts me off. "And *when* did this happen?"

While biting a knuckle, I mutter, "July."

Her face turning red, my mom repeats, "July?"

I gulp. "Yeah."

"Why is this the first I'm hearing about it?"

"I didn't want you to be mad at me." I brace myself for her response.

Repeating Aunt Helen's favorite phrase, my mom says, "Dogs get mad. People get angry."

According to Merriam-Webster's Dictionary, "mad" is a synonym of "angry," and does not only mean "rabid," but years of being corrected have trained me not to use the word "mad" around Aunt Helen. Unless I'm talking about a dog, of course. "I didn't want you to be mad...angry with me for breaking up with him."

My mom shakes her head. "Why would I be ma...angry? Damn, Helen." We both chuckle.

"I know how much you love Doug," I say.

"I thought you did too," my mom says.

"I did."

My mom appears confused, so I spend the next ten minutes rehashing the events of my birthday dinner with Doug and confessing the doubts I had while we were dating. I ask her to please let me get it all out before offering remarks, and she miraculously remains silent throughout. Finally, I let out a deep exhale. "Now you can comment."

"First of all, yes, I love Doug. But I love you more. You're my baby, and I want you to be happy."

"Thanks," I whisper. My heart is still slamming against my chest.

"But I thought you *were* happy. You and Doug were such a wonderful couple—always smiling, always laughing. You share so many interests. Even my friends have commented about what a lovely pair you make."

I flash back to the surprise party Aunt Helen, Cheryl, and I threw for my mom's sixty-fifth birthday, and how Doug and I caught my mom's mahjong buddies sneaking surreptitious glances at us all day and whispering among themselves. Doug insisted they were talking about how handsome he was. I assumed they were gossiping about us living in sin. "I'm actually dating someone else now."

My mom raises an eyebrow. "Oh?"

"Yes. He's a partner at the firm."

"A partner, huh? Nice work."

I wave her away. "Stop it. He's a nice guy."

She purses her lips. "Another young one?"

When I started dating Doug, my mom was concerned about our age difference. She feared Doug might not be as emotionally available and ready to settle down as someone my own age or a few years older. It didn't take long for Doug to prove her wrong, but I was still happy to deliver news she might like. "Philip is six years older than me."

Cocking her head to the side, my mom says, "And never been married?" My mom is old-fashioned and thinks any man over the age of forty who hasn't been married must either be gay or a player. I'm thrilled to ease her apprehension. "No. Divorced. Two kids." I see no reason to clarify that Philip isn't technically divorced yet.

"And he wants to get married again?"

I sigh. "The subject hasn't come up yet. It's a bit premature, don't you think?"

My mom stands up and starts to clear the table. "As long as you're happy. I still think it's a shame though. You and Doug were so—"

I put my hand up and follow her to the sink. "Please, Mom."

Drawing me into a hug, she squeezes me hard. "I just want you to be happy."

"You and me both," I whisper while holding her tight.

After we separate, I return to my seat at the table. "Do you ever wish you got married again?" I take a sip of soda.

"Not once."

Skeptical, I raise an eyebrow. "You were barely thirty-five when Dad left."

"I dated plenty after the divorce, if you recall," my mom says while smiling slightly.

"It rings a bell." Of course I remember being called away from *Gimme a Break!*, *The Facts of Life*, and *The Love Boat* to greet Mr.

Greenberg, Mr. Bowser, and the string of other men who took my mom out on Saturday nights after the divorce. "I wasn't very nice to your boyfriends," I say, biting my lip in shame. Also fresh in my memory is publicly laughing about Mr. Greenberg's receding hairline and Mr. Bower's hairy arms, and privately sharing with Cheryl my anxiety that one of them would become my stepfather.

"No, you weren't," my mom says.

I stand up and bring my dirty dishes to her. "I'm sorry I was such a brat. I hope I didn't drive them away."

"Nonsense. They thought you were adorable. And I was really good in bed."

"Mom!"

Wiggling her eyebrows, she says, "I can't have you thinking your father had all the fun after the divorce."

"That's no joke," I say, shaking my head knowingly. My dad never lacked female companionship, and it's questionable whether he waited until after the separation to take a lover. The one time he invited me to visit him in Dallas, I was twelve and I counted down the days until the trip. I couldn't wait to visit Southfork Ranch and ride rollercoasters at Six Flags, but mostly I yearned to bond with my dad. Instead, I spent the entire week tagging along while he showed off for Kiki, his girlfriend *du jour*. The multiple excuses I came up with to refuse a future invitation were unused as he never asked. "It's not too late, Mom. They have online dating sites for senior citizens."

Recoiling, my mom says, "No thanks."

Pulling her into a hug, I say, "I want you to be happy too."

After a squeeze, she pulls away and points her finger at me. "Don't keep secrets from me, and I'll be ecstatic."

"No more secrets. I promise."

A slow smile breaks across my face when I realize there is no need to cross my fingers behind my back anymore.

*   *   *

A light rapping on my office door causes me to look up from my computer where I'm finalizing the proposed marketing budget for the next year. When I see Philip standing in my doorway, my stomach flips in delight for more than one reason. The proposed budget is more ambitious this year because I'm counting on him to go to bat for me with the management committee. I gesture toward my guest chair. "Have a seat."

Philip shakes his head. "No time. Sorry. Do you have plans tonight?"

I lean my elbows on my desk and look at him from under my eyelashes. "What did you have in mind?"

"I thought maybe we could get some dinner."

"Sounds good. We can stay in if you want." I haven't seen him outside of work in a week and am less interested in dinner than I am in dessert.

"There's a new Greek restaurant near here I've been wanting to try. You game?"

Greek food would not make my top five list of favorite cuisines, but I'm just happy to spend time with him. "Greek works for me," I say happily.

Philip nods. With one foot out the door, he says, "I'll come by and get you later. Around six thirty?"

"Perfect." I glance at the draft budget on my computer screen. "Do you have a minute to—?" I swivel my chair back around to complete my question, but he's already gone.

A few hours later, I'm sitting across from Philip in the brightly lit rear room of Avra Restaurant. I'm certain Philip is mistaken about it being new, but I don't bother to say anything. The décor of the restaurant is understated but elegant—circular tables with white tablecloths crowd the room. Our table is so close to the couple next to us, it almost feels like we're on a double date. I chew my lip as I study the menu, but when I sense Philip's gaze on me, I slowly raise my head. "What are you looking at?" I flirt.

His expression is grim and as I watch his hand fiddle with his napkin, my heart pumps one beat faster. "What's wrong?"

Philip sighs. "I was going to wait until after dinner to do this."

"Do what?"

"We need to talk."

Trying to disguise the tremors in my heart, I say in a light voice, "That sounds ominous."

Philip doesn't say anything as he casts his eyes toward his bread plate, but then he looks up at me and opens his mouth. "Here's the thing—"

"Are you two ready to order?" the waitress asks in a cheery voice.

Philip clears his throat and points to me. "You first."

I say, "I'll have the salmon," even though my appetite has disappeared, and I'm fairly certain it won't return until after I hear what Philip has to say.

"And I'll have the *kota scharas*." He turns to me with his lips turned up. "Fancy way of saying the free-range chicken."

Philip hands the waitress his menu.

I give her mine as well and take a deep breath before facing Philip. "You were saying?"

"I'm not sure how to say this." He averts eye contact but not before I detect sadness in his eyes.

"Spit it out," I say a little louder than intended. Lawyers are usually better at bottom-lining information, and his reluctance to get to the point suggests he's about to tell me I lost a multimillion-dollar litigation. I check to see if the couple at the table next to us heard me, but thankfully, they seem engrossed in their own conversation.

"You're a spitfire, Mags."

"Well, you're making me nervous." With shaky hands, I spread butter on a roll and take a small bite.

"My wife and I have decided to suspend divorce proceedings." His thick eyebrows draw together while he stares at me, awaiting my reaction.

I know my mouth is hanging open, but I can't bring myself to close it. "Oh."

"I just dropped a bomb on you and you say, 'Oh?' Care to elaborate on what you're thinking?"

"I'm waiting for you to go into further details," I say calmly. I swallow hard in an attempt to dislodge the piece of bread, which feels like it's stuck in my esophagus.

"I can't begin to tell you how sorry I am to do this to you. You deserve so much better. I shouldn't have gotten involved with you." He shakes his head.

"But you did," I whisper. I remember the time I was out for drinks with Amanda and the couple next to us was clearly on a first date. It played out like a train wreck when the girl received a phone call and rushed out of the bar due to a "family emergency." Assuming it was really a bail-out call from a friend, Amanda and I had a chuckle at the poor guy's expense. As I glance at the couple next to me again, I wonder if they're finding my public breakup equally humorous. *Karma's a bitch.*

"I know," he says softly. "I should've been more careful. Sheila, my wife, and I spent some time together last week and have decided to give it another go. We have a history, you know? We have two children," he says, as if feeling the need to justify his decision.

I am speechless—literally speechless—as I cannot think of a single thing to say to him. I want to be angry, but he seems sincerely apologetic, and I know in my gut it pains him to hurt me. "It's okay," I say softly.

I'm taking being dumped very well, which is lucky for Philip. I must be in the denial stage of grief. I hope for Philip's sake he is no longer sitting across from me when I reach the anger stage.

"It's not okay. I shouldn't have pursued you until my divorce was final."

"I think I might have pursued you," I say and release a self-deprecating chuckle at my own foolishness.

Philip crinkles his forehead. "What do you mean?"

"I wasted no time in flirting with you when I found out you

were separated. It didn't even cross my mind that separated and divorced are not synonymous. At almost forty years old, I should know better." I release a deep breath.

Philip locks eyes with me. "Mags, I want you to know I didn't plan this. I *need* you to know I wasn't using my separated status to get you in bed under false pretenses. I thought my marriage was over."

"So what changed?" The answer won't make things different, but I'm genuinely curious.

Philip rubs his eyes. "We stopped talking—Sheila and me. Everything was about the kids. We stopped laughing—unless it was about the kids. Our connection tempered until it eventually burnt out. Even the sex was perfunctory."

I cough. I definitely do not want to hear about his sex life with his wife.

"Sorry," he says. "After talking this weekend, we agree it might be worth putting as much effort into our marriage as we have other aspects of our lives, like our careers and our children."

"And you want to try again?" I haven't a clue why I'm asking since I already know the answer.

He nods. "Relationships aren't easy, and marriage is the mother of all relationships. It's remarkably easy to give up. Working on it takes much more effort. But for the sake of our children, we both want to try."

I cock an eyebrow. "For the sake of your children? What do *you* want?" My ego wants him to say he's choosing his wife over me solely for the sake of his children, and I hate myself for it.

"I wish we lived in Utah so I could practice bigamy." He smiles at me sheepishly.

I choke out a laugh. "Sorry, buddy."

"I do love my wife. But you're pretty awesome, Maggie."

"Thanks," I say, but I don't believe him.

The air is silent as our waitress brings over our entrees.

"And don't worry about work. I promise things won't be awkward," he says.

My heart stops. I *really* like my job, but I can't possibly stay there now. I hear Philip's voice talking to me, something about what a talented marketing manager I am and not wanting to lose me, but I'm only half listening. I'm too busy berating my failure to think things through before jumping into bed with a man who is not only technically still married but also technically my boss. I wince inwardly as I mentally add "update my resume" to my to-do list.

* * *

"Picture him dancing to Abba in his tighty-whities," Jodie suggests.

I put my phone on speaker and place it on my nightstand. Chuckling, I say, "Keep going." After struggling through the rest of dinner with Philip, pretending to be okay with being friends and colleagues (at least for the time being), I am finally at home with most of my meal in a doggie bag in my refrigerator. I have no desire to engage in the clichéd behavior of most women who have been dumped—namely pigging out on ice cream while watching cheesy movies. And I also don't want to go to bed and stare at the ceiling counting down the days until my fortieth birthday.

"How about, he wipes his ass with his bare hands?"

"Jodie, that's gross even for you." Back in college, whenever one of us liked a guy who didn't return our feelings or blew us off after a hook-up, we would visualize him in an exceptionally negative light to completely and irrevocably turn us off. Past examples include sitting on the toilet bowl attempting to push through a stubborn case of constipation and floating through space dressed in pink feety pajamas, but Jodie has reached a whole new level today.

"Did it work though? Does picturing Philip with his own shit between his fingers make you feel all tingly down there?"

I clutch my stomach. "Ugh. Not quite." Laughing, I say, "Thanks."

Her voice turns serious. "You gonna be okay?"

I nod as if she can see me. "I think so. I feel more stupid than anything else."

"Why?"

"For thinking it would be so easy to meet someone after breaking up with Doug. He was my most serious relationship, and it took me almost thirty-six years to meet him."

"Would've been awesome if it worked out though," Jodie says.

"What if it takes me another thirty-six years to find someone else?" I whine.

"It won't," Jodie says assuredly.

"How do you know?"

"Because you can't count the first seventeen years of your life when you're under your parents' roof and barely have any free will to make decisions. With that logic, it only took you twenty years to meet Doug."

"Waiting another twenty years isn't much better," I say glumly.

Jodie sighs. "We've been friends since college, and you've never had much trouble getting back on the saddle after a failed relationship. You always found a new boyfriend quickly and without much effort. Don't recreate history now as a way to support your pity party."

To an outside observer, it's true I've had a lot of boyfriends. But, as Jodie knows better than most, the majority of the relationships didn't last beyond the honeymoon stages of the initial six months. Within the first year, we split either because he was bored, I wasn't feeling it, or, in the best cases, a mutual conclusion was drawn that we were not compatible for the long haul. Doug was the first one who really stuck, and Jodie knows this. "Nice bedside manner, bitch."

"I hit my peak with the doody visual. What do you want from me?"

I giggle. "I love you, Jodie."

"Love you too, Magpie. Nighty night."

"Sweet dreams," I say before hanging up the phone and spooning my pillow. I close my eyes, but I'm not tired enough to fall asleep. Without moving from the fetal position, I reach over to my nightstand, grab my remote control, and aim it at the television. I'm in luck as Logo TV is having a *Buffy the Vampire Slayer* marathon. Doug and I planned to watch at least one season on DVD on my birthday weekend, but we broke up instead. I sit up and lean against my headboard.

It's the Thanksgiving episode from the fourth season. I chuckle when Anya, one of my favorite characters, describes Thanksgiving as "a ritual sacrifice. With pie." Riveted to my television set for the next three hours with Buffy, Zander, Willow, and the rest of the "Scooby Gang" as they fight evil, I realize it never would have worked out with Philip. Television is essential to my life, and Philip doesn't enjoy it. Maybe I always knew but was blinded by the butterflies and our mutual appreciation for sex.

After confirming there will be another *Buffy the Vampire Slayer* marathon the following night, I turn off the television and fall asleep with dreams of a man who shares my love of both sex *and* television.

*   *   *

The next morning, when I wake up to puffy eyes and weary bones from lack of sleep, I am tempted to call out sick from work. Philip will either keep his distance to give us time to regroup, or he will make it a point to check up and make sure I'm okay. It's a crapshoot, and I don't want to take the risk. Even if Philip chooses to give me space or simply shares my desire to avoid face-to-face contact for the time being, rarely a day goes by when a business issue doesn't require us to communicate. I have a feeling maintaining a working relationship with him will be difficult considering I've seen him naked and have intimate knowledge of his manscaping habits.

Even though it's November, and I have eight remaining vacation days I must take before the end of the year or lose them forever, I suck it up and get ready for work. If I don't go in, Philip will assume it's because of what went down the night before. He's not so egotistical to take pleasure in my inability to cope, but for the sake of pride, I need to put on a good show. So, after I shower, I put on my cheeriest outfit—a burnt orange wrap dress and my favorite knee-high brown leather boots—and plant a smile on my face. Fake it till you make it. And if all else fails, sneak out of the office early.

* * *

I quietly enter Melanie's office and close the door behind me. She's on the phone but motions for me to take a seat. Relaxing in her guest chair, I flip through the pages of the Zagat guide she leaves on her desk. Avra Restaurant received a food rating of twenty-five—an exceptionally good score—but since I swallowed most of my food the night before without actually tasting it, I have no idea if I agree. I put the book down and observe Melanie as she holds the phone in the crook of her neck while twirling her red locks. She smiles at me and holds up a free finger.

When she finishes her conversation, she hangs up the phone and grins at me. "What's up, girlie?"

"Philip is getting back together with his wife."

Melanie's smile disappears. "Oh."

"The first word out of my mouth too."

She stands up and comes over to my chair. "You okay?"

Standing up to give her a hug, I say, "I'll be fine. But if you know anyone on the prowl for a marketing manager, let me know."

"He can't make you quit. Unless he wants to be sued for sexual harassment." Melanie turns away from me and reaches for a law book on her shelf.

I tap her on the back. "Don't get carried away. He's not firing me. In fact, he wants me to continue to work here."

Melanie releases a sigh and sits back at her desk. Clapping her hands together, she says, "Oh, goodie. I can't bear the thought of this place without you."

I chew my lip. "I think I should search for a new job anyway."

Melanie frowns. "Why?" Motioning towards my chair, she says, "Sit. Talk to me."

Sitting down, I say, "I feel dirty now. It's like a primetime television show. Lowly member of the staff screws a partner."

"You're not a lowly staff member." She shakes her head. "This is all my fault."

"How is it your fault?"

"I told you he was available, and I encouraged you to pursue him." I open my mouth to protest, but she continues. "I should have been more levelheaded. Separated does not mean divorced. I should have seen this coming and warned you."

Shaking my head vigorously, I argue, "It's not your fault. Even if you had warned me about the possibility of him getting back together with his wife, I might not have listened to you."

Melanie frowns. "I'm so sorry, Mags."

"It is what it is." I lift myself off of the chair and walk toward her door. Turning to face her, I say, "I was afraid he'd mention it before I had a chance to fill you in."

"Lunch?"

I nod. "Yeah, and then I think I'll go home early. There's a *Buffy the Vampire Slayer* marathon on Logo TV."

"Team Angel," she says.

"Team Spike," I counter.

Tut-tutting me, she says, "And that, my dear, might be your problem with men. Angel is the better man. Sure Spike has hidden depth, and he's smoking hot, but Angel is solid. What you see is what you get."

"Except when he was evil. You're forgetting the second season."

"And Spike didn't get good until they put a chip in his head."

Laughing, I say, "We'll agree to disagree, okay?"

"Deal. But let's revisit this conversation next year." She taps a finger to her chin. "You should go indoor rock climbing with me at Chelsea Piers after work."

I cringe. "Not a chance."

"You said you wanted to take a break from Doug to find out what made you happy. How are you going to figure it out if you don't try anything new?"

"I was referring to my love life. And I have tried something new—Philip."

Melanie rolls her eyes. "I think it will be good for you."

"I can barely walk without falling." I picture my broken and bleeding body at the foot of a rock wall.

"You'll be in a harness and you'll have supervision. I reserved an open climb with two friends from my runners' group and there's room for one more person. Don't be a wimp, Piper. Do it."

I'm not convinced rock climbing is a wise idea, but Melanie's right that I've been stuck in a work, television watching, cocktails, and repeat routine for too long. Maybe trying something new will be good for me.

* * *

This was a bad idea. My breath is ragged as I grip a green climbing hold and lift a foot to the next one. Even though I'm harnessed in, I don't look down. I'm not afraid of heights when I'm a passenger in a plane or theme park ride, and I've voluntarily climbed to the top of the Empire State Building and looked out the window, but this is different. I'm both the passenger and the ride, and how high I go and how far I fall is in my own hands.

"You can do it, Maggie," Melanie calls from the ground only ten feet beneath me. I've only made it to three climbing holds so far.

Holding onto the climbing rope, the Rock Wall instructor says, "Slow and steady."

I inhale deeply and focus on getting to the next green hold even though the other colors are distracting. My thighs burn and as a bead of sweat drops down my back, I'm grateful I smothered my hands in climbing chalk or I'd lose my grip. I picture my mother cheering me on as I get to the next hold. Then I visualize Jodie stomping her feet and whistling through her teeth as I reach the next one. I can almost hear Cheryl and the kids clapping as I climb higher. My brain assigns my next cheerleader and I freeze in place.

"You okay up there?" the instructor asks.

Doug's face beams with pride and confidence. He says, "Don't give up, Magpie."

With an audible grunt, I take one more step. My body shakes in the workout clothes I borrowed from Melanie and I cautiously look over my shoulder. Afraid to press my luck, I say, "I'm ready to come down now."

* * *

"You were a rock star," Melanie says an hour later over dinner and beers at The Half King, a pub not far from the pier. Her running buddies opted to go straight home.

"More like a rock star's roadie," I joke before taking a bite of my slider.

"They do all the hard work anyway. Did you like it?"

I take a sip of beer while considering her question. I place my pilsner glass on the square faded-wood table and say, "I'm so glad you made me do it."

Melanie beams at me. "I knew you'd love it."

"I said I'm glad I did it. I never said I loved it." In response to Melanie's confused expression, I say, "I'm proud of myself for doing something that scared me even though I feared for my life the entire time." I don't tell her I couldn't have done it without the imagined positive reinforcement provided by my family, friends, and Doug.

"Would you do it again?"

"I might." I would be almost as afraid the second time around, but the sense of accomplishment I feel in this moment is something I want to experience again.

"Awesome. Maybe we can do something else next time. Like the flying trapeze or..." She twists her mouth in thought until her eyes open wide. "Circus lessons. We can learn silks, trapeze, rope—"

"Whoa there lady," I say as I nearly choke on my beer. "Baby steps."

"I suppose I got carried away." Melanie concedes.

I shake my head at her in amusement and take another sip from my glass. Beer never tasted so good.

* * *

As I reach down for another piece of cheddar cheese, my mom calls out, "Don't go crazy on the appetizers or you won't have room left for the main course." I hesitate for a second and then strike a bargain with myself—one more cube of cheese, then I'll sit tight until dinner is ready. I toss the cheese in my mouth and fall back on the couch with a satisfied smile as Cheryl comes out of the kitchen with a platter of pigs in a blanket and a dish of spicy brown mustard.

I groan. "Seriously? How am I supposed to save myself for dinner when you set all of my favorite snacks in front of me?"

"Willpower." Cheryl winks.

With a jumbo pitted black olive on each of her fingers, Cady pokes my leg and asks, "What's willpowow?"

I move the bowl of olives farther away from her. "Something Aunt Maggie doesn't have when it comes to food." I kiss the top of her head before grabbing a mini hotdog and dipping it into the mustard.

"It's a good thing you have a fast metabolism," Aunt Helen says from her spot on the couch. She eyeballs me from head to toe. "Hopefully it won't change once you turn forty. Last thing a single girl your age needs is extra weight."

"I'll take your advice under advisement, Aunt Helen." I recall with pride my recent calorie-burning, rock-climbing adventure and pop another olive in my mouth.

My mom approaches me and wraps me in a tight embrace. "How's my Maggie?"

"I'm good," I say, squeezing her back. "Excited to pig out."

"Come see the sweet potato pie." She takes my hand and leads me to the counter. As she removes the aluminum foil, she says, "Ta da!" Sweet potato pie is absolutely my favorite side dish ever, and my mouth salivates at the sight of the casserole bowl filled with candied yams covered with marshmallows.

Walking by, Cheryl jabs me in the side. "I convinced her to use an extra half bag of marshmallows in your honor."

"Consolation prize for being dumped?" I mumble.

Cheryl rolls her eyes. "Enough with the pity party."

Of all my friends and family members, Cheryl is the least sympathetic about Philip getting back together with his wife. She urged me to focus less on my own disappointment and more on a marriage being saved and two less children growing up in a broken home.

I know she's right, but I'm hurt she gave me the cold shoulder rather than a shoulder to cry on. Dropping the subject, I say, "Bummer Jim isn't here. But at least I don't have to fight him for a drumstick."

"Daddy not here," Michael says, wrapping his chubby arms around Cheryl's legs.

Bending down to hug him, Cheryl says, "Daddy went to Grandma and Grandpa's house this year. You'll see him tomorrow."

"Miss Daddy," he says, rubbing his eyes.

"Oh, I know, sweetheart. We'll call him after dinner, okay?" Patting him on the bum, Cheryl says, "Be a good boy and ask Nana if she wants red or white wine."

Michael toddles away with his ratty teddy bear clutched to his chest.

"What's up with Jim going to his parents' house?" I ask Cheryl.

"What, he doesn't have a right to see his own parents on Thanksgiving?" she asks crossly.

Surprised at being snapped at, I calmly respond, "Of course he does. But don't you guys usually alternate Thanksgiving with Chanukah?"

"Not this year," she says curtly as Michael pokes her leg. Bending down to him, she asks, "What, sweetie?"

"Nana wants white wine."

Cheryl beams at her youngest child. "Good boy. Now go play with your sister until dinner, okay?"

"Aunt Maggie play with me?"

"Can you read to him or something?" Cheryl asks.

Swooping him up in my arms, I say, "Can't think of anything I'd like better." My gorgeous nephew is currently far better company than his mommy. I carry him into the living room, place him on the floor, and immediately start tickling his pudgy belly. He titters uncontrollably and squirms under my touch. Finally, he brings his short legs towards his tummy, obstructing my access. His body still quaking, he says, "Stop, Aunt Maggie."

"Okay, okay." I remove my hands before blowing a raspberry on his stomach. Only I'm horrible at giving raspberries, and the sound is barely audible to the human ear and sounds nothing like a fart.

Leaning her body against my back, Cady says, "Uncle Doug does it bettow."

At the sound of his name, I feel an ache in my gut. Not wanting the kids to sense my discomfort, I say, "Is that so?" before pulling Cady over my shoulder and blowing on her stomach too.

Thirty minutes later, plates are being passed around the table, turkey has been cut for the kiddies, and I'm on my second serving of sweet potato pie when Cady pounds her sippy cup on the table. "I have a 'nouncement," she says.

"What kind of announcement, honey?" my mom asks.

"It's time to go wound the table and say what we aw thankful fow."

I surreptitiously roll my eyes and kick Cheryl under the table. We implemented the tradition when we were little and our moms insisted we continue long after we outgrew it.

"Terrific idea, Cady," Aunt Helen says. "How about you go first?"

Cady smiles, showing a gap where one of her front teeth used to be. "I'm thankful fow Mommy and Daddy, Aunt Maggie, and cwanbewy sauce."

My heart swells with love. Cady and her brother are at the very top of my own grateful list.

"Great job, Cady. But what about Nana Helen, Aunt Doris, and your brother?" Cheryl prods.

"I wasn't finished yet," Cady says as her lower lip protrudes into a pout. "I'm also thankful fow my baby bwotho Michael, Nana Helen, Aunt Dawis, and *Blue's Clues*."

Cady beams with pride as we all offer a round of applause. "Michael is next," she says to her brother.

As all eyes focus on Michael, his face drains of color, a tear lodges in the corner of his eye, and he wails, "Don't wanna."

Holding him to her, Cheryl kisses his head. "You don't have to." As if by magic, the color returns to his face, and he continues to pick at his turkey as if nothing happened. I stifle a giggle.

"I'll go," says Aunt Helen. "I'm thankful for my family, especially my lovely grandkids, and my health." She points at my mother. "Your turn, Doris."

With a straight face, my mom says, "I'm thankful for my mahjong game."

I burst out laughing. My mom cracks me up.

Helen shakes her head in annoyance. "Doris. Be serious." Then she scowls at me as if it's my fault.

"I'm thankful for the love of my wonderful family, and I'm grateful we can all spend another Thanksgiving together. I'm also thankful I didn't dry out the turkey, and last but not least, I am thankful for my mahjong game." She sticks her tongue out at Aunt Helen. Motioning to me with her head, she says, "Your turn, Magpie."

Folding my hands on my lap, I say, "I have a lot to be thankful for. Firstly, I'm thankful for my brilliant and gorgeous niece and nephew." I blow a kiss at Cady who catches it with her hand and holds it to her heart like I taught her. "I'm also thankful for the continued health of my mother." I smile at her across the table and she mouths, "I love you." I continue, "And I'm thankful for the support and encouragement of my friends." I take a deep breath as if trying to swallow enough nerve to say the rest out loud. "And I'm thankful for the time I'm taking to learn about myself and what makes me happy. I'm getting to know myself better with each and every day. I might make mistakes, but hopefully they will lead me in the right direction."

The table falls silent as my family stares at me. My annual proclamations usually include being thankful for my young-looking genes, and I'm sure I've surprised them with the depth of my pronouncements this year. I slide down in my chair as I await their reaction.

With a gleam in her eye, my mom says, "Beautiful sentiment, Maggie."

Aunt Helen nods. "That was very heartfelt. You're finally growing up. With any luck, you'll make your mom a grandmother soon."

"Let's get her married first," my mom says with a wink.

"In her case, I think God would understand if she did things out of order," Aunt Helen says.

Cheryl drops her napkin on her plate. "Not everyone's happiness revolves around getting married and having children," she says.

Aunt Helen waves her hand in dismissal. "Fine. Your turn, dear."

Cheryl pushes her seat back and stands up. "I'm thankful for you," she says kissing Cady on both cheeks. "And I'm thankful for you." She ruffles Michael's hair until he laughs. Then she walks her dirty dishes to the kitchen without another word.

My mom and Aunt Helen seem none the wiser, but I know something is up with Cheryl. I remember standing outside her math class my freshman year in high school the day I got my period for the first time. My friends all assumed I began menstruating a year earlier since that's what I told them, and I didn't want to confide in the school nurse out of fear she would give me an old-fashioned sanitary napkin with a belt. Instead, I told Cheryl, who cut her next class to drive me home. She readily embraced the role of supportive older sister, yet she never relied on me in return. Years later, not much has changed. I want to be there for her like she has always been there for me, but I need to find a way to broach the subject without alienating her.

Sitting down again, Cheryl says, "Who's ready for some pie?"

"I hope we have enough this year," I joke. The year before, Doug brought a pie in every flavor imaginable—apple, cherry, pecan, pumpkin, peach, and chocolate cream—so each of us could have our favorites. "Doug and I were eating leftover pie through New Year's Day last year. We found bits of crust and fruit filling in bed every time we changed the sheets for a month." I smile at the memory until I notice my entire family staring at me. All except Cady, who is having too much fun mashing her leftover sweet potato pie with a fork, and Michael, who appears to be on the brink of falling asleep. "What?"

My mother clears her throat. "Nothing."

Cheryl shrugs. "You've got me."

"Such a shame," Aunt Helen mutters.

I tap my fingertip to the table and sigh heavily. Standing up to bring my empty plate to the sink, I say, "I'm happy with where I am in my life." For now. "Don't go making me feel bad or second guess myself now."

From behind me, I hear Aunt Helen say assuredly, "If you were so happy, we wouldn't be able to."

Later, Cheryl gives me a ride to the train station in her Ford Expedition. I gaze out my window as we drive through the historic center of downtown Peekskill and say, "Did I tell you I tried indoor rock climbing last week?"

Cheryl whips her head in my direction before quickly turning her attention back to the road. "Who replaced my couch-potato cousin with the courageous daredevil in my passenger seat?"

"Ha ha. Melanie coaxed me to step outside of my comfort

zone. She thought it would be a healthy change. And if I do it more often, it might offset the imminent slowing of my metabolism."

"I'll be sure to tell my mom," she says with a smirk.

While wondering how I can segue the conversation to Cheryl's marriage, I stare at the beautiful buttery yellow, amber orange, and burgundy red autumn leaf that has attached itself to my window. Nothing comes to mind so I just say it. "Is everything all right with you and Jim?"

Cheryl peers through her rearview mirror at her sleeping children. "Not now, Mags," she says pulling into the train station.

"When?"

She parks the car and glances at the time on her dashboard. "This clock is three minutes early. You need to run if you're going to catch your train."

I sigh dejectedly and open the door. "Call me?"

She nods. "Get home safe."

"You too." I kiss her on the cheek and take one last look at the napping kids. Then I step out of the car and hoof it up the stairs to the platform. It's only after I'm waiting a good five minutes, I realize Cheryl lied about her clock being early.

* * *

I hastily reach for my office phone and tap the first two numbers of Philip's extension. After months of brainstorming, we finally chose the firm's new tagline—Small Firm: Big Results. My next assignment is overseeing the creation of a new logo. We will eventually employ a logo design company, but first I want to share my ideas with Philip. I don't really want to discuss *anything* with Philip, but since doing so is part of my job description, I don't have a choice. I dial the last two numbers.

Lila, Philip's assistant, picks up. "Hi, Maggie."

I wonder if she knows I used to have sex with her boss. "Hi there. Is he around?"

"One second. I'll check."

I nervously tap my fingers along the laminate surface of my desk while I wait.

"Hey there," Philip says, a little too cheerfully.

I take a deep inhale. "I wondered if you had time to discuss concepts for the new logo." Over the past month, we conducted most of our back and forth regarding the tagline via email, and, fortunately, he was on vacation—presumably with the family—for the last business development meeting. Since our offices are on different floors, I rarely see him, but I fear we won't be able to brainstorm the firm's new logo without meeting face to face.

"Sure. Come around."

"Will do," I say, before placing the phone back on the receiver. My vanity prevents me from not caring about my appearance, so I run a brush through my hair and apply lip gloss. Grabbing my legal pad and a folder of logo examples I printed from Shutterstock, I head upstairs to Philip's corner office.

When I gently tap my knuckles against his open door, I'm surprised to see Brendan, a first-year associate, already sitting in one of his visitor chairs.

Philip waves me in, and when I sit down in his other chair, I glance questioningly at Brendan. "If this is a bad time, I can come back."

"Not a bad time. Do you know Brendan?" Philip says.

"Of course." To Brendan, I say, "Hi."

Brendan, a chubby, baby-faced guy in his mid-twenties, acknowledges me with a nod.

Philip leans his elbows on the desk. "I thought Brendan could help you with the logo."

I stare blankly at Philip, waiting for further information, but none comes. The room is so quiet you can almost hear the dust swirling around. To break the silence, I turn to Brendan. "Are you an artist?" Maybe the firm is trying to avoid outsourcing the work.

"I can draw stick figures. Does that count?"

Philip and Brendan whoop it up while I attempt to lose my "deer in the headlights" expression. I knew the meeting would be uncomfortable for personal reasons, but I fully expected to maintain my professionalism and am not pleased with the Bambi impression I'm currently perfecting. I will myself to take back control. "I'm thrilled to have you on board, Brendan. How can you help?"

Focusing his gaze on Brendan, Philip says, "Brendan is doing his rotation through the intellectual property group. The partners thought working with you on the logo would be good training."

Before I can stop myself, I ask, "Which partners?" How partners make decisions is none of my business, but I want to see how Philip talks himself out of this one. I'm positive the suggestion to delegate the assignment to Brendan under the guise of training was his and his alone.

Philip gives me a quick glance. "The IP partners." He turns back to Brendan. "You can review the search reports with any of the senior associates."

We will have to confirm through trademark searches that any design we want is not confusingly similar to an existing image, but Philip is skipping the first phase of the project entirely. "Terrific," I say. "But first we need to come up with a concept." It's obvious the desire to maintain distance from each other is mutual, but I'm afraid it won't be as easy to avoid as Philip seems to think.

Philip opens his mouth to speak, but no sound comes out. He scratches his Van Dyke beard and meets my eyes.

I wonder if the tension in the room is obvious to Brendan. Through the corner of my eyes, I see him shifting his gaze from Philip to me.

I say, "How about I—" at the same time Philip says, "Why don't you—"

After a nervous chuckle, I say, "You first."

"I assume you have some ideas in there," he says, pointing at the manila folder on my lap. "I trust you. Why don't you show your favorites to the design company and see what they come up with? You can email the results to me, and if I like them, we'll order searches. If I don't, we'll start over."

This is exactly what I was going to suggest, and I nod in Philip's direction.

Philip lets out a deep exhale. "So, we're good?"

"We're good." Rising from the chair, I tuck the folder under my arm. To Brendan, I say, "I'll let you know when I have designs to search."

Without saying anything to Philip, I force myself to assume a normal gait as I walk out of his office and down the internal stairs. When I'm back in my own quarters and safely out of sight, I throw myself in my chair and intake what feels like the first breath of oxygen I've inhaled in days.

December

"The doctor is so guilty. Never trust a ginger!" I scream at my television set while watching the latest episode of *Castle*. I twirl a strand of my own strawberry blond hair with one hand while shoveling microwave popcorn into my mouth with the other. After a particularly busy day at work followed by two hours scouring LinkedIn for possible connections in my job search, I am now sprawled across my couch eating a late, low-maintenance, not-too-nutritious dinner. As the episode moves along, I suspect my initial guess misses the mark. With only burnt kernels of corn left in the bag, I have nothing to chew on except my fingernails as I contemplate the identity of the guilty party. And then it dawns on me. I know who did it. "It's 3XK. He's alive. He's alive!" I place the empty bag of popcorn on my coffee table and stand up at the precise moment Castle and Detective Beckett collectively realize Jerry Tyson, a.k.a. major bad guy "3XK," is alive.

Feeling victorious for solving the crime before it was revealed on screen, I chant, "Be Aggressive. B-E Aggressive." I kick my legs up in a classic cheerleading move, and then in my mind's eye, I see him—Doug—about a year into our relationship, doing the spinning running-man dance after deciphering the twist in *Fight Club* before me. We were always playfully competitive with each other, and that day, even as I pouted in typical sore-loser mode, I had to hold my stomach after roaring so hard watching him dance.

I stop mid-cheer and begin to cry. After pulling my old, stuffed Snoopy doll from the top of my closet, I crawl into bed and weep until Snoopy is soaked with my tears.

*   *   *

Hearing the familiar cackle of laughter, I glance at Jodie across the rectangular bar at Butterfield 8 in White Plains. Her cheeks rosy from drinking multiple glasses of red wine, she's twirling a curly tendril of hair around her finger and in stitches over whatever some guy with a goatee is whispering in her ear. I've never seen him before and wonder if they work together at the bank where Jodie is employed as a financial analyst. It hardly feels like over twenty years since the day I walked into our dorm room for the first time and found her kneeling by the tiny closet we would share, attempting to find space for her not-so-tiny collection of Keds in every color of the rainbow. I still can't believe the girl who taught me how to do a funnel is forty years old, divorced, and the mother of two children. As if sensing me watching her, Jodie turns away from the guy, catches my eye across the room and winks. I wave but her attention is once again stolen by the dude with the goatee. If I didn't know better, I would assume they were dating, or at least contemplating it.

From her leather upholstered seat at the bar, Amanda says, "See anyone interesting?"

Jodie warned me there wouldn't be many eligible bachelors in attendance, but I don't mind. I'm in the mood for a no-pressure kind of night—yummy drinks with friends—nothing more, nothing less. Without even scoping out the attendees, I say, "Nope," and take a sip of my drink.

"You didn't even look."

Cocking an eyebrow, I say, "What about you? See anyone *you* like?"

Instead of answering me, Amanda puts her drink on the dark wood bar and stands up. "I've gotta use the bathroom."

With both amusement and relief, I glance over my shoulder and watch her saunter through the crowded restaurant until her long, wavy brown hair is out of sight before turning back around. I don't want to talk about dating tonight, and a surefire way to motivate Amanda to change the subject is to turn the tables and ask about her own dating situation. And since I haven't been out with anyone since Philip or made any effort to put myself out there, I have nothing worthwhile to share. The one thing I can add to the conversation is the one thing I'm not ready to admit out loud—I really miss Doug.

Since the night I remembered a boastful Doug dancing in my living room, memories of him haunt my every waking moment. But do I truly miss Doug, or is this newborn ache of losing him simply my heart's reaction to being alone and my fear of staying that way? Before I can continue the self-analysis I've been conducting for the past week whenever I'm not otherwise occupied, one of Jodie's friends from high school summons everyone to a table in the back for dinner, offering a temporary reprieve from flashbacks of Doug.

*   *   *

The next morning, the birthday girl insists on making chocolate chip pancakes for Amanda and me, even though I told her I'd be equally happy with a bowl of cereal. "You used to love my pancakes," Jodie says with a frown.

"I still do. But it's your birthday, and you deserve the day off. Especially since your kids are with their dad. Don't you want to take it easy?" Offering to make breakfast for Jodie would be a nice gesture, but I don't say anything. While I can fry a mean egg, Jodie can only stomach them as a hidden ingredient—not the main dish— and French toast and pancakes aren't on the list of things I know how to make. I'm also pretty cozy sitting at Jodie's kitchen table in my pajamas drinking a cup of Gevalia coffee. I curse myself for being lazy, but I don't get up.

Removing flour and a bag of Nestlé Toll House morsels from her cabinet, Jodie says, "I enjoy preparing food for others. It relaxes me." Unlike me, Jodie is already showered and her wet hair is held back from her face with a black cotton headband.

"Then go for it. I don't want to get between you and your

favorite mode of relaxation. And besides, I love your cooking."

Jodie beams. "That's more like it. For a minute there, I thought you were suggesting I no longer possessed the stamina to make you breakfast."

I shake my head. "Not even. You won't be hearing any forty jokes from me." I'm way too sensitive about the subject, and the age difference between the two of us is not big enough for me to feel comfortable poking fun.

Amanda, who was still sleeping when I got out of bed, walks into the kitchen in the yoga pants and t-shirt she wore to bed. With a DVD in her right hand, she joins me at the table. "Me neither," she says. "But I did bring the perfect movie for the occasion."

"Yeah? What movie?" Jodie asks.

Smiling, Amanda holds up the DVD with Paul Rudd and Leslie Mann on the cover. *This is 40.*

My stomach plummets, and I immediately respond, "No way."

Her eyebrows squishing together, Amanda says, "Why?"

"Because it will make me feel worse about myself than I already do."

"I had no idea you felt bad about yourself," Jodie says. Her lips twitching, she adds, "If you must know, I always thought you were a bit conceited."

I grab the first non-breakable item I can find—a napkin—crumple it and toss it at her.

Laughing, Jodie ducks and barely evades being hit by the flying napkin.

Amanda ignores our antics. "Why would watching *This is 40* make you feel bad about yourself? It's supposedly hilarious and totally relatable."

"Exactly. I'm almost forty, and it's not at all relatable to me. Not even close," I say assuredly.

"What's the film about?" Jodie asks. "Not that it matters if it stars Paul Rudd. What a cutie."

"Paul Rudd and Leslie Mann play a married couple who are both turning forty, and it's a comedy about how their relationship has changed since they've gotten older, had kids, and are approaching middle age. Too depressing."

"How is it depressing?" Amanda asks.

"Because it serves to remind me how backwards I am. My life is nothing like that." I look down at myself. "This is thirty-nine?"

Placing a plate of pancakes on the table, Jodie says, "I don't want to watch it either. I might have children, but I don't have an adorable husband anymore. As a forty-year-old divorcée, this is not the movie for me right now."

Amanda rolls her eyes. "Sorry I suggested it."

Perking up, I say, "But speaking of adorable, time to spill about the guy at the bar last night. Goatee man?"

Jodie puts down her coffee cup and raises an eyebrow. "Charles?"

I cut into a piece of pancake and nod. "You completely ignored my note last night." After observing Jodie giggle nonstop at Charles's jokes all through dinner, I wrote "Who is this dude?" on a napkin and slipped it across the table to her. She never wrote back, and I forgot to follow through at the end of the night.

"He's a new friend," Jodie says nonchalantly.

"How did you meet?" Amanda asks, motioning toward the container of Aunt Jemima. "Can you please pass the syrup?"

Jodie slides the syrup across the table. "I met him at the supermarket. Olivia pulled a box of cereal from the middle of the shelf, causing about twenty other boxes to tumble down with it, and Charles helped clean up my daughter's mess." A flush creeps across Jodie's cheeks.

"You like him," I tease.

Jodie blushes. "He's a nice guy. Most men would have run away from the commotion, but he stopped to help the lady with the troublemaking kid." As the rising sun shines through the window, she gets up and closes the shade.

I point at her and repeat. "You *like* him. *Jodie and Charles sitting in a tree,*" I sing.

Amanda jabs me in the elbow. "Leave her alone."

"Ouch," I say, sliding my chair out of touching distance from Amanda. "I'm giving it to her the way she always gave it to me when I started liking a guy. You get what you give."

Sitting down again, Jodie says, "In any event, when I casually brought up my divorced status in conversation, he asked for my number, so I asked him to come last night. We haven't been on an official date yet."

"Yet is the operative word," Amanda says.

Smiling, I agree. "I'm so happy for you." This is the first time Jodie has shown any interest in dating since separating from her ex, despite my frequent prodding. I was beginning to wonder if she was giving up on men completely.

Waving her hand in dismissal, Jodie says, "Let's not get too excited. Like I said, we haven't even gone on a real date. But, yes, I like him." She points at me. "And it supports the possibility of meeting guys who are neither jailbait nor senior citizens after turning forty. My experience should make you feel more optimistic about meeting someone new, right?"

"Right." Except I'm no longer interested in meeting someone new and would much prefer to reconcile with someone old.

"What's wrong, Mags? You don't seem too enthusiastic," Jodie says.

"Of course, I am. I'm totally excited for you." *Truth.*

Narrowing her eyes at me, Jodie says, "But you're sad."

"I'm not sad." *Lie.*

Amanda cocks her head to the side and studies me. "You do seem sad."

"Spill," Jodie says.

I exhale deeply. "I miss Doug."

"I knew it," Amanda exclaims in glee.

Rolling my eyes, I say, "I'm so glad my despair makes you giddy, Amanda."

A blush creeps across Amanda's cheeks. "I'm not deriving pleasure from your pain, I swear. But I'm glad you figured it out before it's too late. You need to call him."

Holding her hand up, Jodie says, "Simmer down. We need to discuss this. No reason to do anything hasty."

"What is there to discuss? Maggie realizes she made a horrible mistake breaking up with Doug. Don't you think she should tell him?"

"Maggie didn't break up with Doug; she asked him for a break. He broke up with her," Jodie argues.

"Ahem. Maggie's here. Please refrain from talking about me like I'm not in the room," I say as my pulse races.

Frowning, Jodie says, "Sorry, Mags. How long have you felt this way?"

I press my fingers to my now throbbing temples and shake my head. "I'm not sure. A few weeks?"

Raising an eyebrow, Jodie says, "Like around the time Philip ended things?"

"What are you getting at?" Amanda asks.

"I'm thinking maybe Maggie doesn't miss *Doug* per se. Maybe what she misses is having *someone*. People often romanticize old relationships when they're lonely. What do you think, Magpie? Could I be on to something?"

Having asked myself the same question at least a thousand times in the last couple of weeks, I sigh. "I don't know, but I guess it's possible you're right." I flash back to the way Doug used to lick the trail of freckles from my ankles all the way up to my inner thighs until I begged him to put me out of my misery.

Interrupting my X-rated daydream, Amanda says, "I think Maggie missed Doug before things ended with Philip. You should have seen the way she hightailed it out of The Apple Store in October."

"I'm merely suggesting you think long and hard about the source of your feelings before you do anything rash," Jodie says.

"But don't think too long," Amanda mutters.

Jodie ignores her. "You already hurt Doug once. If you guys get back together and your old concerns come back, it will kill him. And then I'll have to kill you."

Jerking my head back, I say, "Why would you kill me?"

"Because Doug is one of the good guys."

"But I'm your friend," I argue even though I agree wholeheartedly with Jodie. The last thing I want to do is hurt Doug again.

"Maybe you should join Match.com or something. Get your dating juices flowing," Jodie says.

"I wouldn't recommend it," Amanda says. "I can almost guarantee there is no one online who will be better than Doug."

I force out a chuckle. "Let's change the subject. I promise to think about what you've said." I focus my gaze on Jodie for a moment and then on Amanda. "Both of you."

*   *   *

When I get back to my apartment, I immediately turn on the television in the living room. Then I drop my overnight bag in the bedroom before returning to the couch. Scrolling the channels, I regretfully deduce there is nothing on except repeats of *Law & Order: SVU* which, for the first time since Doug and I spent a winter of Sundays binge-watching seasons one through ten, I'm not in the mood to watch. I turn off the television and call Cheryl. I get her voicemail and tell her to call me back. We still haven't discussed what's going on with her and Jim and her avoidance of the conversation is concerning.

I log onto my computer and after updating my search for job openings on the Legal Marketing Association's job bank, I shoot off my resume along with a tailored cover letter for two legal marketing positions—one for a marketing and business development coordinator and one for a marketing communications manager. True to his word, Philip has made things as comfortable for me at work as possible, starting with making Brendan the go-to person for the logo project. We still have an ongoing email exchange regarding the concepts, but Philip manages to be pleasant without being phony. He has somehow found a way to pretend nothing happened between us while fully acknowledging that something did indeed happen, and I am grateful for his sensitive demeanor. Still, much of the splendor of my current position—one I'd formerly been passionate about—was lost in our breakup. With a milestone birthday staring me in the face, the timing is perfect to start fresh.

My self-imposed hour a day of job searching completed, I tap my fingers on the keyboard aimlessly. I glance at my tiny kitchenette and contemplate making dinner, but I'm not at all hungry. I aim my mouse at the browser and begin to type. I stop after "www" and bite my cheek. Then I peer over my shoulder as if someone can see what I'm about to do. I clasp my hands together, intertwine my fingers, and stretch my arms out in front of me. Then I finish entering the complete URL and find myself on the home page of Match.com.

I'm immediately invited to see photos of singles near me, so I click on "Woman Seeking a Man" in zip code 10016 and hold my breath. I did online dating in my early thirties before I met Doug, but I never took it very seriously. I met a few nice guys and several not-so-nice guys, but I don't recall being overly disappointed when a guy's profile picture didn't match his in-person appearance, or when he didn't call me for a second date. It was merely fun. Today, as I stare at the screen in horror, I wish for even a smidgen of my younger self's nonchalance.

The site won't let me view the results until I provide my email address and birthday, and states that providing the information signifies my agreement to receive promotional emails from Match.com. I'm tempted to close the browser until I read the part about opting out of emails at any time. After providing the requested information, I shield my eyes with my hands as if somehow protecting myself from the profiles I'm about to see. Or maybe I'm hiding myself so the men in the profiles can't see me. I take a deep breath and remove my hand. Staring back at me are rows and rows of pictures of male members of Match.com. I click on a photo of forty-two-year-old Matthew. He's cute with short brown hair and five o'clock shadow. According to his profile, he has no trouble getting dates, but meeting one special woman to settle down with is proving to be challenging. He is a long-suffering Mets and Jets fan, and Key West is his favorite place in the world. He's hoping to meet an attractive, intelligent, and interesting woman with her own opinions and passions.

So far so good. I read further down his profile and freeze—he is searching for a woman between the ages of twenty-five and thirty-five. Seriously? He's a forty-two-year-old *man*, but wants to meet a twenty-five-year-old *girl*? And he won't even consider dating a woman who is over thirty-five, even though she's still several years younger than him.

I close out his profile and continue my casual searching. After about fifteen minutes, I shut down my computer, wishing I hadn't bothered. Of the ten or so decent men in my age range, almost all of them are searching for women who are several years younger than them, and the others included women up to their own age but not even a year or two older.

Not only does it confirm one of my biggest fears about getting older, but it makes me miss Doug even more for never giving my age a second thought. Amanda is absolutely right—I will never meet a guy online who is better than Doug.

I exit the dating website and do a search for indoor rock climbing classes in New York City. I might not be able to freeze time or control what men are looking for, but I'm not completely powerless. I wince when I see the price of the four-week climbing school offered by Chelsea Piers is two hundred and fifty dollars. I chew on a finger nail in contemplation for a moment. Then I reach for the credit card in my wallet, and sign up for the January classes.

*   *   *

Over the edamame we are sharing at Mizu Sushi, my favorite neighborhood Japanese restaurant, Amanda asks me, "Are you sure you don't want to come with us?"

"I'm positive. I truly hate New Year's Eve, Amanda. I have no desire to spend twice as much money for half as much fun." I intend to stay at home with a bottle of Prosecco and a delicious assortment of cheese and crackers and chips and dip.

Amanda frowns. "Well, if you change your mind, let me know. I'm sure Regina can get you another ticket." One of Regina's friends has rented out the top floor of a bar in midtown. "There will be a controlled number of people, so it won't be like The Culture Club, I swear."

I shudder at the memory of paying a hundred and twenty dollars for the privilege of waiting in line outside of the club in below-freezing temperatures for close to an hour before the cocky bouncer let us in, and then tipping twenty dollars to get the bartender's attention at the so-called "open bar" event. I vowed never to attend an open bar party on New Year's Eve again. The following year, I met Doug, who was more than happy to help me keep my promise.

When I was in a relationship, I never realized how few single friends I had. If I wanted to really party for New Year's Eve, it wouldn't be possible without my connection to Amanda. I smile at her. "I do appreciate you being so inclusive though."

"Of course. I worry about you." She glances at the almost empty plate of edamame. "You mind if I take the last one?"

"Go for it," I say. "Why do you worry about me? I'm choosing to stay at home because I honestly detest going out on New Year's Eve. It's not like I'm suicidal or anything."

Amanda grimaces. "God forbid. But don't you think beginning the year alone is a bad omen?"

I tip my head to the side. "Do you truly believe spending New Year's Eve solo will result in being alone for the rest of the year? That's a bit melodramatic, don't you think? And how does your theory explain all the single girls who go out on New Year's Eve, kiss some random guy but still don't find boyfriends by the end of the year? Shouldn't it go both ways?"

Amanda sighs. "I meant it metaphorically, not literally."

I study Amanda fondly. "Well, does your theory work in

reverse? Does your plan of being social on New Year's Eve mean you intend to be social and 'out there' during the year? Because, if you must know, I worry about you too."

Amanda casts her head downward and whispers, "I know. I do too."

I contemplate my next words for a beat before saying them. "Have you talked to someone?"

Meeting my gaze again, she asks, "Like a therapist?"

I nod.

"No," she says, shaking her head. "But it's one of my New Year's resolutions."

My eyes open in surprise, but before I have a chance to say anything, the waiter brings over our order. In a show of support, I reach across the table and squeeze Amanda's hand.

Jerking away from me, she whispers, "Stop. I know it's a good thing, but I don't want to talk about it right now. Okay?"

"Okay," I relent, but I'm doing back flips on the inside.

Placing an extra California roll in front of Amanda, the waiter says, "Complimentary for you."

With a tentative smile, Amanda says, "For me? Why?"

The waiter, an older Japanese man, nods. "You're very pretty." He puts a finger to his lips. "Shh." Amanda blushes as the waiter winks at her and walks back to the kitchen.

"Like I said, you could have your pick of men. You're so pretty," I say, mimicking the waiter.

Rolling her eyes, Amanda says, "Do you still miss Doug?"

"How do you always manage to turn it back on me?"

Amanda sneers wickedly. "You underestimate my talents." Her face turns serious. "Well, do you?"

"Yeah."

She raises an eyebrow. "You gonna call him?"

"I haven't decided. But I did take Jodie's advice. I went on Match.com. Total nightmare." I shake my head in disgust and tell Amanda what my search disclosed.

Amanda nods knowingly. "My friends are starting to have the

same problems. They say if you're a woman between the ages of thirty-eight and forty-three, online dating is a black hole."

Adding more wasabi to my soy sauce, I say, *"No comprende."*

"Apparently, many men on online dating sites avoid meeting women between those ages because they assume they're in a hurry to get married and have children."

I exhale loudly. "Lovely. And not necessarily accurate."

"I know. But it generally only applies to online dating." In a brighter voice, she says, "You can totally meet someone in person. Case in point—Jodie. And Regina meets guys every weekend."

"Because she's easy."

Amanda, who just put a piece of spicy tuna and scallop roll in her mouth, laughs. She covers her mouth with her hand. "There's that."

Not hungry anymore, I drop my chopsticks on my plate.

"But you love Doug, so don't even worry about this stuff."

I don't say anything and dip my chin toward the floor.

When Amanda's hand covers mine, I slowly lift my head to face her. She locks eyes with me.

"All I'm suggesting is you think about it," she says. "And if you want to call him, don't let pride stop you. If he loves you, he'll understand. You'll work things out."

"What if he doesn't love me anymore?" I swallow hard as the possibility stings my insides.

Giggling, Amanda says, "Then you can come to therapy with me."

"Well, if that isn't incentive, I don't know what is."

January

Thoroughly enjoying my New Year's Eve party of one, I stumble to my kitchen and place the empty bottle of Prosecco on the counter. After drunk calling my mom to wish her a Happy New Year, texting Cheryl, Jodie, Amanda, and Melanie, and dancing around my living room to "Breakout" by Swing Out Sister, I fall back on my couch and continue to scroll the music channels on my television set. I switch between the various options—Heavy Metal, Top 40, Classic Rock, 70s, 80s, and 90s—stopping only when a song moves me to get up and dance.

I pass over "Animal" by Def Leppard, "Umbrella" by Rihanna, and "Turn it on Again" by Genesis, stopping momentarily to sing along to "I'd Really Love to See You Tonight" by Dan & John Ford Coley, until I decide I'm not feeling it. I finally hit pay dirt when I catch the beginning notes of "Carry On Wayward Son" by Kansas— the song Doug and I sang together at karaoke at his thirty-fifth birthday party. I stand up and sing along into a purple Sharpie but sit down again when I realize the only words I know by heart are the chorus.

I wonder how Doug is celebrating. Last year, we went out for early drinks with Melanie and Barry and then ate a private dinner for two at home. Doug made us lobster tails and key lime pie martinis. After drinking several martinis, I was itching to go out to a bar, but Doug had no interest. After calling him lame, I walked around the corner to Rodeo Bar in time to witness a drunk girl stumble out and puke on the sidewalk. I took one whiff of the sweat-filled bar, turned around, and went home to find Doug passed out on the couch.

I often complained Doug was too much of a homebody, and here I am—home. I muse at the irony and pick up my phone. I question the wisdom of calling him drunk on New Year's Eve. I wonder if I'll regret it in the morning, but I honestly believe it's the right thing to do and fear I won't have the guts unless I'm under the influence. As the phone rings, my heart pounds against my chest.

"Maggie?"

My hand shakes at the sound of Doug's voice, and I open my mouth to speak, but nothing comes out. I should have rehearsed it.

I hear Doug's voice again on the other side of the phone. "Hello?"

I clear my throat and ponder my next words. Should I say "Happy New Year?" Or is a simple "Hi" the way to go?"

I'm still debating what to say when the phrase "Who is it, babe?" echoes in the background in a high-pitched and obviously female voice. I end the call and drop my phone on the floor.

*   *   *

"You're such a showoff," I say to Melanie as she takes a bow. While I hold onto the edge of the ice skating rink in Bryant Park with white knuckles, she is literally skating circles around me. "Next, you'll show up at work with the Dorothy Hamill haircut."

Melanie does a figure eight and stops in front of me. "I could never pull off the Dorothy Hamill." Offering her hand, she says, "C'mon, I won't let you fall." In exchange for going ice skating with Melanie after work, she agreed to a post-skating glass of Glühwein at Celsius, the adjacent restaurant/bar.

I glance down at her hand as it twitches towards me. My ice skating routine usually includes staying close to the perimeter for a few more laps before venturing out. Deciding the sooner I skate a few circles around the rink, the sooner I will have a steaming cup of mulled wine in my hands, I say, "Okay. Don't let go of me until I'm ready." My fingernails dig into her palm. "I'm serious. Don't let me fall."

"I promise. I've taught two little boys to ice skate. I think I can handle you, Mags. Besides, skating is easy peasy compared to rock climbing, something you're voluntarily paying hundreds of dollars to learn." I know she's right, and before I can change my mind, she drags me to the center of the rink, and we get behind two handholding teenagers who are gliding gracefully on the ice. I stare at the back of their down jackets and concentrate on skating at the same pace. I pray they don't speed up. I also pray Melanie won't lose patience with me. She is singing along to "Best Day of My Life" by American Authors, and I can tell she is itching to let go of me and turn our predictable forward circular movements into a choreographed dance number.

"You doing all right?"

I gently nod my head, afraid to make any sudden movements. It would be better if ice skating came with a harness. "Yes."

She loosens her grip. "Your hands are super clammy, Mags."

I slow down but don't come to a full stop and remove my hand from hers. I think I'm good now.

After two or three more laps, I'm feeling significantly more confident. My facial muscles are noticeably more relaxed, and I've even attempted easy conversation. By the time Pink's "Blow Me One Last Kiss" comes on, I'm smiling and singing along.

Someone taps me on the back, and I whip my head around in surprise. My eyes open wide.

"Doug!"

And *splat*, I'm down. The hard ice jabs the spot on my lower back where it meets my ass.

I glance up at Doug, who is standing over me. The apples of his cheeks and his nose are red from the cold, but his green eyes are wide with concern. Offering me his arm, he says, "Are you okay?"

I don't want to let go of his warm hands, but once I'm up and stable on my feet, he releases me, and that's when I notice the girl standing next to him. From the way she is leaning into him, I know she's the girl from New Year's Eve. Appearance-wise, she's attractive but not gorgeous. Average height, long straight brown hair, thin. But she's young. Definitely younger than me, and probably a few years younger than Doug.

I wipe my hands against my jacket. They sting from the fall. "I'm fine." Flattening down my hair, I say, "A blow to my fragile ego is all." I'm thankful I had my hair touched up a couple weeks ago. Even though I'm the oldest person in my present company, I don't want to look the part.

"I've seen you fall before, Mags. Nothing to be embarrassed about," Doug says with a teasing smirk. He nods at Melanie.

Drawing him in for a hug, Melanie says, "Good to see you, Doug." She glances at me, furrowing her brow. "You sure you're not hurt? I have bandages in my bag if you're bleeding."

Unable to focus on anything except the girl with Doug, I mutter, "I'm fine." Then I glance at her with a timid smile. "Hi. I'm Maggie."

"Oh. Sorry for my lack of manners." Doug jerks his head toward the girl. "This is Lindsay." Motioning to Melanie, he says, "And this is Melanie."

"Nice to meet you guys," she says, grasping Doug's hand. Tilting her head to the side, her dark eyes probe my light ones. "I've heard a lot about you."

I study her, wondering what she's heard about me, and then shoot Doug a questioning glance. Did he tell her I called on New Year's Eve? I hadn't told anyone. Sharing the news would make it real. Although no more real than bumping into them at the skating rink.

"Small world seeing you here," he says quietly.

Lindsay smiles brightly, revealing a set of straight teeth. "And we weren't even going to come. We both took the day off from work and went to a horror movie marathon. Doug thought being outside would be good for us after sitting in a dark theater all day."

There's a dull ache in my gut as I imagine Doug and Lindsay at the movies. If it was a horror movie, they would be hunched close together. The last time Doug and I saw a horror movie, it was at a drive-in theater in Warwick, New York, about sixty miles from New York City. We watched *The House on Haunted Hill* starring Vincent Price. I clutched Doug so tightly the entire time, fearing the psychotic murderer was going to tap on the window with an ax at any moment.

As I listen to Lindsay describe with enthusiasm their afternoon of *Paranormal Activity* movies, I avoid making eye contact with Doug. I wonder what else he does with Lindsay that he used to do with me. Besides the obvious, as I can't even go there. Do they watch back-to-back episodes of *Criminal Minds* together? Has he made her watch every Marvel Comics movie stored on his computer? Was she his plus-one at any events at The Paley Center? As Lindsay continues to babble on, I question whether she's even thirty years old. She has the energy of a twenty-something. I force myself to look at him, afraid to find him beaming in the direction of Lindsay. But his gaze is not directed at her. He is watching me. Lindsay and Melanie have somehow gotten on the subject of John Hughes movies and are discussing the similarities between *Pretty in Pink* and *Some Kind of Wonderful*. I drown them out as I lock eyes with Doug. He gives me a closed-mouth smile before bending down. "You lost this in the fall," he says, handing me one of my green mittens.

My heart beating rapidly, I take it from him, rubbing my thumb against his for an instant before breaking away. "Thanks."

Turning to Lindsay, he says, "We should get going."

Wrapping her arm around Doug's waist, Lindsay agrees. To Melanie and me, she says, "Nice meeting you guys."

"You too," I say absently.

"Good seeing you, Melanie. Tell Barry and the kids I said hi." With one last glance at me, Doug murmurs, "Take care, Maggie."

I gulp. "You too."

*   *   *

Twenty minutes later, I bring my mug of Glühwein to my mouth. The steaming drink is not nearly as comforting as I thought it would be, I note with disappointment.

"What was *that* about?" Melanie asks.

I blow on the mulled wine in an attempt to cool it off. "What was what about?"

"Between you and Doug before. There was some serious tension."

I put the mug down and plant my elbows on the festively-decorated table overlooking the skating rink. "What did you expect? We haven't seen each other since we broke up, and he's there with his new girlfriend."

Melanie nods. "Awkward situation, for sure, but you handled it pretty well. Aside from the falling part." She giggles. "Anyway, I'm impressed." I told Melanie about missing Doug a few days after confessing my feelings to Amanda and Jodie.

I shake my head. "Don't be impressed. I already knew about her."

Melanie's green eyes open wide. "How? And why didn't you say anything?"

"I called him on New Year's Eve in a moment of weakness. I heard her in the background and hung up."

Her jaw falling open, Melanie says, "Did he know it was you?"

"I called him from my cell and didn't bother with star sixty-seven. I thought he'd be happy to hear from me. I never imagined he would be with another girl." I take a deep exhale. "There should be a warning on bottles of Prosecco that drinking too much causes delusions of grandeur."

"Poor Mags." Melanie frowns.

I stare into my drink. "Yeah, poor Mags is about right."

"If it's any consolation, he doesn't seem to be very into her."

I regard her cautiously. "Based on what?" I will her to say something hopeful so I can latch onto it.

"She did all of the talking. He was watching you the entire time."

This is true, but I say out loud what I have been telling myself for the past thirty minutes to avoid making a self-serving assumption that Doug still loves me. "He was probably concerned for my feelings. You know Doug. He would never hurt me on purpose." I hold my breath, awaiting Melanie's response and praying she won't agree with me. She looks thoughtful as she takes a sip of her Hot Toddy.

She puts the glass down. "Perhaps."

My stomach drops.

"But it seemed like more to me."

My lips involuntarily curl upward, and I feel a flutter in my belly. "You think?"

Melanie nods. "Why don't you give him a call and talk things through?"

I jerk my head back. "And hone my skills as a homewrecker? In case it's escaped you, he's dating someone now. Wouldn't it be messed up to call a guy with a girlfriend?"

"All's fair in love, and he was your boyfriend first."

I chew on my lip as I ponder her words. "Maybe I'll call him."

*   *   *

I am going to call him, and I'm going to do it soon—before the end of the month. After February 1st, all of the television shows will air their Valentine's Day episodes; the Lifetime and Hallmark movie channels will broadcast back-to-back romantic comedies; and every other commercial will be for Kay Jewelers or Godiva chocolates. If we get back together, I don't want Doug to think I chose the timing because I'm hoping he'll go to Jared's. More importantly, if I do it soon, and we don't get back together, I have a better chance of being done crying about it by Valentine's Day. And I have to do it before whatever he has with Lindsay gets serious. God, I hope it's not already serious.

Someone taps me on the arm. "Maggie?"

Everyone in the conference room eyes me expectantly. I'm at a business development meeting and obviously being negligent in my job. My face hot with shame, I clear my throat. "Apologies. I was somewhere else for a second. Can you please repeat the question?"

Thankfully, Neil Black is an easy-going guy—as far as managing partners in law firms go—and he chuckles before replying, "We were wondering if you had a chance to run the report of last year's new matters."

"Yes. I ran a report for all new clients and matters opened last year. I organized it by originating partner. I didn't bring it with me, but I can email it to everyone when I get back to my desk."

"Please do," Neil says.

I exhale a sigh of relief I was able to answer the question. Makes being caught daydreaming at a meeting a lot less worrisome. A few minutes later, I'm asked to summarize where things stand on the rebranding issue, which I do with poise and composure.

The meeting continues as each partner goes around the room discussing billable hours, clients who haven't paid in months, and all the other things lawyers talk about when they assemble. I put my plans to phone Doug on the back burner.

Every so often, I sense Philip's eyes on me from the other side of the table—the way you just know when someone is looking at you. I resist making eye contact for as long as I can and try to behave as if I am oblivious to his glances, but I'm not the smoothest cat in the kennel and find myself fidgeting in my seat and playing with my hair. I am unpracticed at acting normal in front of an ex-lover, as Philip is the only man I ever slept with whom I had to see repeatedly after we broke up. As I contemplate whether there are any all-female law firms I can cold call for a position, I vow to never shit where I eat again.

After several minutes of consciously avoiding moving my head in Philip's direction, my neck begins to ache, and my anger builds at being such a coward. If anyone should be shamefaced, it's Philip; not me. I didn't play games or make false statements to get Philip in bed. He fell for my charm and sass. Purposely or not, Philip is the one who misled me into believing his split with his wife was permanent. While many women would have caused a scene in the restaurant, stalked his wife, or boiled rabbits on his stove, I handled it like the first-class lady I am by accepting the news, forgiving Philip, and moving on.

I am discernibly cooler than I'm behaving today in the conference room, and I wonder if it's a delayed reaction to seeing Doug with Lindsay. In any event, I am no shrinking violet. As Neil concludes his closing remarks and people get up from the table, I spy Philip glance my way through the corner of my eye, whip my head in his direction, and meet his gaze head-on. I pause for a beat and then flash him a dazzling smile even Julia Roberts would envy. I know I've surprised him when his head jerks slightly back. Before he can recover, I grab my legal pad and walk out of the conference room.

I am definitely ready to call Doug.

*   *   *

It's the following day, and I'm at work in my office with the door closed. I want to call Doug during the day because I would rather catch him when he's with colleagues than with Lindsay.

I take a deep breath and close my eyes for a pause. Then I open them and find Doug's number on my cell phone. I continue taking calming breaths while the phone rings once, then twice.

He answers on the third ring with a cautious tone. "Hello?"

I will my heart to stop slamming against my chest, and in a pitch slightly higher than my normal one, I say, "Hey, Doug. It's Maggie." I'm completely unaccustomed to feeling ill at ease around Doug and think I might vomit.

"Unless someone took your phone hostage, I figured as much."

Since he responded in a somewhat friendly manner, my confidence goes up half a notch. Or maybe a quarter of a notch.

"It was, uh...good to see you the other day," I say.

"Yeah. Small world, huh? Of all the ice skating rinks in the city, you had to fall at mine," he jokes.

I chuckle. "I'm fairly certain I would have fallen even if we were at the rink in Central Park or Rockefeller Center."

"I tend to agree with you. But falling is part of your charm," he says in a soft voice.

Warmth floods my belly. I should have known awkwardness between Doug and me wouldn't last long.

He clears his throat. "To what do I owe the pleasure of your call?"

I cross my fingers. "I was wondering if you wanted to meet for a drink." Maybe coffee would have been the safer option, but he doesn't drink it, and asking him to meet for a cup of tea sounds too British. There is silence on the other end of the phone, and I take the opportunity to drink from the water bottle on my desk.

Finally, he speaks. "Can I ask why you want to meet?"

I haven't anticipated this question, and I am momentarily stumped. "I wanted to talk to you about a few things."

"Did I leave anything at the apartment? I thought I got everything, but it's entirely possible I left some stuff behind accidentally," he says, apologetically.

"No. You didn't leave anything as far as I know." I add the latter half of the sentence because I'm not the tidiest of people, and it's possible he left something in places I skipped in my weekly apartment cleaning. "But maybe you can come by and double check," I say, hopefully.

"I trust you. If you find something, let me know."

The awkwardness is back in high gear. I make one last go of it. "So, about that drink?"

Doug sighs. "Maggie, what is this about?"

I know some people would consider having the conversation over the phone the easier option, but I much prefer talking in person so I can gauge his reactions by his facial expressions and body language. "Like I said, I just want to talk, and over the phone is too formal."

"Okay," he relents. "When?"

I exhale for what feels like the first time in an hour. "Whenever is convenient for you."

After a brief silence, Doug says, "What about after work today?"

My stomach rumbles nervously. This is moving faster than I thought, but it's a good thing. "Tonight is good. Can you meet at I Trulli?" Only a few blocks from my apartment, the wine bar was one of our favorite local hangouts.

"Can we meet somewhere further uptown? How about the Oyster Bar in Grand Central?"

"Sure. Six thirty?"

"Six thirty is perfect. See you then." He disconnects the call before I have a chance to respond.

I rub my fingers against my lips as I stare at my computer. Throwing myself into work would be the best way to push the drink with Doug out of my mind. On the screen is an Excel chart of our most coveted clients and the names of the partners who have relationships with key players. It is my job to evaluate the data and eliminate some of the companies on the list, namely those we have close to zero chance of acquiring, in order to improve the efficiency of our business development efforts. But I can't make any sense of the information and fear having a productive day is going to be challenging. And it's not even lunch time. In the battle between productivity and time-suckage, the latter wins, and I head to Melanie's office for a distraction.

She's got her head in a file but looks up when I knock lightly on her door. "Hey," she says wearily.

Leaning against her doorway, I say, "Is this a bad time? You busy?"

Melanie lifts her arms in the air in a stretch and yawns. "I'm always busy."

"Want me to come back later?"

Her eyes drift down to my right foot, which I don't realize I am tapping until she points it out to me. "Is everything all right?"

I take her question as my invitation to sit in her guest chair. "I called Doug."

Melanie pushes her file to the side and leans toward me across her desk. "And?"

"And we're meeting for a drink tonight." My lips twitch nervously.

"You don't waste any time, do you?" She gives me a once-over. "Is that what you're wearing?"

"What's wrong with my outfit?" I'm wearing navy dress pants, a white silk button-down shirt, and red patent leather Mary Jane wedges—basic business casual attire.

Melanie scrunches her face. "Not wrong exactly. But it's nothing special."

I roll my eyes. "It's Doug. He knows what I look like. I don't think what I'm wearing will have a bearing on the outcome of our conversation."

Shaking her head at me, Melanie says, "Maybe so. But he *is* dating someone else now, so it wouldn't hurt to put in more effort and show him what he's been missing." Reaching into her desk drawer, she pulls out a blue and white polka dot silk scarf and extends it across the desk. "Undo one button on your shirt and put this on. It adds a little something-something."

Laughing, I take the scarf. "I'm beginning to think you're Sabrina the thirty-something witch, able to conjure up a matching scarf with the wiggle of your nose."

Melanie smirks. "You'll thank me later."

"I'll thank you now—thank you." I stand up. "I should get back to my office and try to be productive."

"Good luck, Magpie. Please keep me posted."

"You know I will." I blow her a kiss and let her return to work.

*   *   *

Seven hours later, I'm sitting across a table from Doug in the iconic Oyster Bar in Grand Central Station. Tourists dine here for the vaulted ceilings and legendary architecture, but I'm merely interested in reuniting with my ex-boyfriend. As I drink him in, it strikes me he is the only person I know with that particular shade of sea-green eyes. We've already ordered a round of beers and have covered the basic conversation starters like "How's work?" and "How's your mom?" From the way Doug is fiddling with his watch, it's evident he's impatient for the real reason I asked him to meet me.

I take a sip of my beer and lick my lips. "Lindsay seems nice."

"She is nice." He offers no other information and simply raises his own glass to his mouth.

"Is it...is it serious?"

Doug narrows his eyes at me. "What do you want, Maggie?"

Part of me wants to make up a stupid lie about why I insisted on meeting him, but it's Doug. We shared a bed, a bathroom, a life. I owe it to him to be honest. With my legs shaking under the table, I bottom-line it for him. "I miss you."

Doug draws in a breath and slowly releases it. "What do you miss?"

I chew on my lip. "Everything. We had so much fun together and I...well, I miss it. I miss us."

He sighs dejectedly. "I miss us too, Maggie."

I resist the urge to hold his hand across the table.

"But what is this about?"

I swallow hard. "I was hoping maybe we could try again."

Doug shakes his head slowly. "You're the one who didn't want to be with me anymore."

Raising my voice, I say, "That's not true. You broke up with me."

Narrowing his eyes again, he says, "Right. You wanted a break, not a breakup. I forgot."

"I just wasn't sure. I was confused."

"About what?"

I wrack my brain to put it into words, but can't. "I don't know."

Doug pinches his lips together. "If you can't put your finger on exactly what concerned you then, how can you be sure it won't come up again later?" He takes another sip of beer and places it roughly on the table, spilling some onto the red and white checkered tablecloth. "This is what I think. I think you're feeling the pressure of turning forty and being single, and you're wondering if you made a mistake letting go of your steady, comfortable boyfriend. But I don't want to be your consolation prize."

My pulse accelerates as I try to defend my motivation. "I've never thought of you as a consolation prize. I miss you. I miss *us*."

"And what about your lawyer boyfriend?"

I open my eyes wide. "Wha...?"

Cocking his head to the side, he says, "The world is smaller than you think, Maggie. The new accounting guy at my company used to work at your firm. News travels."

"He...uh...we're not seeing each other anymore, but he has nothing to do with my feelings for you." Convincing Doug my connection with Philip paled in comparison to what we had together is significantly more important to me than finding out to what guy in my firm's accounting department Doug is referring.

With a slack expression, Doug says, "I believe you think this is what you want, but I don't believe it truly is. There was a reason you didn't want to commit to me, and it will rear its ugly head again eventually. I don't want to be the cause of your unhappiness, and I definitely don't want to go through this again."

"Is it Lindsay? Are you in love with her?"

"This has nothing to do with Lindsay. It's about you and me. I still have feelings for you, Maggie. I've never lied to you before, so I won't do it now. But you broke us, and it can't be fixed. I'm sorry."

Since I don't have any fighting words, I look at him pleadingly, hoping he'll see in my eyes that I'm serious.

Instead, he throws a twenty and a five on the table, enough to cover both of our drinks and a generous tip. He stands up and regards me with sad eyes. "You're a special person, Magpie. I've no doubt you'll meet someone who makes you one hundred percent happy."

As I watch him walk out of the restaurant, I'm hit by the full effect of his words, and my world feels like it's crashed into a million pieces. It's over.

*   *   *

After Doug leaves the restaurant, I stare straight ahead, unable to get up from the table. The waiter comes back and asks if I need anything else, and I barely glance his way when I order a vodka tonic with lime. I reach into my bag for my cell phone and call Melanie. I pray she didn't pick tonight to leave work at a reasonable hour.

"I didn't expect to hear from you so soon. How'd it go?"

I open my mouth to say something as tears fall down my face. My voice cracks as I choke out, "Please come."

"Are you okay?" Melanie asks.

My nose is running, but since I don't have tissues, I wipe it with a cocktail napkin. "No. Please."

"You're scaring me. What happened?"

"Can't talk. Please come. Downstairs at the Oyster Bar." I disconnect the call and take a big gulp of the drink the waiter has placed in front of me. I shiver at its strength and take another sip.

I'm detached from myself, as if I was merely an observer and not an active participant in the conversation with Doug. But the loss I feel is palpable. Doug has rejected me. The concept is so foreign that I can't wrap my brain around it. I always took Doug's acceptance of me—warts and all—for granted, but I underestimated his threshold level. I crossed it. Like he said, I broke us, and it can't be fixed.

Fifteen minutes later, the tears have stopped flowing by the time I see Melanie run into the restaurant and frantically sweep the room with her eyes. I can't find my voice, but I raise my arm and wave it around in an attempt to get her attention.

When she sees me, her face falls. "Oh, sweetie, you've been crying. Stand up and give Melanie a hug."

I shake my head. "I don't have the energy to stand up," I say flatly, gesturing to the chair where Doug sat less than an hour earlier. "Sit."

I recap what happened the best I can, but each word tastes like poison, and I have to take several pauses before I finally complete the story.

Neither of us speaking, I watch Melanie regard me with pity until I see Amanda and Jodie walk into the restaurant with the same sense of urgency Melanie had. "What are they doing here?" I ask, jutting my chin toward the entrance.

Melanie turns around as they approach our table. "I called for reinforcements."

As they sit down and Jodie calls the waiter over, I bury my head in my hands. When I lift my head, I say, "It's bad enough I dragged Melanie into my shitty night. Now all of you are going to have crappy nights too."

"That's what friends are for," Amanda says before placing her glove-clad hand on mine.

Amanda and Jodie stare at me expectantly until I, once again, summarize the night's events. When I'm finished, I take a deep exhale and reach for my now-empty glass. Jodie pushes a fresh one in my face. "How do you feel about everything now, having gotten over your shock, cried, and gone through the story twice?"

I say simply, "Sad. Very sad."

Jodie leans forward and locks eyes with me. She purses her lips before saying, "Do you think Doug could be right about you being afraid? Please don't hate me for saying so. You know I like to play devil's advocate."

I rub my eyes, vaguely aware I probably look like a raccoon as well as every bit of my thirty-nine years. "I really don't think so, Jodie. But..." I shrug. "Who the hell knows?"

"Time will tell," Melanie says.

Placing a piece of hair behind my ear, I say, "I guess so."

Amanda frowns. "I shouldn't have encouraged you to do this. I was so positive Doug would want to get back together with you. If anyone should advise caution under these types of circumstances, it's me."

I squeeze Amanda's hand. "Not your fault at all. And it's better this happened now. At least I know he's no longer an option."

Amanda nods. "Better to try and fail than to wonder."

"What now?" Melanie asks.

"I guess I try to move forward. It occurs to me I haven't spent more than a few months without a boyfriend or some sort of male company in a very long time. Maybe the time is now." I'm trying to be brave, but in truth, I'm scared shitless I'll be alone forever, and the only guy who ever truly loved me for me no longer trusts that I love him back. I take another sip of my drink. "Since I've already disrupted your nights, tell me what's going on with all of you. Jodie, who is with the kids?"

Jodie says, "You can reimburse me for the emergency babysitter, and we'll call it even."

I chuckle. "Deal. What about the rest of you?"

"I worked the after-school program today and was planning to go shopping, so you might have saved me several hundred dollars," Amanda says.

Melanie waves me away. "Barry would have had to make the kids dinner anyway."

I make eye contact with each of them again before saying, "One of you please share something personal so I can get my mind off of Doug."

Melanie blows her bangs out of her eyes. "I billed over three hundred hours this month so far."

"How are you still standing?" Jodie asks. "Better question, how are your children not starving and in desperate need of a bath?"

Chuckling, Melanie says, "It's called a husband."

Rolling her eyes, Jodie says, "Hence why you're still married and I'm not."

"Speaking of which, any developments with Goatee Man?" I ask.

"He's in Vegas shooting a wedding," Jodie says. It turns out,

Charles, a.k.a. Goatee Man, is a wedding photographer. He took several candid shots at Jodie's birthday party, including one where Jodie, Amanda, and I were twerking. We made an agreement not to post the picture on Facebook under any circumstances and, instead, leave it stored safely in the cloud for nostalgic purposes to laugh over when we're in our sixties.

Her voice barely louder than a whisper, Amanda says, "I've got news."

"Do tell," Jodie says.

Amanda bites her lower lip and gives us a sheepish grin. "I'm signing up for a speed dating event."

As my jaw drops, Jodie and Melanie say in unison, "Really?"

A blush creeping across her cheeks, Amanda nods. "It was my therapist's idea. She thought it would be a good way to ease into dating."

"Your therapist considers meeting a gazillion guys in one night easing into dating?" I ask doubtfully.

"My first reaction too," Amanda says. "But she claims the short duration of the dates—five minutes each—is a lot less pressure than an hour or two with one guy. And a bad conversation with any one guy is less likely to have a lasting effect on me since I'm meeting so many at once."

Melanie nods. "Makes sense."

"But she suggested I ask one of my single friends to do it with me to further alleviate my anxiety," she says, locking her eyes on me.

"Good idea," I say encouragingly.

Amanda smiles at me.

I smile back.

"So you'll do it?" she asks.

Ruh roh. I knock back the rest of my drink as a wave of panic splashes through my center. "Why me?" I turn to Jodie and Melanie, hoping they'll help me.

"Count me out. I'm married," Melanie says.

"What about you?" I ask Jodie.

Not making eye contact, Jodie says, "I'm seeing Charles."

"I thought you were casually dating. Your sudden exclusivity is very convenient," I mumble. "Did anyone hear what I said less than ten minutes ago about taking a break from dating?" Neither Melanie nor Jodie jump to my rescue.

"Please, Magpie. I'm finally trying to meet someone again, but I'm scared to do it alone." Amanda cocks her head to the side and protrudes her lips in a pout.

I want more than anything to say no. Well, almost more than anything. But when she ogles me with her puppy-dog eyes, I can't do it. With a loud sigh, I relent. "Fine. But I'm only doing it for you."

Clapping her hands, Amanda says, "Thank you."

I'm genuinely moved by Amanda's enthusiasm to attend a singles event. This time last year, and probably even last month, she would have flat out refused to even consider it. It's a big step for her, and I'm proud she's taking it, even though I would prefer she find someone else to go with. I catch Jodie's eye across the table, and she winks at me. I roll my eyes. "When exactly are we doing this?" I ask.

"February 15th. The theme is Valentine's Day for singles. I'll email you the signup link."

"Swell," I say, not even trying to disguise my sarcasm. "What's the age range?"

"Women twenty-nine through thirty-nine, and men thirty through forty," Amanda says.

"Another reason I can't do it. I'm too old now," Jodie says with a chuckle.

My muscles tense. "Why are the women younger than the men?"

Amanda says, "I don't know. They're almost all like that."

"I'll be the oldest girl there, and almost every guy will be younger than me. This is getting better and better." I assume Amanda is unfettered by the age discrepancy because at thirty-four, she won't be the oldest or the youngest in attendance.

Squeezing my hand across the table, Amanda says, "If you focus on it being a favor for a friend, it will go down a lot easier."

"You owe me one," I say, only half joking.

"And people always mistake you for being younger. I guarantee you won't stand out," Jodie says.

"And you like younger guys," Melanie says, after which her face immediately drains of color.

Staring into space, I say, "Correction: Younger *guy*. I liked one younger guy." My lips begin to quiver as I think about Lindsay and how she's probably close to ten years my junior. "And now he's dating a younger girl."

*   *   *

I sling my gym bag over my shoulder and take one last look at the enormous rock wall. I'm wistful after completing my final class.

"You've come a long way since I supervised your first climb."

I turn to Ralph, my instructor, and smile. "I bet you never expected to see me again after that first time."

He cocks his head to the side. "If I remember correctly, you were a little hesitant initially, but then something pushed you forward."

My stomach drops. It wasn't something. It was someone—Doug. His imaginary support got me to the final hold the first time, but since our disastrous meeting at the Oyster Bar, I've had to rely on my own strength to keep me going. "And now I'm hooked."

Ralph waves to a group of climbers on their way out. "See you next time," he says before turning back to me. "I hope that means you'll sign up for our advanced beginner class."

I haven't thought about taking my rock climbing to the next level, but I tell Ralph I'll consider it before thanking him for all of his help and heading home.

On the cross town bus, I chew over the option of signing up for another set of classes. Rock climbing has been a great outlet for my stress. My favorite escape used to be television, but lately it's a reminder of Doug and what I lost. I'm not sure I can afford the fees right now, but I know if it's not rock climbing, it will be something else. I recall Melanie's suggestion that we try the flying trapeze. Perhaps it's not such an outrageous idea after all.

February

I stare at my closed office door, biting back my curiosity about the condition of the secretarial desks lining the hallway today. Are they teeming with long-stemmed roses? Even when I had a boyfriend, I never made a big deal of Valentine's Day. I didn't go out of my way to dress in red. Doug never sent me flowers to the office, though he always brought them home for me, along with a bag of assorted candy since I prefer sugar to chocolate. The mood was a bit more romantic on Valentine's Day than random nights, but we didn't make dinner reservations at a crazy expensive restaurant or take a mini-break to a bed and breakfast for the weekend. Yet today, I am veritably aware of my single status on a holiday made for lovers. I make a conscious effort to stay enclosed in my office all day in order to avoid observing the mail guys delivering bouquets of flowers to the romantically-attached women in the firm.

It's not like I'm the one kid in class who didn't get any Valentine's Day greetings. I did receive one—from my dad. If there is one thing I can credit to my father, it's always remembering me on special occasions, whether it's my birthday, Chanukah, or Valentine's Day. The pink and red card he sent me this year depicts an image of an owl and the words, "Whooos the Sweetest?" A personalized note was written in my father's scribbly handwriting: *Dear Freckles, Happy Valentine's Day. Love, Dad.* As much as I appreciate my father's attempts—however half-assed—to demonstrate his love, the card does nothing to ease the loneliness in my heart.

Cheryl invited me over for dinner, which I find strange since she's married and should spend Valentine's Day with Jim, but I accepted the invitation without hesitation. Last time we spoke on the phone, I told her about meeting with Doug, but she conveniently ended the call, claiming the kids needed a bath, before I had a chance to press her about Jim. For a while now, I've been worried something is wrong, so I hope she'll confide in me tonight.

I glance at the bottom of my computer screen to check the time. I have a phone interview with a headhunter in less than ten minutes. This is my first phone interview ever—in my previous job searches, I always met my prospective employer in person from the get-go. My lazy side is happy I don't have to leave the comfort of my office for this screening call (or wear pantyhose), but I know my best impressions are usually made face to face. I assume she'll ask the basic questions about my skills and experience history, even though both are listed on my resume.

Maybe she'll ask about my salary requirements. I'm not pining for a substantial pay increase, but I wouldn't turn it down either. My rent has doubled since Doug moved out, and it would be nice to earn enough to make up for it. The ideal position would be one where I can put my existing skills to use with room to learn and grow. Access to an assistant would be sweet too.

My final deal-breaking requirement is that the firm not employ anyone I've had sex with. It shouldn't be too difficult, since I've been a serial monogamist since I lost my virginity the summer between high school and college and have slept with a total of eleven men—all boyfriends, with the exception of two casual hook-ups in college and two since.

I *do* wish the motivating factor for instigating a job search was more substantial than having nailed a married partner who was also technically my boss, but I can't think of much I would want from a different employer that I don't get from the one I already have. It might be cool to branch out from the law firm environment and utilize my marketing skills in a different setting. I close my eyes and try to visualize myself at my ideal job, but all I can picture is a comfy couch and a giant flat screen television. My model job shouldn't resemble a sick day off from work.

The phone rings, drawing me out of my daydream and back to the real world. I take a deep breath and answer, "This is Maggie Piper."

* * *

After work, I hop on the train and lean against my window seat. I close my eyes, hoping to drown out the conversations taking place among all the couples in the rows directly in front of me. When I arrive in Yorktown, Cheryl and the kids are waiting in her SUV to drive me back to their house. I tell the kids I have a gift in my overnight bag for them to share, but I don't tell them what it is. This pisses Cheryl off, because Cady and Michael spend the entire ride taking turns guessing what it is and bouncing as much as they can while restrained under their seatbelts. The gift is from one of Melanie's clients, a toy company. I don't see the appeal, but it was rejected as evidence in a case Melanie's working on and is apparently popular with the under-ten crowd. Melanie's boys are also under ten, but I took advantage of my sadness of late to convince her to give it to me so I could maintain my status as the best aunt in the world and infinitely better than Joyce, their only other aunt and Jim's sister.

As soon as we're inside the house and our jackets are off, I pull the game out of my bag. Cady and Michael squeal in delight and beg Cheryl to let them play with it immediately. Cheryl says yes, but only if they take it upstairs. Then she winks at me and slickly motions her head toward the two wine glasses on her kitchen counter.

I realize this is her ploy to give us some peace, quiet, and alone time. These strategies rarely work since the kids are usually more inclined to hang on our every word (and every limb) when we most want them to go away, but this time, Cady grabs the game, and she and Michael race up the stairs with no argument.

A few minutes later, Cheryl hands me a glass of wine. "I was thinking we could order a pizza. What do you say?"

"I'm game. Good wine, though I should cut down. I drink way more single than I did when I was in a relationship," I say, before heading to the living room and plopping myself on Cheryl's black leather couch. Cheryl keeps her house cold, like her mom and mine did when we were growing up, so the first thing I do is pull the black and white afghan that Aunt Helen knitted over my legs. "What's going on?"

Cheryl sits next to me on the couch and glances up at the stairwell leading to the second floor of her three-bedroom high-ranch-style house. I assume she's listening to confirm Cady and Michael are still alive, because she doesn't answer me until we hear them tittering together. "Not much. How's everything with you?"

I know she's lying, but I decide to wait it out. "Things are good. Well, things are fine. I had a phone interview today with a recruiter."

"How did you do?"

"Aside from saying 'um' every other word, it went all right. She said my experience and skill set work in my favor, but the limited job market works against me." I take another sip of wine before placing it on the cherry wood coffee table. "She's going to try to set up some interviews."

Cheryl nods. "Sounds semi-promising." Grabbing the end of the afghan and covering her own feet, Cheryl asks, "Are things still awkward with Philip?"

"No, he pretty much ignores me. Except when I catch him staring at me."

Cheryl's eyebrows go up. "He stares at you?"

"Staring might be an exaggeration, but each time he passes by my office, he peeks inside, whereas I go out of my way not to walk past his office at all. And he checks me out at all of the biz dev meetings." My stomach growls. "Where are the hors d'oeuvres?" Cheryl is usually a much better hostess, putting out a plate of cheese and crackers or chips and dip before the main course.

"Biz dev?"

"Business development," I say with a smile. "Appetizers?"

"Interesting," Cheryl says, still ignoring my inquiries about the food situation.

"It's not interesting at all. It's awkward. I wonder if he pictures me naked whenever he sees me." I also wonder if he has visions of me bouncing on top of him with my tits in his face, but I'm too embarrassed to say this to Cheryl.

"Do you picture him naked when you look at him?"

"Of course. Which is why I only do it when we have work-related one-on-one conversations." I can also hear his loud groan right before he comes, but again, I don't say this to Cheryl. In contrast, my memories of Doug are not all sexually driven, probably because our relationship was not almost entirely physical in nature. Of course, now I'm thinking about the faces and sounds Doug used to make when we had sex and trying not to imagine him with Lindsay. "I'm starving."

Cheryl stands up. "You're as bad as my kids. I'll call the pizza place now. We can order bread sticks or garlic bread with cheese too."

"Garlic bread with cheese," I declare happily. Growing up, Cheryl and I always ordered garlic bread and cheese at the local pizza places, even though it was overkill on cheese and carbs from a nutritional standpoint. We didn't care then and I don't care now, even though, as Aunt Helen loves to warn me, my metabolism might slow down when I turn forty. I rummage through Cheryl's cabinets searching for chips or pretzels, but aside from several liters of soda, boxes of cereal, and various cooking staples like sugar and flour, it's barren. "You don't have any junk food."

"Sorry, Magpie. Didn't have time to stock up."

I decide the time has come to confront her. I wait for her to call in our order to the pizza place and then I pounce. "What's going on with you? And do not turn it around on me." Cheryl opens her mouth to speak, but I hold up my hand. "And don't tell me nothing is going on. I haven't seen Jim in months. You snap at me whenever

I mention his name. And...*And*," I repeat with emphasis, "you invited me over for a girl's night on Valentine's Day. What the hell is going on?"

Cheryl's eyes bug out as she puts two fingers to her lips. "Shh. The kids are upstairs," she whispers.

My face gets hot in shame. Cursing in front of the twerps is a bad habit. "Sorry," I whisper back.

Cheryl finishes her wine and pours another glass. Gazing at the glass with a guilty expression, she says, "I shouldn't drink this much until the kids are in bed." Then she turns to me. "Jim and I are taking a trial separation."

My stomach drops in dread even though I predicted it was something like this. "Oh, Cheryl. I'm so sorry." I follow her back to the living room where we resume our seats on the couch, both under the warmth of the afghan. "What happened?"

"We grew apart. Or maybe we didn't grow at all and have nothing new to talk about. It's like we're going through the motions of being a couple, but the romantic bond is broken. Or at least cracked."

I recall Philip's explanation of what happened with his wife, and it sounds eerily similar. I also remember Cheryl attempting to show me the positive side of Philip and his wife trying again, even though it meant he had to dump me in the process. "Are you going to work on it, or are you talking divorce?"

"We're in therapy, but we thought it made sense to live separately while we figured things out." She regards me with sad eyes. "Neither of us wants to get divorced."

I'm happy to hear this. "Good."

"But we also don't want to be in an unhappy marriage. We're too young to settle into a ho-hum, uninspiring existence."

Her association of the early forties with being too young for *anything* pleases me. "I'm so sorry, Cheryl. I don't even know what to say except I'm here for you, and pulling for you guys to get through this. Do you like your therapist?" My mind flashes to Miranda and Steve's therapist in the first *Sex and the City* movie.

"Yeah, we both do. Jim was afraid a woman would automatically take my side, and I secretly hoped he was right." She pauses and gives me a sheepish grin. "But she's completely impartial. We'll see."

When the doorbell rings, Cheryl stands up and heads to the kitchen where she left money for the pizza. She pays the guy as the kids come racing down the stairs, shouting "Pizza! Pizza! Pizza!" I laugh at them as Cady drags me by the hand to the kitchen table. "You sit next to me, Aunt Maggie."

"I wouldn't have it any other way," I say until I notice Michael standing off to the side with his full lower lip curled in a pout. Approaching him, I ask, "Will you sit on my other side, Michael?" Michael's eyes light up like a sparkler on the Fourth of July.

"I guess I'll eat mine in the basement since no one wants to sit next to me," Cheryl says with a frown.

"Mommy, you can sit on my othow side," Cady says.

"I wanna sit next to Mommy too," Michael wails.

"Oh, now I'm Miss Popular," Cheryl says dramatically, and while the kids giggle, I wonder if I'll ever have children of my own. Sometimes I'm positive I don't want to be a mother, but other times, like when I witness the bond Cheryl shares with Cady and Michael, unique to mothers and their children, I ache for a little boy or girl to call me mommy and love me unconditionally.

After dinner, Cheryl and I give the kids their baths and get them ready for bed. I read them not one, but two bedtime stories, then find myself back on the living room couch with Cheryl and a tall glass of water.

"I'm reluctant to bring it up, but how are you holding up?" Cheryl asks, her eyebrows creased in concern.

As much as I hate what Cheryl is going through, it's almost a relief to talk about her problems instead of mine for a change. "I'm trying not to think about it. Which means I think about it all of the time." My mind wanders to the thought of Doug and Lindsay celebrating Valentine's Day, and I blink my eyes to keep from crying.

"I'm sorry, Maggie. I honestly never thought he would find someone else so fast."

Not ready to accept Doug replacing me so easily, I jump on the defensive. "He said it had nothing to do with Lindsay. Just because he's dating her doesn't mean he's in love with her."

Cheryl places her hand on mine. "Of course it doesn't. I didn't mean to suggest it did. I imagined Doug moping over you while zoning out to stupid videos on YouTube. I'm just surprised he's even dating someone."

"He's a catch," I whisper.

"He sure is," Cheryl agrees. She pauses before saying, "To be honest, I never understood why you had doubts in the first place, Mags. What was the problem?"

"Doug asked me the same thing."

"And what did you say?"

"I told him I didn't know. I could never put it into words, but I suppose it was lacking the oomph."

Cheryl narrows her eyes. "Oomph?"

I give her a timid smile. "You know. Drama. Angst. Challenge." I'm on a roll. "It was so easy."

Cheryl gawks at me like I'm crazy. "That's a bad thing, why?"

I stare back at her blankly. "I have no idea."

"Were you bored?" she questions.

I shake my head. "No." Doug and I always had fun, even when we were doing nothing. We were only bored when we wanted to be.

"Was the sex bad?"

"Not at all. It was good." The sex wasn't new and exciting, and we weren't particularly experimental after the first year, but we knew what the other one liked, and it was always more than satisfying. I close my eyes, remembering the last time we were together. Way too long ago.

Cheryl sighs loudly. "Here's what I think about challenges, drama, and angst." She pauses dramatically and locks eyes with me. "If Doug was a challenge, you would constantly worry he'd dump you. You would be afraid every girl he spoke to would steal him away from you. You would spend your entire relationship anxious and paranoid. The drama would come from you accusing him of cheating on you and the angst would come from makeup sex. Makeup sex is fun, but not if it's the only sex you ever have." Cheryl's face turns a shade of red as she shakes her head and regards me with something resembling disgust. Before I can defend myself, she continues. "Doug wasn't a challenge because he was in love with you and committed to your relationship. There was no drama because you were compatible, and there was no angst because you didn't need to constantly prove yourself worthy of his time and attention. It was easy because it was right. You have no idea how lucky you are...*were*."

By the time she is finished, my body has shrunk into the couch and when I swipe my fingers across my cheek, there is dampness caused by tears I had no idea I'd shed. I struggle to find my voice and all I can manage is, "Okay." Unable to meet Cheryl's eyes, I stand up and say, "I'm going to bed. Work tomorrow. Sorry." I hate being scolded, especially when I deserve it.

As I grab my overnight bag and head to her guest bathroom, Cheryl says, "I'm sorry, Magpie. You know I love you. I left two towels on top of the laundry machine in the bathroom, and there's a fresh tube of toothpaste."

I mumble, "I love you too," and close the bathroom door behind me.

*   *   *

The wine I drank induces sleep, saving me from a restless night of tossing and turning while hearing Cheryl's voice in my head telling me what an utter fool I am. I sleep uninterrupted until the sound of Cheryl trotting down the stairs and flicking on the light switch in the kitchen wakes me up. My first waking thought is: "Shit. I have to go speed dating tonight."

After I shower and blow-dry my hair, I sit at the kitchen table silently drinking a cup of coffee. It is unnervingly quiet, and the only sounds are the kids chomping on their toast with peanut butter. I guess none of us are morning people. Must be genetic.

After breakfast, Cheryl drives me to the train back to the city. Out of the side of her mouth, presumably so the kids don't hear, she says, "Are you mad at me?"

I stare at the line of cars ahead of us. "Only dogs get mad, remember?"

"Why ow you mad at Mommy, Aunt Maggie?"

I shift to face Cady. "I'm not angry at your mommy, sweetie." Turning back to Cheryl, I say, "I'm not mad. It stung, but you were right."

Gripping the steering wheel so tightly her knuckles have turned white, Cheryl whispers, "I'm sorry. It's challenging for me to empathize with you when I would do anything to be as happy with Jim as you were with Doug. We're in therapy hoping to recapture what you guys had all along."

"I get it, but it's not fair to compare my three-year pre-marriage relationship with Doug to your relationship with Jim. You've been married for a decade. Things change. Ebb and flow, right?"

Cheryl glances through the rearview mirror at the kids, who are both bopping along to a One Direction song playing out of the back speakers of the car. "I sometimes wonder if we were ever truly compatible. Even at the start. Getting married later in life is not such a bad idea. At least you're fully developed."

I look down at my breasts. "Darn it. I was hoping I was still developing."

At the same time, we chant, "*I must, I must, I must increase my bust*" from our favorite Judy Blume novel and burst out laughing. ،

* * *

That evening, after moaning to Melanie *again* about being suckered into going speed dating (I complained all through lunch too), she wishes me good luck and promises to send positive romantic vibes my way. I tell her to save her vibes for Amanda, since I'm only going for moral support and have no interest in finding my own love connection.

An hour later, Amanda and I walk into the World Bar in the United Nations after enjoying a pre-event drink at Press Box, a dive Irish pub a few blocks away, to calm our nerves. A peppy woman sitting at a desk by the entrance signs us in and hands over name tags and a pink piece of note paper. She then encourages us to go to the bar and mingle before the official event commences in approximately twenty minutes. I have no desire to mingle, but would like to get another drink in my hands as soon as possible. I express this to Amanda, and she chuckles nervously.

"After you," she says, straightening her above-the-knee black pencil skirt. She paired it with a simple black and white striped shirt, and with her hair flowing in waves well past her shoulders, I'm certain she looks sexier than she realizes.

After I order us both a significantly more expensive drink in the World Bar than the ones we purchased at Press Box, we take small sips and casually glance around the dimly-lit room for a sneak peek at who we will be meeting for six minutes a pop, as well as our competition. So far, there are significantly more women in the room than men, and it reminds me of an episode of *The Bachelor* with pockets of multiple women vying for the attention of a single man. Only the people are far less attractive than those on *The Bachelor*, I think. Then I mentally scold myself for pre-judging the men before the mini-dates, but it's difficult not to notice how many men are bald, chubby, and shorter than me. I'm having trouble believing some of them are not well over the age of forty, even though they're supposed to be between thirty and forty. Most of the women, on the other hand, are cute and in shape. The green pleated skirt I'm wearing with a black fitted sweater is comfortable, but very slimming, and even though a part of me wishes I could blend into the crowd unnoticed, I'm glad I had the foresight to pack a flattering outfit in the overnight bag I brought to Cheryl's house.

I plant on a smile, determined to make this a positive experience for Amanda. "You ready for this?" I ask her.

"I guess." Leaning in closer to me, she whispers, "I'm only using this as practice. I seriously doubt I'll like any of these guys."

"Keep an open mind," I advise, even though I'm thinking exactly the same thing.

Waving her pink piece of paper at me, she says, "Yeah, yeah. Whatever."

Before I can respond, the peppy hostess ("PH") taps her microphone and asks for our attention. The room goes silent as she welcomes us all to the event and explains how it will work—the women will remain at their assigned table for the entire evening, and the men will join the women for the six-minute dates and rotate around the room until every man has met every woman. According to my pink paper, I am assigned to table nine, which is by the window. Amanda is assigned to table eleven, which is directly opposite table nine. I'm not sure if this is a good thing, as I'm afraid eye contact with Amanda in the middle of a date will result in a giggling fit.

Besides providing the pertinent seating information, the pink paper also contains a chart we can use to take notes on each guy we meet. PH gives us examples such as "has bad breath, funny, wearing orange sweater, looks like George Clooney." In response to the last example, I catch another girl's eye and we exchange a knowing look. Then PH explains that beginning tomorrow morning, we will be able to login to the website and complete an online form indicating which guys, if any, we are interested in (a) going out with again, (b) pursuing a platonic friendship with, or (c) networking with on a professional level. We are told if two people choose each other for the same type of relationship, and only the same type of relationship, the dating service will provide the other's contact information. Upon hearing about option (c), I allow my hopes to soar at the possibility of coming out of this night, perhaps not with a potential love interest, but with new job prospects.

I wish Amanda good luck and head over to table nine. I

attempt to make myself comfortable on the couch as I wait for my first date. When he stands above me, the first thing I do is glance at his name tag. It says, "Dave R."

"Hi, Dave R.," I say. "Have a seat."

After he sits down, he glances at my name tag and scribbles on his blue piece of paper. I assume he's writing "Maggie P." and hope he's not including a comment about how unattractive he finds me. If I'm being honest with myself, I'm not at all attracted to him either. He has brown wavy hair, dark eyes, a very fair complexion, and is average height with a lanky body. He's not bad looking, but his baby face suggests he's young—so young that if I brought him home with me, I wouldn't know whether to take him to bed or tuck him in. I write, "Dave R. baby face" on my pink paper.

Once we've both jotted down our notes, we lock eyes and greet each other at the same time before chuckling. His face turns red, and I'm sure mine does too.

"Have you done one of these events before, Maggie P.?" he asks once we stop laughing.

"This is my first time," I confess. "What about you?"

"Mine too. We can pop our speed dating cherries together."

Struggling not to spit out the drink I haven't finished swallowing, I snort. "Sounds like a plan. Be gentle with me, okay?"

"Of course. So, Maggie P., what do you do for fun?"

"I spend a lot of time with my friends—going out for dinner, having a few drinks. I've recently taken up indoor rock climbing. And I'm not ashamed to admit that television is the love of my life."

"Oh, I'm a major television junkie too. What's your top show?"

"There are so many shows I like, it's difficult to choose. *The Following* was up there before it was cancelled."

Dave's eyes brighten. "One of my favorites too. Seriously creepy but addictive."

"To be honest, I originally watched it only because Kevin Bacon was in it."

Dave touches his finger to his chin contemplatively. "What movie is he famous for again?"

"*Footloose*," I say without hesitation.

"Never saw it, but I think it came out the year I was born."

According to my calculations, if I'm barely young enough to qualify for this event, Dave is barely *old* enough. I let this sink in as a bell rings, and PH calls out, "Time's up."

Dave stands up and holds out his hand. "Thank you for a terrific first experience. It was a pleasure."

I shake his hand. "Same here." It was not a bad way to spend six minutes, and I'm hopeful the rest of my dates will be equally pleasant.

The next several dates leave me feeling more or less the same. I don't find myself longing to extend my six minutes with any of the three guys, but they are all easy to talk to and the time passes swiftly.

When John K. sits down, I write "John K. Tall, bushy eyebrows, *The Office*" since he resembles a less attractive John Krasinski and even has the same initials.

John leans back in his chair and crosses his arms over his chest. "How's your evening coming along, Maggie?"

"I'm enjoying myself so far," I respond, truthfully. "How about you?"

"Not bad." He leans forward. "Where are you from originally?"

"Westchester. Peekskill, specifically," I say. "How about you?"

"Also from Westchester. Rye Brook. I think we were football rivals," he says with a twinkle in his dark blue eyes.

"I don't think Peekskill had an official rival, but I suppose any team we played was technically the enemy."

"Were you a cheerleader, by any chance?"

"Nope. But I did go to all of the games." My high school boyfriend was on the football team.

Cocking his head to the side, John says, "I'm surprised."

Mirroring his body language, I say, "Yeah, why's that?"

"You're a cutie. I bet you would have made a great addition to the squad." He leers at me.

Even though my gut says John is a bit of a douche bag, my face heats up at his compliment. "Why thank you. I'm not sure I was quite as cute back in the early nineties."

John squints his eyes. "Early nineties? When did you graduate high school?"

Estimating John at close to my age, I answer without any shame. "1995."

Jerking his head back, John says, "So you're almost forty?"

"I'm thirty-nine."

Leaning against his chair again, John says, "Oh, wow."

Taken aback by his strong reaction, I say, "When did you graduate?"

"1993," he says before blatantly checking out the rest of the room.

"Making you...?"

Focusing on me again, John says, "Forty-one."

"I see." Older than me and technically too old for this event.

John inches closer to me. His face serious, he says, "Listen, we're almost out of time, but can I give you a piece of unsolicited advice?"

I raise an eyebrow. "Go for it."

"You seem like a nice girl, Maggie. And very attractive. But you might want to focus on an older age range. Guys in their fifties would flock to you like alcoholics at an open bar. I'm not sure how much luck you'll have here."

I'm attempting to pick my jaw off of the floor when the bell rings, and PM yells, "Time." Saved by the bell.

"Nice meeting you," I mutter, still in a semi-state of shock.

John has already stood up, but he turns around and absently says, "Yeah, you too." Then heads to the next table. I give his current date the once-over and hope for both of their sakes she's younger than she looks. I write "Asshole" on my paper by John K.'s name.

Two dates later, I have mostly wiped the memory of John's insensitive comments out of my mind. I try to convince myself his ageist attitude is the exception rather than the norm, but find myself flashing back to the many profiles I read on Match.com with the same mindset.

I snap out of it as the next, and thankfully last, guy sits down across from me. I take note of his name, "Ben C.," and write it down on my paper. Then I focus my gaze on him and smile softly. "Hi. I'm Maggie."

Ben returns my greeting with a wide grin before taking a sip of red wine. As he carefully places the glass back on the table, I inspect him more closely. He has freckles like me and eyes the same color as mine. I wonder if I would look like him as a man.

"I can't believe this is the last date," he says.

"Are you happy it's almost over?" I ask.

"Not happy, exactly. But it's exhausting, you know?"

And how. "Totally. Have you done this before?"

"Nope. What about you?"

"This is my first time too. Although after seven dates, we're sort of experts now, huh?"

"And I saved my best material for last."

"Did you now?" I surprise myself with my flirtatious tone.

Ben runs a hand through his short, light brown hair. "I sure did. I have all sorts of party tricks in my repertoire."

I lean forward. "Like what?"

"Well, for one, I'm a talented juggler. And I can swallow fire."

"And where did you learn these tricks?"

"I trained for the circus."

"Really?"

Ben nods in response, his face expressionless.

I narrow my eyes at him. I assume he is pulling my leg, but he looks so earnest. And according to Melanie, there are places in the city that offer circus classes. "For real?"

Ben leans forward as if to tell me a secret and then whispers, "Not for real. I'm not a fan of the circus. I hate clowns."

Giggling, I say, "So do I." I conclude Ben is kind of adorable, even if he can pass for my brother. I hope that doesn't make me conceited.

"Do you live in the city, Maggie?"

I nod. "In Gramercy. How about you?"

"Murray Hill. We're practically neighbors."

Murray Hill is notorious for being a very young neighborhood, but I would peg Ben for at least thirty-five. "How do you like Murray Hill?"

Ben crinkles his nose. "Well, it's convenient since I work in midtown, but to be honest, it's got a post-college vibe."

I laugh. "We refer to it as Fraternity Row." I realize a second too late the "we" in question is Doug and me.

Ben chuckles with me. "Yeah, that's about right. I'm thirty-nine, so sometimes when I grab a beer at a local pub after work, I worry I'll be mistaken for someone's dad."

"I know what you mean. I'm thirty-nine as well." I hold my breath in anticipation of his disappointment, but none appears.

"Maybe we can head to one of those teeny-bopper bars together and show them how it's done," Ben says with a wink.

My heart beats faster as I wonder if it was a rhetorical question, or if he is asking me out. Since I have no idea how to respond, I'm relieved when PH interrupts with, "Time!" before I have a chance.

As she continues speaking—something about the bar remaining open if anyone wants to hang around—I say, "It was nice meeting you," to Ben.

Ben stands up. Making eye contact with me, he says, "Same here, Maggie. A great way to end the evening."

I spot Amanda heading my way with her coat already on and put on my jacket as she reaches my table. Once Ben is out of earshot, I say, "What'd you think?"

Amanda gives me a timid smile. "It could have been worse. Let's grab something to eat and swap stories."

My stomach rumbles, reminding me I haven't consumed solid food since lunch. "Do you mind if I ask Melanie to join us? Since we're near the office, she told me to text her if we went out to dinner." I glance at my watch. "Although she might have left already." It's almost nine thirty p.m., which is late to be in the office even for a workaholic attorney like Melanie.

"I don't mind," Amanda says.

Then I remember that this was Amanda's first single's event in over a decade, and she might not want to discuss it with Melanie. "Are you sure? I don't have to call her if you'd rather discuss this in private."

Amanda pats my arm. "No worries. But let's go. I'm starving."

I text Melanie to tell her we're heading over to Public House on 41st Street if she's interested. She responds a few seconds later to confirm she'll join us. I put my phone in my purse. "She'll meet us there soon."

A few minutes later, the three of us are perusing the menu at Public House. The pub is crowded, but most of the patrons are hanging around the bar watching basketball. We easily secure a table in the restaurant section. Melanie wastes no time on pleasantries, jumping on us the minute the waitress is finished taking our orders. "So...spill."

I glance at Amanda. "You first, since this was your gig and I was merely your sidekick and chaperone. How'd it go?"

Her lips curling up, Amanda says, "I actually had fun. It was so low pressure, and all the guys were relatively normal."

"Did you make a love connection?" Melanie asks with a questioning gaze.

Amanda smirks. "No love connection was made, but I'm seeing my therapist tomorrow morning. I'm afraid she's going to encourage me to pick some of the guys anyway for practice dates. I'm hoping she'll say attending the event was good enough."

Beaming at Amanda, I say, "You shouldn't do anything you're not comfortable with. I hope you're proud of yourself for going in the first place. It was a huge step, and you didn't even complain."

"Unlike this one," Melanie mutters, shaking her head at me. The conversation halts momentarily when the waitress appears with our food, but when she leaves again, Melanie immediately turns to me. "And you, my dear? Anyone you liked?"

I sigh. "Besides the guy who kindly suggested I was too old for him but would be a hit with the over-fifty crowd?"

Melanie has a forkful of salad at the opening to her mouth but drops it into her bowl. "You're kidding me."

Amanda's eyes widen like saucers. "Someone seriously said that to you?"

"Pretty much verbatim." I nod solemnly.

Amanda asks, "Which guy?" Her face is as white as fresh snow, and I can tell she's as horrified as I was.

"John K.," I say.

"How old was he?" Melanie asks.

"This is what kills me. He was older than me by two years."

Chomping on lettuce, Melanie says, "What a dick."

I remove my pink piece of paper from my bag and point to where I wrote "asshole" next to his name. "But dick works well too," I say.

I chuckle with Melanie until I notice Amanda gazing off into space. "You all right?"

Snapping to attention, Amanda says, "Yeah, I'm fine. I knew you were afraid you'd be the oldest girl there, but I never dreamed someone would throw it in your face. I'm so sorry."

"It's okay. Not your fault," I insist. "And besides, the rest of the guys were totally cool." I pause and then clarify, "Well, maybe not *totally* cool. But not dicks."

"Besides, Maggie isn't even forty yet, so to suggest she should hook up with men more than ten years older is bullshit," Melanie says.

I wave a hand. "Honestly. I was upset for about five minutes until I realized the source of the comment was no one I had any desire to go out with anyway. Or even be friends with."

Amanda nods in agreement, but she seems uncomfortable.

Narrowing my eyes at her, I say, "What?"

"It's just..." Amanda stops and lowers her gaze. "John K. was the one guy I was going to let my therapist talk me into choosing."

Melanie nearly chokes on her salad. "Oh my God."

I feel my face drain of color. "You are full of surprises, but if you like him, I'll learn to like him too," I lie, crossing my fingers behind my back. I take a bite of my sandwich to avoid direct eye contact with her. I know the girl hasn't dated since her twenties, but she needs to sharpen her jerk-radar big-time. Then again, I'm sure John poured on the charm with Amanda. She's beautiful and at only thirty-four meets his age requirements.

Whipping her head back, Amanda says, "Not a chance. I would never date a guy who would think such an unsolicited comment was appropriate or even remotely helpful."

I tip my head in her direction. "You sure?"

"I'm positive. It's not like I wanted to marry the guy. I figured if my therapist forced me to pick at least one guy, I'd choose him. He was the cutest."

"You think?" I ask in surprise. "I thought Ben C. was way cuter." As the table falls silent, I realize I admitted to liking one of the guys and curse myself. I attempt to back pedal. "Relatively speaking, of course." I spoon some soup into my mouth, hoping my friends will let the subject drop.

Leaning forward in interest, Melanie asks, "Who was Ben C.?"

No such luck.

I wipe my chin with a napkin. "He was the last guy I met tonight. I thought he was kind of attractive," I admit.

Smirking, Melanie says, "You don't say? *Interesting.*"

I roll my eyes at her.

"What did you think of Ben C.?" Melanie asks Amanda.

"He was the first guy I met. I was too nervous to pay much attention for the first couple of dates. All I remember is him spilling red wine on the table," Amanda says.

"Sounds perfect for our girl, Maggie," Melanie joshes.

"No one is perfect for me," I say. "Except maybe Doug." I managed to go almost the entire night without thinking of him, but the ache in my gut has now re-emerged with a vengeance.

Melanie frowns. "We're not trying to replace Doug, but if you felt something for this Ben dude, why don't you pick him?"

"I didn't feel anything for him," I say, a decibel too loud. Lowering my voice, I continue, "He was nice and cute. Although maybe I only think so because he resembles me."

Melanie raises an eyebrow. "Seriously?" Turning to Amanda, she asks, "Do Ben and Maggie look alike?"

Giggling, Amanda agrees. "I didn't notice it at the time, but they do have the same coloring and freckles."

"How sweet," Melanie mocks.

"Stop it," I plead. No longer hungry, I place my napkin on my plate.

"I think you should pick him," Melanie says. "What do you think, Amanda?"

Amanda sighs. "I'm the last person who will force you to choose this guy if you really don't want to."

"Thank y—"

"But, you don't have anything to lose. He might not even pick you back, and then you won't have to worry about it. And if he does, you can always change your mind. But if you don't pick him, the choice will be taken from you. Remember, interest has to be mutual or no contact information will be exchanged."

"I second Amanda," Melanie says.

I remove my napkin from my plate and pop a potato chip in my mouth. To appease them, I say, "If we can change the subject, I promise to sleep on it, okay?" I hate to lie to Amanda and Melanie, but in all honesty, I'm not too keen on taking their advice. They encouraged me to call Doug.

* * *

I try my best to avoid Melanie at work the next day. I don't want to give her the opportunity to ask what I've decided about Ben C. Unfortunately, I haven't decided anything, despite going through the pros and cons of both options while tossing and turning in bed the night before. One con is I'm not over Doug, and nowhere near ready for another relationship. Would it be fair to lead Ben to believe I'm emotionally available when I'm not? A valid point, but agreeing to go on one date is not the equivalent of telling the guy I want to marry him.

Ben C. made me laugh, and I *did* think he was cute. A point in favor of my going out with him is the high likelihood of enjoying his company, even if the date doesn't lead anywhere. But what is the purpose of going out with the guy if I have no interest in taking it to another level?

Every argument I have to go out with the guy comes with an equally credible reason *not* to go out with him and vice-versa. Time I should have spent sleeping was instead used up engaging in an internal debate, and I have puffy circles under my eyes this morning to prove it.

As I rub my tired eyes, I hear a scuffle of feet and glance in the direction of my office door in time to catch Philip walking by. He raises his hand in a wave, giving me full view of his wedding ring in the process. As I unenthusiastically return the gesture, minus the wedding ring display, my stomach drops.

What am I going to do if Doug marries Lindsay?

Before I can chicken out, I login to the speed dating website. Scrolling through the list of the men I met the night before, I spot the name "Ben C." and click "Interested in a second date."

March

My hands shake as I lock the door to my apartment. I might be late for my first date with Ben C. We're meeting in ten minutes at Terroir Wine Bar, and while it's only four blocks from my building, I always underestimate how long it takes to wait for the elevator. If it's a local—stopping on every floor—getting to the lobby could take me close to ten minutes. Then again, even if I'm late, it will only be by a couple of minutes, and I suppose it's less awkward than being early.

I needn't have worried. The wait for the elevator is not even enough time for me to check my iPhone for new emails, and before I know it, I'm outside and crossing from the south side of 27th Street toward the bar located between 30th and 31st. The gusts of wind smack me in the face with force, and I pull my knit hat over my ears in retaliation.

I can't tell if I'm nervous or merely dreading the evening ahead of me, but my stomach is in knots. Ripping the mitten off of my right hand, I pull my phone out of my bag and call Jodie. She answers on the first ring.

My bare hand is already frozen from exposure to the cold, but willing myself to stop thinking about it, I say, "I need a pep talk."

"They call me Peppy McGee for a reason. What can I do you for?"

Even though I fear losing a finger to frostbite, I slow my step to avoid arriving at the bar too early. "Why do people call you Peppy McGee? Your last name is Anderson."

"I'm being silly. What do you need a pep talk for?"

"I have my date with speed dating guy tonight."

"He's gonna love you," she squeals enthusiastically. "Did I live up to my name?"

"And how. But I'm not sure I want him to love me."

Jodie doesn't say anything, and I can almost hear her thinking through the phone before she speaks again. "I don't follow you."

I'm approaching 29th Street and slow my pace even more in order to miss the light. "I don't have much time."

"When are you meeting the guy?"

"I'm less than two blocks from the bar."

She blows air out of her cheeks. "Jeez, Mags. You might have thought of calling me earlier."

"I know. I didn't realize I would be so nervous." I duck under an awning and stop walking. "I'm not predicting a nightmare date or anything, but I don't know if I'm ready for a great date either. I thought going out with Ben would make me feel like I was moving on. Like Philip and Doug moved on. But I'm not sure I'm ready to move on, or if I even want to. But I can't spend the next four months sitting at home waiting to turn forty. And unless I move to Sedona, there are only so many rocks I can climb." I pause for a response, but when none comes, I say, "Do you think I'm crazy?"

"For shizzle. But it has nothing to do with this silly predicament you've gotten yourself into."

I chuckle.

"Listen to me, Maggie. It's just a date. If you don't like the guy, it's not your last chance saloon. You'll meet someone else eventually."

I nod but don't say anything.

"I swear you will."

"I believe you," I say, even though the act of falling in love with someone other than Doug seems very out of my grasp right now.

"And if you *do* like the guy, it doesn't mean you have to *love* him or even think about loving him anytime soon. Stop putting so much pressure on yourself, for the love of God. It's one date. It doesn't have to change your life."

She has a point and so I allow a modicum of stress to leave my body. "You're right. It's just one date."

"Now go have fun."

"Thanks. You have lived up to your name, Peppy McGee."

"And don't forget to use a condom."

My mouth drops open. "I'm not—"

"Ciao, Magpie."

After giving my phone one last glance to check the time, I return it to my bag and hurriedly put my mitten back on before walking the final block to the bar.

I spot Ben sitting at a table in the back of the long, narrow bar, and he stands up when he sees me. He's wearing a midnight blue sweater and gray work pants. My face gets hot as I note how adorable he is. I was concerned the lighting in the World Bar favorably altered everyone's appearance—like the skinny mirrors in the dressing room at Macy's. Or that my memory of the Ben I met more than two weeks ago wouldn't match the reality of the one I'd meet tonight.

I reach over to kiss him on the cheek. "I hope I didn't keep you waiting." His face is still cold—a good sign he hasn't been here long.

"I just got here a couple of minutes ago."

Removing my hat from my head and smoothing down my hair, I say, "Glad to hear it." I let my hands wander under the table and feel around hopefully, searching for hooks.

Ben sits back down, and, as if reading my mind, says, "There are hooks for your bag and coat."

I place my handbag on one of the hooks. "Great," I say, while pulling on the zipper of my jacket. I bite down on my lip and jerk the zipper harder, but it doesn't budge.

Ben's eyebrows draw together. "Are you all right?"

I yank my zipper in one last attempt and then shake my head in embarrassment. "I'm sort of stuck."

His blue eyes widen. "Stuck?"

"I can't get my jacket off." I curse inwardly at whatever higher power decided now was a good time for my jacket zipper to break.

Ben stands up. "Maybe I can help."

As he moves closer to me, practically in kissing distance, and starts manipulating my zipper, I consciously lean my head back trying to create more room. I can feel the blood rush to my face. I watch him tugging earnestly, and I wonder if he hates me already. He glances up at me. "Almost got it."

I force a smile. "I'm such an idiot," I mutter.

"No worries," he says before returning to his mission.

As I stand there helplessly, I imagine it is Doug—and not Ben—coming to my rescue. I remember the time I got a brush stuck in my hair, and Doug spent almost half an hour extricating it. And the time he used an entire Tide Stain Stick on one of my skirts when someone accidentally spilled tomato sauce on it at a dinner party. Those things never fazed me as I considered it part of his job. But this is different. I don't even know Ben's last name, except that it starts with a C.

"Got it."

I snap out of my nostalgia as Ben guides my arms out of my jacket. "Thank you. I'm so sorry."

Ben winks. "It was nothing."

A few minutes later, the ice has been broken, and we're chatting easily over a glass of wine. I tell Ben how I spent thirty minutes the previous night screaming at my remote control for not working before I realized it needed new batteries. "If something breaks in my apartment, I'm better off replacing it than trying to fix it." This reminds me that the hook Doug glued to the bathroom door to hold our towels fell off. Since I have no idea how to fix it, I'll be throwing my towels over the shower rack for the foreseeable future. "And I break things a lot, which doesn't help." I shrug sheepishly and take a sip of my wine.

Ben clinks his wine glass against mine. "Welcome to my world. I'm totally accident prone too, but I compensate by being pretty decent at putting things back together."

I open my mouth to tell Ben he is welcome to come over to my apartment to fix my towel hook, but stop myself. At this point, I would be saying it facetiously. I wouldn't want to give him the wrong idea, so I change the subject. "How long have you lived in the city?"

"I moved here not long after graduating college."

"Where are you from originally?"

"Pennsylvania. It was a big transition. Especially not having a car."

"Do you miss having a car?"

"Not at all. I have a license and everything, but I don't particularly like driving."

"Me neither. And I'm not a very good driver. It took me three driving tests to get my license." Why I admit this, as if it's something to be proud of, is beyond me. No wonder no one ever wants to take a drive with me on the rare occasions I borrow my mom's car.

Ben's face gets red. "Me too."

I chuckle. "We have a lot in common. Both accident prone and shitty drivers."

Pointing at his face, Ben says, "And we both have freckles."

I smile at Ben while making a mental note to ask my dad if a half-brother from another mother is among the many secrets he's kept from me. Then I think of something. "When's your birthday?"

Ben raises his eyebrows. "Why? Thinking about what to get me? Remember, anything besides tickets to the circus."

Giggling, I say, "Just curious."

"December 7th. What about you?"

"July 12th." I'm relieved he's not my long-lost twin brother separated at birth.

Twenty minutes later, Ben and I are exchanging stories about our respective careers over a cheese plate when the volume of music increases and "Reign in Blood" by Slayer blasts over the speakers. Ben and I stop speaking and lock eyes for a second before laughing. "Interesting choice of music," Ben says.

"Heavy metal isn't exactly what I would expect to hear in a wine bar," I agree.

"I think I heard both Black Sabbath and Anthrax earlier."

Layering a slice of Manchego cheese between two small pieces of raisin and nut bread, I say, "Personally, I prefer the glamour rock bands like Guns N' Roses and Def Leppard."

"I love Def Leppard. Saw them at PNC—"

"Art Center," I interrupt excitedly. "So did I."

The corners of Ben's lips rise. "You weren't the chick who streaked across the stage, were you?"

"Probably."

"Funny. Okay. Time to get personal."

I bite my lower lip. "Okay..."

Ben lightly taps his hand over mine. "Don't look so scared. I just wanted to ask if you'd ever been married."

"Nope. Never been married. What about you?" I hope the answer is also "no" so Ben doesn't feel the need to bombard me with a list of questions to determine how a seemingly normal, attractive, and well-adjusted woman such as myself made it to thirty-nine without getting hitched.

Lifting his glass of wine to his lips, Ben says, "Never been married either. I did live with a girlfriend for several years, though."

"So did I." Then I correct myself. "Of course, in my case it was a boyfriend."

"No way," Ben says, his eyes opening wide. "When did you guys break up?"

"Last July."

Ben stares at me. "So did we. This is super freaky."

The twin theory re-forming in my brain, I'm about to ask to see Ben's driver license to make sure it says December 7th and not July 12th when my eyes catch his hand precariously placing his wine glass back on the table. I think he's too busy marveling over our parallel lives to pay attention to the actual location of the table, because the glass lightly hits the corner before slipping off the edge. Ben manages to catch the glass before it hits the ground. But not before a significant amount of wine spills onto the floor. His cheeks blush charmingly. "I'm a bit clumsy."

Not at all surprised by this confession considering all of our other similarities, I say, "Me too."

As it approaches ten o'clock, I barely suppress a yawn. Ben's eyes twinkle, and I know I'm busted. "Nothing personal."

"I'm beat too. Shall we call it?"

I thank Ben for picking up the tab, and he follows me to the exit. Before heading outside, we stop to arm ourselves for the brutally low temperatures. Ben studies me putting on my jacket. "You going to be able to zip it?"

"I'm not even going to attempt it and risk not being able to get it off later." I slip my arms through the sleeves. "I'll use the snaps and skip the zipper for now."

Grinning, Ben says, "Snaps are snaptastic."

Tightening the belt around my waist, I say, "True that. One of the reasons I bought this coat." I throw my neck warmer over my head and face Ben. "You ready?"

"Whenever you are."

Once outside, we stand face-to-face on the sidewalk. My heart pumps one beat faster as the awkward conclusion of the date approaches.

"I had a great time," Ben says.

"Me too. Thanks again," I say truthfully. I *did* have a nice time. But I'm not ready to kiss him.

"I hope we can do it again."

"Me too," I say with a nod of my head. In all honesty, I'm not sure where I stand with respect to a second date. I am happy for the safety of my bed and the comfort of time before I have to commit to one.

"Great. I'll be in touch," Ben says before leaning down and planting a quick kiss on my mouth. With a wave, he crosses to the other side of Third Avenue, and I head south in the direction of my apartment.

Even though it was a fleeting kiss, devoid of any passion, I can still feel it on my lips as I walk home. I'm not sure if it feels good or bad.

*   *   *

Cheryl and I exit the Broadhurst Theatre first and stand off to the side to wait for my mom and Aunt Helen. We took them to see *Mamma Mia* for a very early Mother's Day celebration.

"Such a cute show, though I'm sure my mom will have some constructive criticism to offer," Cheryl says with a chuckle.

I concur but keep my mouth shut. It's one thing for Cheryl to say something negative about her mother, but it's another for me to agree with her. Unlike real sisters, we don't have the advantage of openly and honestly commiserating about our mothers, and we're both highly protective of our respective female parent.

"Oh my God, they are beyond slow," I complain. This is one point on which we always agree, and I sigh loudly in frustration as I watch nearly every theatergoer walk onto the street except our mothers. The cold air seeps through the snaps of my coat since I haven't found the motivation to get the zipper fixed yet. Waiting in below-freezing temperatures might be the push I need.

"I know. My mom likes to stay through the credits at the movies, but unless she's waiting for an encore performance of 'Take a Chance on Me,' I have no idea what's holding them up now."

"Maybe my mom wanted to use the bathroom," I say just as I spot them walk out. Their heads are close together, and I bet they're discussing the highs and lows of the show, or maybe where we should go for dinner. Either way, they appear seemingly clueless that we're waiting for them in the brutal cold. My mom spots me and her eyes light up. She is instantly forgiven.

When she approaches, I say, "Did you like it?"

Squeezing me in an embrace, she says, "I loved it. Thanks for treating me, sweetheart."

"My pleasure. What did you think, Aunt Helen?"

Aunt Helen smiles, revealing a lipstick-stained tooth. "Wonderful. So much better than the movie. Merry Streep was so poorly cast."

I glance over at Cheryl and try to maintain a serious

expression. Cheryl shakes her head at her mother and points to her mouth. "You've got lipstick on your tooth."

Aunt Helen wipes her tooth with her finger. "Where are we eating?"

Cheryl says, "Maggie recommended Le Rivage on Restaurant Row. It's a French place."

"Maggie has taken me there before," my mom says. "They have duck with orange sauce on the menu."

"Sold," Aunt Helen says.

The restaurant is only one avenue and two blocks away, but between the number of tourists crowding the sidewalks and our mothers' inability to walk more than three steps a minute, it takes us close to a half hour to arrive and be seated.

There are more off-limit topics of discussion than usual, so once we've exhausted conversation about the show and what each of us is ordering for dinner, there is an awkward silence. Cheryl and I make eye contact across the table, and I silently pray the meal will proceed without anyone getting insulted.

"Your mother tells me you went on a date the other night," Aunt Helen says.

My mom busies herself spooning French onion soup into her mouth and pretends not to notice me glaring at her. Unlike most daughters, I like sharing personal information with my mother, and it was a relief to get my breakup with Doug out in the open. But she should know not to share my business with Aunt Helen unless I authorize it. Thankfully, Cheryl knows this, and I never have to remind her. I don't discuss Cheryl's marital difficulties with my mother for the same reason.

"Yes, I did." I take a sip of water, hoping my failure to elaborate will clue her in to my preference to drop the subject.

"Did you like him?" Aunt Helen asks.

Thanks for playing. Try again. "He was very nice."

"Are you going to go out with him again?"

"I haven't decided yet," I mumble. I give my mother a pleading look.

My mother smiles at me softly. "Let's leave Maggie alone, okay?"

Aunt Helen smirks. "Oh, I get it."

I raise an eyebrow. "What do you get?"

"He didn't ask you out again."

My eyes bug out as Cheryl says, "Your assumption is based on what, Mom?"

Keeping her stare on me, Aunt Helen waves her hand in dismissal. "Well, did he?"

"Yes, he did." Ben *did* ask me out again, but if he hadn't, I would hope Aunt Helen wouldn't be so pleased about it.

Aunt Helen mumbles something I can't hear.

My face burning up, I say, "You don't believe me?"

Aunt Helen drops her spoon into her bowl of lobster bisque. "I believe you, dear."

My gut tells me she thinks I'm lying and is merely trying to placate me. Determined, I pull my iPhone out of my bag and locate his latest email. I shove the phone in her face. "See?"

Aunt Helen lets her glasses rest on the bridge of her nose while she reads the email. Then she glances at me from under her eyelashes. "I told you I believed you."

She takes another spoonful of soup while I stare at her with my mouth gaping open. It boggles my mind that Aunt Helen insists on being a supporting player in my dating performance but takes only a backstage role in Cheryl's trial separation. If I weren't so loyal to Cheryl, I'd be tempted to tell Aunt Helen to worry about her own daughter's floundering marriage and stay out of my love life.

"Of course he asked her out again. Who wouldn't want to date my Maggie?" my mom says while beaming at me.

"Thanks, Mom," I whisper.

"I never said Maggie wasn't lovely. But why aren't you sure you want to go out with him again?" Aunt Helen asks.

"I'm afraid I'm not emotionally available for another relationship yet," I confess.

"Well, your biological clock is not going to wait for you to be ready. What if this man meets someone else? Aren't there more single women than men in this city?"

"Mom," Cheryl says in a warning tone.

Aunt Helen's blue eyes widen. "Well, aren't there?"

"I guess," I mutter.

Cheryl mouths, "I'm sorry," from across the table.

"Well, don't shoot the messenger," Aunt Helen says. "I was merely stating a fact. If this man fancies you, and you think he's nice, don't you think you should give him another chance before someone else catches his eye? Doug moved on. You should too."

Since I can't think of a valid reason not to—at least one good enough to satisfy my aunt—I elect on the spot to go out with Ben again.

Some say peer pressure is the biggest motivator for people to do things they aren't sure they want to do. I say those people never met my Aunt Helen.

*   *   *

It's my second date with Ben, and we're feasting on ribs and cold beer on the top floor of Blue Smoke, a barbeque restaurant near my apartment. Since I don't typically make a man privy to my messy eating habits and propensity to get food stuck in my teeth until I'm certain he likes me enough to let it pass, I assume my agreeing to eat ribs with Ben so soon means I'm either truly at ease with him or his opinion of me doesn't matter. As I take a sip from my pint of Sierra Nevada, I contemplate which one it is.

"Have you ever been to the jazz club downstairs? Jazz Standard?" Ben asks.

"A few times, actually. I live so close, and my ex loves live music." I second guess mentioning the ex while on a date, but my comfort level with Ben makes it difficult to remember proper dating etiquette. "You like jazz?"

"I do. Not as much as glamour rock though," he says matter-of-factly. Then he smiles. "Obviously."

I chuckle. "Obviously."

"What do you think about getting tickets to the show tonight? It doesn't start until eleven thirty."

My heart immediately jumps into my throat as if he suggested we fly to Las Vegas and get married by Elvis. Listening to live music in a dark lounge late on a Saturday night strikes me as very intimate. When I channeled my inner cheerleader to psych myself up for a second date, I told myself it was just dinner. No big deal. I'm not prepared for Ben to change the rules on me.

Apparently I'm taking too long to answer, because Ben lets out a laugh. "Or not."

I mentally chastise myself for getting so flustered, and the heat rises from my neck to my forehead. "No, it sounds fun. I'm not sure whether we can get tickets on such short notice, but if so, let's do it." I will leave it in the hands of fate. Going to a jazz club with the guy doesn't obligate me to let him hold my hand under the table while he caresses my palm with his thumb to the beat of the music. Like Doug used to do.

Ben beams at me. "Great."

When the waitress comes over, Ben asks about the show, and she suggests going downstairs as soon as possible since it's first-come, first-served, and if you don't have a reservation, an available table is unlikely.

Ben pays the tab, refusing to accept my offer to take care of the tip, and we hurry down to the club. The coat check girl says there are no tables available, but there is room at the bar. I try to contain my relief. A bar stool is much more casual than a dark table in the corner. Feeling more at ease, I try to tune out my inner Jodie, who is mocking me for getting so worked up over a second date.

An hour and a half and a top notch performance by Freddy Cole later, we make our way out of the bar onto the street. March is making its slow metamorphosis from lion to lamb, and I breathe in the brisk, clean air. It is welcome after being in a dark basement.

"What a phenomenal show. The acoustics were amazing," Ben says.

"Definitely a great venue."

"I'm glad the show wasn't sold out. One more thing I can cross off my bucket list."

Ben starts walking in the direction of my apartment, and I follow him, trying not to worry about whether he expects an invitation to come inside. "Was seeing a show at Jazz Standard really on your bucket list?"

"Not my bucket list per se. But my to-do list."

I stuff my hands in my pockets. "I'm glad I was able to help you strike something off of your to-do list. If you can help me find a new job, we'll be even." I stop in front of my building. Looking up, I say, "This is me."

"I didn't know you were on a job hunt."

"Yeah. It's not urgent or anything. I think a change could do me good."

Ben cocks his head. "Is that so, Sheryl Crow? I don't know anyone in marketing, but I'll keep my eyes and ears open."

"Much appreciated."

He takes a step closer to me. "I had a great time. Thank you."

"I had a great time too. Thank *you.*"

"Do it again?"

"I'd love to." As I say the words, I realize they're mostly true. I very much enjoy Ben's company. Hopefully, that's enough for now. Like Jodie said, I don't have to worry about loving him anytime soon.

"Great. I'll call you."

Ben leans forward and kisses me. He applies more pressure than last time, and I open my mouth against his and kiss him back. With tongue. We stand under the awning of my building, kissing for a few moments. My knees don't go weak, and I don't hear fireworks, but I'm not repelled.

It's a start.

When I get home, the first thing I do is kick off my chestnut leather boots and peel my form fitting dark blue jeans over my ankles. I throw on a pair of sweat shorts, not bothering to remove the long-sleeved white V-neck t-shirt I wore out, and wash off my makeup. After pouring a glass of water, I crawl into bed and replay the evening in my head. I conclude the date was a success.

Still, it's Doug I think about when I hug my stuffed Snoopy and close my eyes for the night.

*   *   *

Amanda places her menu on her lap and takes a sip of her peach bellini. "Is this the first time we've all gotten together since Maggie's birthday in July?"

I consciously fail to remind them of our reunion at the Oyster Bar after my ill-fated attempt to reunite with Doug, but Jodie does it for me. "We all saw each other in January. At least, I think it was January." Squinting her eyes at me, she says, "Was it January when you and Doug met up?"

I nod.

"Oh, yeah. I guess I wiped it out of my memory," Amanda says.

"You and me both," I mumble into my mimosa.

Artfully changing the subject, Melanie asks, "Do you guys know what you're getting?"

After a dozen emails back and forth over the last month, the four of us finally managed to nail down a date for a girls' brunch. We're at the Flatiron location of the trendy Sarabeth's restaurant. The average age of the diners is thirty, and I'm guessing there are fewer than five people over the age of forty-five. Packed with couples and groups of girls, we waited fifteen minutes for a table despite having made a reservation.

"I'm getting the pumpkin waffle," Jodie says. Cocking her head to the side, she says, "You guys ever notice how often we meet in Maggie's neighborhood? A coincidence, or strategic planning on Maggie's part?"

"There are some great restaurants in my hood," I say.

There is no shortage of quality restaurants in other neighborhoods, but since I'm the common thread of this group of girls, I don't complain when one of them suggests meeting someplace convenient for me. "I've never refused to go uptown, by the way."

Jodie points her finger at me. "I've got your number, girl."

I playfully kick her under the table. "I'm bummed they don't have steak and eggs on the menu. I was craving some red meat. I think I'll get the scrambled-egg-stuffed popper and a side of bacon. Or maybe the sausage." I crinkle my nose in indecision.

"Why don't you get both?" Amanda suggests.

"So glad you said it and not me," I say.

We place our orders with the waitress, and I take Amanda's advice and request sides of both bacon and sausage.

"How you're not four hundred pounds is beyond me," Jodie says. "Remember when you used to eat an entire turkey hero from Mr. Sub in one sitting in college?"

I would also wolf down a family-sized bag of Smartfood White Cheddar Cheese Popcorn by myself and not worry about working out to burn the calories. "Those were the days. When I turn forty..." I fake a shudder. "I plan to watch my calorie intake. I'll probably add strength training to my workouts too. Until then, I will enjoy my youthful metabolism to its fullest."

"You're blessed you can get away with only cardio. Running keeps me from gaining weight, but it doesn't do anything for flab. After thirty, I noticed the skin would jiggle when I moved my arm, so I started lifting weights to increase muscle tone. Check out these babies." Melanie proudly lifts a toned arm and points to her tricep. "I agree you should add weights to your workout, if for no other reason than it's good for your bones, but you don't honestly think your metabolism is gonna turn a switch the second you turn forty, do you?" she says with more than a hint of doubt in her voice.

"According to Aunt Helen."

"Screw Aunt Helen," Jodie says.

"Maybe if someone *did* screw Aunt Helen, she wouldn't be so mean to Maggie," Amanda says with a giggle.

"A flawed theory since, according to Aunt Helen, it's more

difficult to get laid after you turn forty," Melanie says, rolling her eyes. "Isn't she pushing seventy?"

While my friends unite in *Project: Attack Aunt Helen*, I figure someone should defend her honor. "I don't think she lies awake at night thinking of ways to make me feel bad about myself. She's just..." I try to find the right words. Giving up, I say, "She's just Aunt Helen. She can't help herself. Can we please change the subject so I can eradicate the visual of Aunt Helen fornicating?"

"Sorry about that." Amanda says with a wry expression. "How are things with Charles, Jodie?"

"They are progressing nicely, thank you," Jodie says as a blush paints her cheeks.

Raising an eyebrow, I joke, "Not doing much vacuuming lately, I gather?"

This time it's Jodie who kicks *me* under the table while Amanda and Melanie exchange confused glances. "No comment. But no, I haven't felt the need to vacuum as much as usual." She smiles at me. "What about you, Mags? How's *Benjamin*?" She says this with a strong Spanish accent, imitating Javier from *Felicity*, one of our favorite old television shows.

"Ben is fine," I say, happy the waitress conveniently comes over to deliver our food.

"Just fine?" Amanda asks after the waitress leaves.

"He's a nice guy. Funny too. I like him," I say, cutting into a piece of sausage.

"You've been out twice now?" Amanda asks.

"Three times," I correct. We went to the movies on our third date the week before. "The movie starred Justin Timberlake, and I tried not to squirm in discomfort when he had a sex scene with the European actress playing opposite him. Kind of awkward watching a sex scene with a guy you're sort of dating but never slept with."

"What base have you gone to?" Melanie asks.

Smirking, I say, "Base? Really? Did we jump in a time machine back to high school?"

"I'm curious too. Has he felt your boobs yet?" Jodie asks.

"Have you touched his penis?" Amanda says with a giggle.

For a girl who hasn't kissed a guy in God only knows how long, Amanda has no problems teasing me about sex. I shovel a spoonful of eggs in my mouth and swallow. "No. All we've done is make out." I turn to Melanie. "Making out is first base."

Melanie rolls her eyes at me. "I know."

"He's been a gentleman so far," I say.

"Is that a good thing?" Jodie inquires.

"What do you mean?"

"Are you happy to take it slow, or are you itching to move it up a notch?" she asks.

"I'm not ready to sleep with him," I say.

"Do you think you ever will be?" Jodie asks.

I crumble my napkin. "I don't know," I snap.

"Okay," Jodie says. "Sheesh."

I give her a fixed stare, and in a raised voice, say, "We've only been out three times. Is not being ready to get naked in front of him so bizarre?"

Melanie places her hand over mine. "Not at all, sweetie. Not at all."

"Absolutely, take your time," Amanda agrees.

I lock my eyes onto Jodie's baby blues. "Is that okay with you?"

"Of course it is. I'm just teasing you," she says.

I nibble on a piece of crispy bacon. "Please stop."

Jodie nods. "Consider it done."

Brunch continues at a leisurely pace, and I engage fully in the conversation, which ceases to include Ben. Behind the scenes, however, there is a one-man show playing in my head—all Ben all the time. Although it's not unusual for singles to have sex even on the first date, waiting more than three dates isn't unheard of either. I keep this to myself, but not only am I not ready to be intimate with Ben, I don't want to. And despite finding him attractive and fun to be around, I have no idea when, or even if, I ever will.

April

"Maggie, right?"

At the sound of my name, I turn away from the display of Smashbox cosmetics at Sephora and find myself facing the last person I expect to see—Lindsay. Her expression is friendly, but caught off-guard, I instinctively keep watch for Doug. I don't think I can face seeing them together when I'm alone.

"You're Maggie. Doug's ex-girlfriend, right?" Lindsay repeats herself, presumably because I have yet to utter a word.

In an effort to compose myself, I smile. "Hi there. Lindsay?" Through my peripheral vision, I continue my lookout for Doug, but since there are two girls standing on either side of Lindsay, I assume she is with girlfriends. I hope this means they broke up, but it probably means nothing.

"How are you?" As if reading my mind, she adds, "Doug's not here. He's with his brother, Connor."

I'm well aware that Doug's brother's name is Connor, but I let it go. "I'm doing well." I motion to the display case in front of me. "Bare Minerals stopped making my favorite eye shadow color, so I'm hoping another brand carries a similar shade."

Lindsay frowns. "I hate when brands discontinue my favorite products. So annoying, right?"

And *I* hate that she's so peppy, that she's already ended two sentences with "right?", that she's probably ten years younger than me, and that she's dating Doug. But I agree enthusiastically with her statement. "It's totally annoying."

Lindsay introduces me to her friends. "Maggie dated Doug before me. For like a year," she tells them.

"It was actually three years," I mutter.

"What?" Lindsay asks gently.

I bite my lip in embarrassment and say nothing.

Lindsay scrunches up her face. "Sorry. I didn't hear what you said."

Waving my hand in dismissal, I say, "We dated for three years, not one. But it's no big deal."

Putting her hand to her mouth, Lindsay says, "Oh. Sorry. I didn't know."

Her ignorance regarding how long Doug and I were together stings, as I assume it's because Doug never told her.

"In any case, Doug was still grieving your relationship when we met. And kind of pissed at you." She gives me a crooked smile. "But now he realizes you were right, and you guys weren't meant to be." She pats me on the shoulder. "So, thank you."

Trying to disguise the sinking feeling in my stomach, I jokingly say, "Yeah. I drank much more than him. Apples and oranges."

"Exactly," Lindsay says with a giggle. "And if you guys had stayed together, Doug would have missed out on being a dad. We were talking the other night about how badly we both want kids."

I jerk my head back. "In truth, we hadn't decided either way on the issue of children." And if Doug wants them badly, it's news to me. As Lindsay's friends awkwardly avoid my gaze, I wish Melanie or Jodie was with me to cut the tension with a witty retort.

Lindsay's eyes open wide. "Oh my God. I didn't mean to insult you by implying you *can't* have kids. I just thought you didn't *want* them, and he does." Her eyes scan the store before meeting mine again. "Can we forget I said anything? Did I stick my foot in my mouth or what?"

Until then, I didn't realize she was referring to the possible challenges that come with having a baby at my age, and I'm pissed. I want to ask her to take this outside, but choosing to play the role of mature grownup, I smile warmly at her. "Don't worry about it."

She frowns apologetically. "Thanks. I'm so glad Doug is in my life, and it wouldn't have happened if you hadn't broken up with him is all I meant to say."

I'm itching to scream, "I wanted a break. Not a breakup!" I'm still thrown by Doug's sudden desire for a household of rugrats, but I'm in no position to challenge Lindsay. I try to muster an appropriate response but come up short. Suddenly needing fresh air, I realize my new eye shadow will have to wait. "It was nice seeing you. Tell Doug I said hi." After a nod of acknowledgment to the other two girls, I weave my way through the crowded store and onto the street as fast as my feet will take me.

It is a typical Saturday afternoon in New York City: a swarm of tourists are walking up and down 42nd Street with seemingly no place to be as they stop mid-step to gawk at a tall building or stare into a store window. I summon the patience of a priest to avoid pushing them out of my way as I race to the subway. I'm almost happy for the clouded vision caused by the tears pouring down my cheeks so I can avoid making eye contact with anyone on the train platform. People say New York is a cold city where strangers don't make conversation, but people in the Big Apple are as nosy as anywhere else, and a grown woman crying is bound to garner curious stares.

The tears are still flowing freely by the time the train stops at 28th Street, and I half-jog to my building. I have so far managed to suppress the pathetic wails dying to escape my gut, and I pound the elevator button repeatedly and with force as if doing so will make the door open faster.

When I enter my apartment at last, I toss my purse on the floor, throw myself headfirst onto my couch, and let it rip. I weep over the ending of my relationship with Doug, and the children we won't have—the children I never even knew he wanted. I cry over losing him to Lindsay, a woman who probably won't mourn her twenties until after I'm already in my forties. I scream in frustration for not knowing what I wanted was exactly what I already had until I didn't have it anymore. And I gasp for air in between questioning out loud in my empty living room why in the world I ever craved a relationship filled with angst and drama—"oomph" as I foolishly described it to Cheryl. I imagine this is what Amanda felt like after she realized the mistake she made breaking up with Noah.

Perhaps because I've exhausted myself and lack the energy to create more tears, I abruptly stop crying and sit up on the couch. My phone alerts me to a text message. I wipe my eyes with the back of my hands and take a deep breath in and out before placing my palms on the couch and lifting myself to a standing position. Pulling my phone out of my bag, I wonder for a second if it might be Doug. I say a tiny prayer for it to be Doug, but of course, it isn't.

Leaning over my kitchen table, I swallow hard and read the text. It's from Ben. He wants to know if I'm around this week for dinner—sushi—as he's determined to revive my taste for eel which mysteriously disappeared after years of feasting on dragon rolls. I picture his friendly blue eyes and boyish grin, and I am happy to hear from him despite the events of this afternoon. I *do* like Ben. And Ben likes me. I'm not Amanda. I can't afford to waste a decade playing over my mistakes like a broken record, and I won't let them paralyze me from pressing forward. Moving my thumbs swiftly, I send a return text to Ben, making plans for dinner on Tuesday.

*   *   *

I let the piece of dragon roll slide down my throat, grimace at the slimy texture, and quickly take a shot of warm sake from the ceramic glass in an attempt to drown out the residual taste of eel from my mouth. I raise my palms up. "I still don't like eel. Sorry."

Grabbing a piece of the roll with his chopsticks, Ben says, "No need to apologize. I should thank you, since there's more for me now." Then he grins. "At least you tried."

I was dubious my taste buds would reverse over dinner with Ben at Amber, a trendy sushi restaurant in my neighborhood, but I'm glad I took the risk. "I promised you I would, and I always keep my promises."

Ben winks. "Nothing ventured, nothing gained, right?"

"Precisely," I say, nodding.

Testing my palate for eel after so long is not the only risk I have planned for the evening. Viewing Ben across the table, I doubt he has any expectations of getting laid later, but like most guys, I'm sure he hopes so. I'm relying on the theory that the oxytocin released during sex will strengthen my feelings for him—essentially doing exactly what books on dating warn women against. The way I see it, I already like Ben as a friend, but I'm not sure the physical chemistry is there. Since there is only one way to find out, I spent much of Sunday afternoon tidying up my apartment, and thankfully Anna, the only woman I trust to wax my bikini area, had a last-minute cancellation yesterday.

Ben gestures at the plates on our table. "Is there enough food for you without the dragon roll? We can order something else."

"I think we have enough," I say as I remove a piece of shrimp tempura roll from the plate and place it in my mouth. "But I'll let you know if I'm still hungry. I'm not bashful when it comes to food."

Since we met for dinner at seven, it's not even nine o'clock when we finish eating and pay our bill. Standing on the sidewalk outside the restaurant, Ben points to the bar next door. "What do you say to a beer at Van Diemen's?"

I cock my head in the direction of Baskin-Robbins across the street. "I'm craving ice cream. I always do after sushi. Any interest in grabbing some and heading back to my place? I have beer and wine there too if you still want to drink."

"Ice cream at your place sounds great," Ben says casually.

I can tell he's trying to play it cool, but the slight twitch of his lips gives him away. *Men.* Even the most patient and gentlemanly of them turn into horny schoolboys when invited inside a girl's apartment for the first time.

After I treat us to a scoop of ice cream (Oreo Cookies n' Cream for me and German Chocolate Cake for him), we walk over to my apartment. Since beer doesn't go well with ice cream, I tell Ben to make himself comfortable on my couch while I pour us each a glass of Baileys Irish Cream on the rocks. After I join him, I kick off my shoes, put my feet on the coffee table, and take my first spoonful of ice cream. I close my eyes and moan as the creamy deliciousness slides down my throat. "Nothing hits the spot after sushi like ice cream." When I open them, I see Ben smiling at me in amusement and immediately feel my face flush. "What?"

Ben shakes his head. "Nothing. It's nice to see a girl enjoy dessert."

I angle my head towards his cup. "How's yours?"

Ben takes a spoonful of ice cream and closes his eyes. "*Mmm. Delicious.*" He opens his eyes and laughs.

Swatting him gently in the leg, I say, "Stop teasing me."

Ben slides closer to me on the couch. "Okay. I'll stop. You're cute, though."

Facing him, I smile shyly. "Thank you."

Ben inches his face closer to mine. "You're welcome." His eyes roam from my mouth to my eyes and back to my mouth again before he kisses me.

This is the moment in a date most women anticipate—when the talking stops, and the action begins. I've always felt this way in the past, most recently with Philip—I couldn't remove his clothes fast enough. It was the same way the first time Doug and I got hot and heavy. After going out to dinner, we spontaneously ended up at the Pine Tree Lounge, a watering hole in Murray Hill which looked more like a log cabin in the Adirondacks than a dive bar. We lost track of time singing along to Top 40 hits on the jukebox and were completely surprised by—and unprepared for—the hurricane-like rainstorm waiting for us outside. Even today, I can practically feel the lack of oxygen in my lungs from sprinting to my apartment a few blocks away. Once inside, it took us several moments to regain our bearings as we stood shivering and dripping rain all over the wood floor of my studio. And then we locked eyes and cracked up until I asked if he wanted to join me for a hot shower. The rest, as they say, is history. *Just as Doug and I are now history.*

I yank myself out of the past and try to concentrate on the present and Ben, the man I am kissing while our ice cream melts into liquid, and the Baileys Irish Cream dilutes in ice. We have now shifted positions so I'm lying horizontally across the couch, and Ben hovers above me. His lips are soft, and I feel his warm breath as he moves his mouth along my neck in between kissing my mouth. I slip my hands under his wool sweater and run my fingers along his smooth and, thankfully, hairless back. There is a hint of cocoa fragrance in his cologne, and I inhale deeply. I know I can enjoy this if I give myself a chance.

Ben stops kissing me and moves a hair from my face. His complexion is ruddy, and he's slightly out of breath. "Are you okay here, or should we move this to your bedroom?"

And this is when I know I can't go through with it. I can't sleep with Ben in an attempt to force romantic feelings for him I don't have despite how well we get along. Einstein said the definition of insanity is doing the same thing over and over again and expecting different results. Last July, I questioned my feelings for Doug. We broke up because I said I wanted to "get my ducks in a row" before I turned forty. Nine months have passed, and my ducks are not lined up. Instead of taking the time to sort myself out, I'm a layer of clothing away from jumping into a relationship with Ben—not because I'm crazy about him, but because I'm afraid of entering my forties as a single woman. I'm not sure my behavior is insane, but it's definitely stupid.

Ben is staring at me expectantly with his brow furrowed, and I know I have to say something. I exhale deeply and bite my lip. "I'm so sorry, but I can't do this." In a cowardly move, I close my eyes for a moment before meeting his glance again.

"Is it too soon?" He sits up, his facial expression one of both disappointment and concern.

I position myself so we're sitting side by side on the couch. "In a way, yes, but I don't think a few more dates will resolve it." I run a hand through my hair and blurt out, "The truth is, I'm still in love with my ex-boyfriend."

Ben's eyes open wide.

"I had no intention of meeting someone at speed dating. I only went to support my friend. But you were so nice. And we had so much in common. We even look alike. And I really like you. But..."

"But you're not over your ex," Ben says.

I shake my head. "No."

"I get it," Ben says softly.

He's a great guy, and I hate hurting his feelings, but I know it's better to end it now. "I'm so sorry, Ben. Maybe under other circumstances it would be different, but I don't think it's fair to get involved with you when my heart is with someone else." Even as I say the words, I know they're not true. Ben is an attractive, interesting, kind man, but even if I was ready to fall in love, I don't believe my affection for him would ever extend beyond a fondness or a strong like. Despite Aunt Helen's harping about my biological clock, I would rather be alone than settle. This was my mindset the morning after I broke up with Doug, when I was still doubting whether he was the one. I was ready to separate from Doug, a man I truly loved, because I wasn't certain it was right. Surely I am strong enough to break it off with Ben after only four dates. "I never meant to lead you on. I swear." I recall Philip saying the same thing to me when he broke things off. The J. Geils Band said it best—love stinks.

"Don't worry about it. It's not like you left me at the altar or anything. And I've barely spent any money on you yet," he jokes.

I grin. I wish I had someone to fix him up with, but Amanda didn't find him attractive at speed dating. Which in a strange way makes me question how fetching she thinks *I* am.

"You wanna have sex anyway?" Ben says, one eyebrow lifting suggestively.

Chuckling, I say, "It's tempting, but I think I'm gonna be a good girl for a change."

"Just my luck, you decide to turn over a new leaf now." Ben shakes his head from side to side.

With an apologetic frown, I say, "Sorry." I drop my gaze to the floor and then back at him. "Thanks so much for being so understanding." I am drenched in guilt and relieved he isn't verbally attacking me for being a tease.

Ben stands. "I'm a nice guy. Nice guys finish last."

Rising too, I say, "Nice guys are underrated. If it's any consolation, my ex is a nice guy too, so maybe there is an ex-girlfriend somewhere out there who regrets losing you."

Ben grabs his jacket, and I follow him to my front door. "Excuse me if I'm being nosy, but are you going to tell him how you feel?"

"I did." I offer no further information. It would be way too awkward discussing Doug with a guy I almost slept with a few minutes ago.

Ben leans his back against my door, holding his jacket against his chest. "Gotcha. I hope we can still be friends." With a crooked smile, he says, "Even if we're just fake friends on Facebook."

"Sounds good. I'll search for your page. By the way, what's your last name, Ben C.?"

"Covington."

My eyes bulging, I repeat, "Covington?"

"Let me guess, you watched *Felicity*?"

"The answer is a resounding yes. I guess it's something you've heard before?"

"I hate to break it to you, sweetheart, but you're not the first girl I've ever met."

"Yes, Ben was a hit with the ladies, me being one of them. But Noel was the better catch. Despite sharing Ben's name, you have more in common with Noel, and that's a good thing."

"I'll take it as a compliment." Ben plants a kiss on my cheek, says, "Be good, Maggie," and walks out, letting the door close behind him.

May

Reaching across the coffee table toward Cheryl's empty glass, I say, "More wine?"

With a handful of M&Ms in her mouth, Cheryl nods. "Yes, please."

I fill Cheryl's glass and observe Amanda, who is sitting on my living room floor. Wearing a silk purple pajama set, she's riveted to the television screen on which the scene where Mark Ruffalo kisses Jennifer Garner for the first time in *13 Going on 30* is playing out. "How about you, Amanda?"

Amanda takes notice of me, says, "Huh?" and then returns her attention to the screen.

I resist the urge to laugh, since I'm positive Amanda has seen this movie at least five times already. "Do you need a refill of anything?"

"Prosecco, please," she mumbles.

I walk to my kitchen where an unopened bottle of Prosecco is chilling in the refrigerator.

The three of us are in the throes of a girls' night meant to help us embrace our single status by doing all the "chick" things that would threaten the masculinity of our significant others if we had one. We're spending the evening watching back-to-back romantic comedies, skimming fashion magazines, eating copious amounts of mini cupcakes from Baked by Melissa, and Cheryl even painted my toenails earlier.

Most important, however, is the requirement that all alcoholic beverages consumed be pink in color. I purchased bottles of White

Zinfandel (perfectly acceptable to drink in the privacy of one's own home) and Rose Prosecco. We are a cliché of the girls-night-in experience, but that's the fun of it.

After filling Amanda's glass and my own, I inspect the box of cupcakes, remove one with a peanut butter cup on top, and toss it in my mouth before returning to the couch next to Cheryl. We watch the movie until it ends, and then I mute it while the credits run. "Best chick flick ever," I say.

"I have to disagree, though it's definitely in my top ten. *When Harry Met Sally* is better," Cheryl says.

"Do not fear. We have *When Harry Met Sally* in the house too," I say, patting the pile of DVDs on the end table next to me. "I also have *Bridget Jones's Diary* and *Clueless*."

Cheryl yawns.

"Don't even go there," I say. "It's not a real slumber party if we don't stay up late into the night talking."

"No offense, but one of the best things about not having the kids around is eight uninterrupted hours of sleep without a crying child crawling into my bed in the middle of the night," Cheryl says.

"I promise not to get in bed with you, but I might paint your face with markers while you're sleeping." Amanda snickers.

"And I might stick your hand in warm water to see if it makes you pee in your pants." Crinkling my nose, I say, "Or maybe not. I could do without the smell of urine in my apartment."

Cheryl narrows her eyes at me. "You wouldn't dare. I have my ways of inflicting torture on you. Or have you forgotten?" She gives me her best evil face, taking me back to the 80s and early 90s when she outplayed me each time I tried to one-up her in anything. And the few times I managed to pull one over on her, I regretted it. Like the time I manipulated a ride home from a party by convincing her Jason Priestley was the birthday girl's cousin and visiting for the weekend. Cheryl pissed off her friends by persuading them to bail on a movie and join her in picking me up, and of course, "Brandon Walsh" wasn't there. Her friends laughed their asses off. In my defense, I didn't know she would bring her friends along, and it was a cockamamie story she shouldn't have fallen for. She was obsessed with *Beverly Hills, 90210* at the time, and I ran with it. She enacted revenge by delivering the medicine I *accidently* left at home, Monistat, in the hallway at school in front of my freshman year crush and his friends. These days, having cute guys think I have a yeast infection wouldn't faze me, but I was a fifteen-year-old-girl who had never even used a tampon yet, and I avoided all social interaction for over a week.

"Point taken," I say. I decide to change the subject before adult Cheryl devises a genius way to torment me in my own home for the fun of it. "Time for girl talk. What should we talk about?"

"Boys, of course," Amanda says.

"I don't have much to contribute. But at least it's self-inflicted abstinence," I say.

"Jim is moving back in," Cheryl says matter-of-factly.

I sit up straighter. "When were you planning on sharing this pertinent turn of events?"

"I thought I just did," Cheryl says with a smirk.

"And we had to force it out of you." I mock glare at her.

"I don't recall any forceful measures taken," Amanda says.

I roll my eyes. "In any event, I'm so happy for you guys. The twerps must be over the moon." I picture Cady and Michael in my mind's eye, and my heart swells knowing they won't have to grow up in a broken home. They are part of a small minority of children whose wish for their mommy and daddy to get back together will actually come true.

"They don't know yet," Cheryl says.

I refill her wine glass. "Glad to know I'm not the last to know, but why haven't you told them, and when is the big family reunion taking place?" Motioning to her glass, I say, "Drink up. It's a celebration."

Cheryl smiles and takes a sip of her wine. "Sunday night. Jim's going to pretend like he's dropping the kids off as usual, but instead of leaving, he'll stay for dinner and tell Cady and Michael he's moving back in. We thought it would be fun to surprise them.

Tomorrow will be the last time I have the house to myself for a while. Of course, I'm not complaining."

"That's seriously fantastic. It's nice to have a happy ending for a change," Amanda says, beaming.

I stand and motion for Cheryl to join me. "A hug is in order."

Cheryl stands up and I pull her into an embrace. When we separate, she sits down and says, "It's great news, yes. But the marriage still needs work."

"What type of work?" Amanda asks.

"We have to make sure we don't lose ourselves in the kids again. They're still so young. It would be very easy to fall back into bad habits."

I recall Cheryl's earlier apprehension regarding her compatibility with Jim outside of the children and their initial attraction, and I try to wipe away the twinge of doubt I have as to whether they can be truly happy together. I hope they're not staying together solely for the sake of Cady and Michael, but I don't want to bring up something so sensitive and potentially negative, especially in front of Amanda.

"At least for the time being, we'll still meet with our counselor once a month," Cheryl says. "We'll also have a date night at least one night of the weekend and a mini-date during the week. The mini-date consists of spending time truly engaging with each other once the kids are asleep. And merely sitting in the same room watching television or reading won't cut it."

"*Bow chicka bow wow*," I sing, giggling.

Cheryl mutters, "So immature," and shakes her head at me in amusement. "It has to be more than sex. We're obviously encouraged to have sex, but only after we have a conversation about something other than the kids."

"Like, for instance, sex?" Amanda asks.

I chuckle, and Amanda joins me.

Cheryl points at Amanda and then at me. "You two."

"I'm trying to get all of my childish behavior out in the next two months," I say.

"As if we're supposed to believe you'll grow up once you turn forty?" Cheryl asks.

"Of course not. But it sounded good," I say.

"Speaking of which, any thoughts on how you want to celebrate your birthday?" Amanda asks.

"By turning thirty-nine again?" I suggest, looking at Cheryl and Amanda hopefully. My suggestion is met with silence. "It was worth a shot. I have no clue. I still have two months."

Amanda releases a resigned breath. "Fair enough. We'll follow up with you in a couple of weeks."

"Make it a month. At least," I mumble.

Amanda waves her hand in dismissal. "Fine. Back to man-talk. Guess whose online dating profile is seeing a lot of action?" Not waiting for us to answer, she says, "Mine!"

My eyes opening wide, I blurt out, "Wow."

Between this news and Cheryl's imminent reconciliation with Jim, I get the distinct impression I'm being purposely left in the dark in matters regarding love and sex. As thrilled as I am for my cousin and close friend, I can't help but wonder if my recent dating hiatus is the reason my friends and family seem reluctant to share their relationship news with me. And I hate that this neurosis is taking up space in my overactive brain, since I should be one hundred percent devoted to being happy for Amanda and Cheryl.

I smile. "Who knew this girl's night would reveal so many previously unknown developments in each of your love lives? I had no idea you'd gone on any dates, Amanda."

"I haven't," Amanda says.

Confused, I say, "But you just said—"

Amanda grins sheepishly. "I said my profile has seen a lot of action. I didn't say I went out with anyone. But I'm communicating with a few guys who seem decent, and I'm having fun."

"Fantastic, Amanda. Keep me posted." With a furrowed brow, I add, "I mean it."

"I promise," Amanda says.

I say, "Since I have no love life to speak of, I'm going to buckle down on my job search. I signed up for four more rock climbing classes for next month and it's not cheap. I'd love to make enough money to justify joining Chelsea Piers as a member. I'd have unlimited access to the rock walls and their state-of-the-art fitness center."

Cheryl whistles. "Check out my cousin the fitness addict."

"Let's not get carried away, but I do need to do something to make up for the calories I'm not burning by having sex," I joke.

"Won't you miss your job? I thought you loved it," Amanda says.

"I might not be a master of relationships, but I think I'm a champion of marketing. I enjoy my job, do it well, and they think highly of me there, but I'd like to explore non-law-firm environments before I'm pigeon-holed. I think of it as a new direction for a new decade." I scoop up a handful of M&M's. "It would also be nice not to come face-to-face with my mistakes on a regular basis."

"Mistakes being Philip?" Cheryl asks.

I nod. "He's perfectly nice to me, but each time I see him, it's a painful reminder of how stupid I was to think for one second he was somehow better for me than Doug. He didn't even watch television. Can you imagine me getting serious with a guy whose time on the boob tube is limited to CNN?" I roll my eyes at the absurdity.

"Speaking of boobs, er, in a roundabout way...you don't plan on giving up men forever, do you? It gets old after about a decade," Amanda says with a knowing look.

I wave her away. "Of course not. I like sex way too much to live like a nun. But I don't trust myself to date right now."

"For what it's worth, I think you did the right thing about Ben," Cheryl says. "A little alone time will do you good."

I smile at Cheryl gratefully. "I'm relieved you think so. Part of me agrees. I'm glad I'm not letting fear drive me, and I have faith everything will work out in time. But threatening my faith is the stubborn fear that I totally blew it and will regret my decision when years go by and I'm old and alone." I blink to prevent the onset of tears. "What if Ben is the last decent guy who will ever like me, and I pushed him away? He's nice, handsome, age-appropriate. Maybe I should have gone with it, even though I mostly liked him as a friend. Better than waiting until I'm fifty and settling for a sixty-five-year-old widower with a saggy ass and a prescription for Cialis."

Cheryl wraps her arm around my shoulders. "You're being silly, Magpie. The right guy will find you if you don't find him first. I promise."

Amanda tilts her head to the side. "The way you felt about Ben...I thought you described your relationship with Doug the same way." Biting her lip, she clarifies, "That it was more of a friendship."

Shaking my head, I say, "No. I never thought of Doug as just a friend. My romantic feelings for him were never in question. It was more of the excitement factor." I look cautiously over at Cheryl, afraid of part two of her wrath. "Life with Doug was fairly predictable, and I guess I wasn't sure if we had what it took for the long haul. As if the novelty of a covert office romance would have more staying power." Disgusted with myself, I drop my gaze to my wood floor and try to drown out Lindsay's upbeat voice in my head telling me how excited Doug is to start a family. "I still can't believe he downplayed his desire to have kids for so long."

"I'm surprised too," Cheryl says. "You guys used to talk about the places you would visit. Doug would talk about eating haggis in Scotland and blood soup in Vietnam, and riding the Tower of Terror rollercoaster in Australia, but he never mentioned kids. I assumed he was like you, with an 'if it happens, it happens' attitude toward children."

My night to celebrate all things single has taken a dangerously depressing turn and in a desperate attempt to change the subject, I make a statement I doubt will come to fruition, but should provide the desired shock value. "Once I master rock climbing, maybe I'll train for a triathlon."

June

From the visitor's chair in my office, Melanie frowns. "I can't believe you're leaving us."

"I'm leaving the *firm*, yes. But I'm not leaving you." In a high-pitched cheerleader voice, I say, "Maggie and Melanie, friends foreva."

"Promise?"

I extend my hand across my desk and jiggle my pinky at her. "Pinky swear. And besides, I'll be here for two more weeks." I'm still in a semi-state of denial over quitting my job, but even though I'm going to miss having one of my closest friends in an office down the hall from me for impromptu lunches, emergency happy hour drinks, and all-too-often needed distractions, I know I've made the right decision from both a personal and professional standpoint.

"Are you going to meet the cast of the *Veep*? It's one of my favorite shows and the reason I pay for HBO. Please get me an intro to Tony Hale. I've loved him since *Arrested Development*."

Chuckling, I say, "I'll see what I can do, but I'm not sure how often HBO's Manager of Advertising & Promotion meets the actors of their Original Programming." As much as I'm playing it down, I'm every bit as psyched to be working for HBO's marketing department as if I was hired to star in *Girls*. I can't think of a cooler way to incorporate my honed career skills with my devotion to the medium of television.

Melanie scrunches her forehead contemplatively. "True. Maybe I can be your plus one at the Christmas party."

"I wish I could say there would be others vying for the

invitation, but—" Before I can finish, I am interrupted by a light tapping on my open door.

"Hi, Philip. Come on in," I say with as much nonchalance as I can fake. It's not like I'm surprised by his appearance, but I'm glad we're doing it on my turf. I'd been waiting to be beckoned into his office since I left notice a few hours earlier.

Melanie rises from her chair. "I was just leaving. Hours to bill and all." As Philip replaces her in my guest chair and faces me, she mouths, "Good luck" before walking out of my office and closing the door behind her.

My eyes meet Philip's across the desk, and I try not to fidget.

Crossing one leg over the other, he says, "I hear you're leaving us."

"Yes. It's a great opportunity."

Philip nods. "HBO's gain is our loss."

Fighting the urge to apologize for quitting, I say, "Thank you."

Not meeting my eyes, he says, "A little out of your comfort zone though, no?"

I silently count to five in my head. I am practiced at answering this question after three rounds of interviews. "It's not a law firm, no. But my experience with media planning and developing promotions will transfer to the entertainment arena. And I was in need of a new challenge, and HBO delivered."

"I've no doubt you will deliver as well."

Ever original, I say, "Thank you" again.

Philip swipes a finger across his eyebrow and closes his eyes for a pause. When he opens them, he studies me for a moment before saying, "I have to ask."

"Ask what?" My heart beats rapidly as if anticipating an awkward moment. As if every moment between Philip and me hasn't been uncomfortable since we stopped dating.

He leans forward in the chair. "You're not leaving because of me, are you? Because of what happened with us?"

I bite my lip, trying not to look at his wedding band. Of course, since I'm consciously attempting to avoid darting my eyes towards his left hand, I make contact at least twice before opening my mouth. "Honestly, it did play into my initial decision to switch jobs, but the more I thought about it, the more excited I became at the prospect of spreading my wings outside of the legal arena. And once my headhunter told me about the opening at HBO, and I met with the team, I was hooked. I'll be managing the development and execution of consumer advertising and promotion plans for all of their Original Programming. I'm already extremely passionate about the work, and I haven't even started yet."

Philip grins. "You're beaming. You can't fake that."

"I'm excited, Philip. I think it's a good move for me." I hesitate before adding, "Regardless of what precipitated the decision."

"I hear you. But if it's about money, I've already been given authorization to counter their offer. I...we really don't want to lose you."

Before I can stop myself, I blurt out, "Wow." When I met with Neil Black earlier in the morning to leave notice, he didn't do a happy dance around his office, but he didn't seem particularly fazed by my resignation either. In my experience, senior partners in law firms, especially those on the management committee, regard all non-legal personnel as dispensable. "I'm shocked and flattered."

"Meaning you'll consider it?"

His brown eyes are wide and hopeful, and if I didn't know better, I'd question whether he genuinely valued my marketing skills or if it was my *other* skills he hoped to keep close. "Truthfully, the salary increase is not life-changing, especially since I'm lacking some relevant experience." Giving him a wry smile, I confess, "I sort of charmed them into giving me a shot."

Philip looks at me fondly. "I wish I could have observed you in action."

"That makes one of us. I was nervous enough without an audience."

"So, the answer is..."

"Thank you so much. But, no. I'm sorry." I knew an apology would slip out at some point in the conversation.

Philip stands up. "Well, in case you change your mind, the offer is good until your last day." Winking, he adds, "And probably even longer."

"Thanks, Philip." I flash him a genuine smile, grateful for his counter-offer and his kindness under the circumstances.

When he's gone, I take a deep breath and remove a fresh legal pad from my left desk drawer. I'm not sure if my successor will start or even be hired before my last day, and I want to create a cheat sheet to make her transition as smooth as possible. I have pen in hand, ready to jot down my first set of notes when my phone rings. Answering it, I say, "Maggie Piper."

"Time's up, Maggie Piper. The moment to plan your birthday bash has arrived," Amanda says.

My lips part to protest, but I'm all out of excuses. I will turn forty in a month, and there is nothing short of death to prevent it. Giving in, I say, "Fine. Let's talk."

July

My eyes open the moment my alarm goes off. Unmoving, I stare at the ceiling and blink a few times until it sets in. *I'm forty.*

I expect to be overwhelmed with dread in the pit of my belly, but I mostly feel resigned. I have been praying to find a loophole to ending my thirties short of death for well over a year, but since I've been talking about *turning* forty for so long, *being* forty is kind of anticlimactic.

I commence my morning ritual as usual, taking a few sips of water from the glass on my night table before stepping out of bed and heading to the bathroom to pee and brush my teeth. After soothing my dry eyes with a drop of Visine in each, I scrutinize my reflection and check for signs I've aged overnight. The face staring back at me in the mirror is the same face I wore the night before, only the slightest of lines at the corners of my eyes. No brown spots, no deep wrinkles, no parentheses around my mouth. Lifting my chin, I touch the skin of my neck with my fingertips—just as taut as it was yesterday. I breathe a sigh of relief and roll my eyes at my mirror image for foolishly worrying I would morph into a matronly woman on the eve of my fortieth birthday.

Of course, this doesn't stop me from stripping off my pajamas and searching for evidence of sudden sagginess in my body. My breasts are no less perky than they were the last time I checked them out. Unfortunately, they are no bigger either. Pinching the small amount of flesh directly under my belly button confirms the absence of six-pack abs or a completely flat stomach I would be comfortable flaunting in a string bikini. Nevertheless, standing sideways in front of my mirror evaluating my profile, I am pleased to note I can still rock a modest two-piece bathing suit better than many women in their twenties and thirties, despite my foray into my forties. Those who say bikinis are for women thirty-nine and under can kiss my ass.

Speaking of my ass, I drop my panties down to my ankles and step out of them, prepared to stand on my toilet bowl to take a closer look at it. I have one foot on the bowl and the other mid-step when I change my mind. Mother Nature has been kind to me so far this morning. I don't want to push my luck.

The tune of Maroon Five's "Pay Phone" blasts from my cell, convincing me I made the wise choice to forego climbing on my toilet bowl to do a thorough examination of my *derrière*. The sudden sound in my otherwise silent apartment might have caused me to career headfirst onto my cold porcelain floor. Still naked, I run back to my bedroom and retrieve my phone. I smile when I see "Mom" on the display. "Hi, Mom."

"*Happy birthday to you. Happy Birthday to you. Happy Birthday dear Maggie, Happy Birthday to you.*"

My eyes well up at the sound of her off-key but cheerful voice. "Thanks, Mom."

"How's my baby today?" There is a catch in her voice as if she's not certain who she's talking to—her baby or a woman who has maturely accepted it's time to grow up.

"I'm forty," I say, torn between which role to assume. I sit on the edge of my bed, my lower lip quivering dangerously.

My mom laughs. "I wish I was calling to tell you there was a mistake on your birth certificate, and you're actually turning thirty-nine and not forty, but then you'd have to go through another twelve months of awaiting the inevitable. The day of reckoning is upon us. Tell me the truth: isn't it a bit of a relief?"

"It is. When I woke up this morning, being forty years old didn't hit me too hard since I had been dreading the day for so long."

"Exactly. And would you really want to go through the last year again?"

"No." I think back on the last twelve months of my life and know I wouldn't want to experience it a second time unless it included a do-over equipped with my new-found wisdom.

"And now you can show everyone how young, vivacious, and beautiful forty can be," my mom says proudly.

Choking back tears, I say, "Thank you. You always know what to say."

"I speak the truth. Are you excited for tonight?"

"Totally." When Amanda finally cornered me into planning my birthday party, I told her my ideal celebration consisted of dinner with my family and closest friends. "How are you getting into the city?"

"Cheryl and Jim are driving me, Helen, and the kids. Cady is already calling dibs on sitting next to Aunt Maggie."

Picturing my "mini-me"—as my friends have taken to calling Cady—I say, "I can always count on my favorite niece to make me feel special."

In a stern voice, my mom says, "You *are* special. And everyone coming to dinner loves you."

"Which is exactly why I want to spend my birthday with them." I glance at the time on my television set. "Crap, I need to jump in the shower. I haven't been at this job long enough to be late." And since there's no way I'll accomplish anything at work before I've read all of my "happy birthday" posts on Facebook, I need to get going if I have any intention of being at all productive.

"I'll let you go. Have a great day and I'll see you later."

"Thanks, Mom. I love you."

"I love you too. To the moon and back."

I hang up the phone, basking in her unconditional love. When I read the birthday texts sent by Cheryl, Melanie, Jodie, and Amanda while I was on the phone, a sentiment I didn't predict experiencing on my fortieth birthday washes over me—happiness.

*   *   *

Clink. Clink. "May I have your attention, please?"

I turn my focus away from Jodie and direct it toward the end of our round table, where my mother is standing with a glass of champagne in her hand. I'm grateful for her timing, as Jodie was about to rehash to my Aunt Helen how I celebrated my birthday last year by giving pedestrians in Union Square a peek at my undies. Jodie thinks these stories are endearing, as she should after over twenty years of friendship, but I'm afraid Aunt Helen will cite my klutziness as another strike against me finding a husband.

"I want to make a little toast," my mom says. She is wearing a new dress in a shade of purple, which brings out the blue of her eyes, and her cheeks are flushed with happiness. Or maybe it's the champagne. Whatever the cause, she is beautiful.

The clatter at the table at Otto, Mario Batali's Italian restaurant in the West Village, slowly ebbs until my mom has everyone's rapt attention. I'm fairly certain all of the neighboring tables are equally beguiled by the raucous we are causing. It's a Wednesday night, but Otto is notoriously booked to capacity almost every day of the week, and we have to project our voices to hear each other above the din of other diners.

"Forty years ago tonight, I was in agony," she begins. "My contractions were coming every two minutes, and I was begging for an epidural."

At this, my mom puts her hand to her stomach and distorts her face in mock pain. Everyone chuckles while I bow my head in embarrassment.

My mom continues, "But at 10:18, I was blessed with the most precious gift of my life—my Maggie. Of course, she was covered with white greasy vernix and resembled a plucked chicken, but she was *my* plucked chicken, and I loved her at first sight. And I have loved her every day since." She shakes her head at me. "Even when she thought she was doing a good deed and did a load of laundry with Clorox bleach instead of detergent."

"I remember that day," Aunt Helen shrieks.

"What's Clawax bleach?" Cady asks.

Covering my eyes, I say, "I didn't realize this was a roast. I might need something stronger than champagne."

Glancing knowingly at Amanda, Jodie whispers, "We'll get you something stronger later. Don't you worry, Magpie."

"I will keep this brief because I don't want our food to get cold." My mom's eyes sweep the table, which already holds the various dishes we ordered for our first course. "Thankfully, cheese plates and assorted salads are generally eaten at room temperature. We're all here to wish my baby a happy birthday, and I know she is thrilled to have you celebrate with her, as am I." Locking eyes with me, she says, "Maggie, you might be forty, but you'll always be my little girl. I love you and I'm so proud of the woman you've become and continue to become with every passing year." She raises her glass. "Cheers. To Maggie. To another forty plus years of good health, happiness, and love."

Most of the table echoes, "To Maggie," except Jim, who adds, "Don't forget money."

Blowing her a kiss, I say, "Thank you, Mom. I love you too." Unable to resist, I stand up and squeeze her into a tight embrace.

She whispers into my ear, "This is your year. I can feel it."

The next hour whizzes by while we inhale assorted gourmet pizzas and pastas, and before I know it, coffees and desserts are being ordered. I've played musical chairs around the table to spend time with everyone. Even Aunt Helen has been on her best behavior. She hasn't made a single comment about my father being a no-show or me being a dried-up middle-aged spinster. Yet—the night ain't over 'til it's over.

My phone rings, and when I see, "Kenneth Piper would like to FaceTime" on the screen, along with the still image of my father, I allow a breath of relief to escape my lips.

I received his birthday card earlier in the week, but when I didn't hear from him all day, I came up with a list of the only circumstances under which it would be acceptable for him to forget his only child's fortieth birthday. I didn't get far—Alzheimer's disease, amnesia, and sudden death.

I click "accept" and smile into the phone. "Hi, Dad."

My dad gives me a wide grin, displaying a set of straight, white teeth that I imagine melted many hearts back in the day. According to him, they still do. "Happy birthday, Freckles."

I thank him, raising my voice to be heard over the boisterousness of the restaurant.

Mimicking the volume of my speech, my dad practically shouts, "Are you at your party?"

Aunt Helen asks, "Is that your father?"

I turn from the phone to my guests, who have all halted their own conversations and focused their curious attention on me.

I mouth, "One minute" to them and excuse myself to the only quiet spot in the restaurant—the bathroom. Once inside, I say to my dad, "Yes, we're all here. I'm sorry you couldn't make it."

My dad runs a hand through his salt and pepper (mostly salt) hair and gives me an apologetic frown. "I'm sorry, Freckles. I really wanted to be there, but I had an important meeting today. Next year, I promise. Did you get my card?"

I nod. "I did. Thanks." The card said, "You have a very special place, that no one else can fill...because you mean so much to me and you know you always will! Happy Birthday."

"I love you, baby."

"I love you too, Dad."

"I'll let you get back to your party, but have a wonderful time."

"I will. Thanks."

"Send my best to your mom." He flashes me a devilish grin. "Aunt Helen too."

Laughing, I say, "Will do. Bye, Dad."

"Bye, baby."

I disconnect the call and return to the table. "That was my dad." To my mom, I add, "He sends his best."

My mom smiles softly. "You can send mine back next time you speak to him."

I consider telling Aunt Helen my dad sent her his regards as well, but decide against it. She'd know he was being facetious, and I want a peaceful evening.

Cheryl clears her throat. "I'd like to say a few words, if you'll give me your attention."

This is a surprise. As my likely matron-of-honor, I would expect Cheryl to make a toast at my wedding, but I didn't expect anything for my birthday. I can't help but hope the two are not mutually exclusive.

The table quiets, and Cheryl locks eyes with me. "Maggie. Growing up, we shared the same room—I forced you to make my bed. We shared the same toys—I took all of the good ones. We shared the same dinner table—we couldn't even look at each other without cracking up. We shared secrets—you kept mine, as far as I know. I confess to not always being as loyal. While we didn't share the same parents, you are my little sister in every other sense of the word. I pushed you around as often as I had your back. You know I never sugarcoat things for you, and so when I tell you how much I admire you—your quirkiness, your big heart, your willingness to try new things, your fun spirit, your sense of humor. Your..." She hesitates as if she's run out of qualities to admire.

"Her graceful coordination?" Jodie suggests.

Melanie chuckles. "Her talent for getting clothes dirty?"

Holding my hand up, I laugh. "I get the gist."

"Exactly," Cheryl says. "Your ability to poke fun at yourself, to admit when you've made a mistake, and your determination to learn from your screw-ups."

"And there have been a lot of those," Aunt Helen says, snorting.

At this, Jodie meets my eye and winks.

"In summary, I will say this one time and one time only. You, my pesky sister, are my hero, and if you ever repeat this to anyone outside of this table, I will deny, deny, deny. And then I'll exact revenge." Pointing her finger at me, she says, "And you know I will."

I smirk. "Do I ever."

"I love you, Magpie," she says with a slight nod of her head.

Rushing to her chair, I pull her into a bear hug.

"Happy Birthday. You give forty a good name," she whispers.

Still locked in our embrace, I blink back my tears and whisper back, "Thank you."

When we separate, she glances over at Jim, who is bouncing a giggling Michael on one leg and a dozing Cady on the other. I point at him. "I know it's not a great time for a long talk, but things are good at home?"

Cheryl's lips curve upward. "Yeah. They are."

"I'm so glad. I need to believe people can be happily coupled over the long haul." Biting my lip, I add, "Not that it's all about me."

"Tonight, it's all about you. If I can say one thing, it's this— even the healthiest relationships are not easy, but they shouldn't be *hard* either." She cocks her head to one side. "Do you know what I mean?"

I answer with a nod. It took me forty years, but I know exactly what she means.

*   *   *

And then there were four. After Cady almost fell nose-first into a bowl of melted gelato, and Michael's eyes turned the shade of red velvet from rubbing them so hard, Cheryl and Jim begrudgingly departed for Westchester, taking my mom and Aunt Helen with them. I invited Barry and Charles to dinner, but Melanie and Jodie insisted if I was single on my fortieth birthday, they would be single on my fortieth birthday too.

The four of us are standing at a table in the front bar area of the restaurant, and after we order a bottle of Lambrusco from the sommelier, Jodie says, "I think a round of shots is in order too. Lemon drops?"

Protesting, I say, "I have work tomorrow. And you have to drive home."

"No, I don't," Jodie says.

"Are you taking the train?" I ask.

Jodie grins. "Nope. I'm staying in the city."

I jerk my head back. "Where?"

"My college roommate's bachelorette pad."

Raising an eyebrow, I say, "I'm your college roommate."

"And I'm staying over. So are they," she says, pointing at Amanda and Melanie.

I look at Amanda and Melanie. "You are?"

They both beam at me and say, "Yes" at the same time.

"If you'll have us," Amanda says.

"Of course I will. I generally tidy up my apartment before having guests over, but as long as you don't care about the less-than-immaculate living conditions, I'm thrilled for the company."

Rolling her eyes, Jodie says, "I have experience cohabitating with you under the best and worst of circumstances."

"Oh, and you're taking the day off tomorrow. We're having a spa day. Our treat," Amanda says.

Before I can argue, Melanie says, "And don't worry about missing a day of work. Leave a message now with your boss telling him your friends are kidnapping you for your birthday, and if there's an emergency, you'll make yourself available."

"I suggest mentioning you turned forty. Anyone with blood running through his veins will understand how bad it sucks to turn forty," Jodie says.

"Honestly, I couldn't ask for a better birthday. Turning forty has been pretty terrific," I admit. "Only one thing would have made this birthday better."

"Let me guess—a boyfriend?" Amanda asks.

I shake my head and look down at the marble table top. "Close. A phone call, text...*something* from Doug. More than almost anyone, he knew I feared turning forty as some sort of official entrance into middle age."

Melanie reaches across the table and places her hand on mine. "I'm sorry, sweetie."

"Me too," I say. "I didn't expect to hear from him. But I wanted to. I wonder if he even remembered it was my birthday."

"I'm sure he did," Melanie says as Jodie and Amanda nod in agreement.

"I suppose I'll never know," I say. "Anyway, I can't thank you guys enough for throwing me such an amazing birthday party. Single or attached, boyfriend or no boyfriend, I'm incredibly blessed to have friends like you." It's true. As grateful as I am for a speedy metabolism and youthful skin as I enter my fifth decade, I am immeasurably more thankful for the unconditional love and support of my girlfriends.

Her eyebrows, raised, Jodie says, "So...shots?"

Caving, I say, "Yes to shots."

"I have another thing to celebrate," Amanda says, her voice bubbly.

"Do tell," I insist, while Jodie summons the bartender.

With a twinkle in her eye, Amanda says, "I'm kind of dating someone."

I slap a hand against my cheek as Melanie and Jodie yelp.

"Details, now," Jodie demands.

Amanda's eyes light up. "His name is Greg. I met him on eHarmony. We've been out three times already." Raising her hand in the air, she adds, "And before you yell at me, I'm sorry I didn't confide in you earlier. It was killing me, but I was afraid to jinx it. I also wanted to trust my instincts without any advice—solicited or not."

Blinking, Jodie says, "When have we ever given unsolicited advice?"

I playfully nudge Jodie and then grin at Amanda. "We understand. And I speak for all of us when I say we are so pleased for you."

Always a loyal friend, Amanda allowed the spotlight to shine on me on my birthday dinner, but if I hadn't been enjoying holding court, I would have tuned into her secret hours earlier. She is radiating happiness from within, and even though she is always beautiful, her smile is wider, her hazel eyes shine brighter, and even her posture is straighter.

The bartender brings over our shots, and after the girls toast to my birthday (and to Amanda's new man), we count to three before slamming them.

As we take turns hugging Amanda afterwards, it dawns on me that I'm currently the only one without a boyfriend. If I said the realization didn't leave me with a twinge of envy, I'd be lying. But I'm happy for my friends, and I am confident my turn will come around again. I just have to keep the faith for as long as it takes, no matter how many disappointments or false starts I encounter along the way.

"So, birthday girl, since I'm not using my *vacuum* much these days, you're welcome to it," Jodie says, bumping me in the shoulder.

"Sharing *vacuums* is nasty." I distort my face in disgust and bump her right back. Lowering my voice, I say, "But if you insist on treating me to a new one, I won't turn it down."

Much later, my eyelids heavy and ready for sleep after hours discussing sex, bowel movements, reality television, most embarrassing moments, and every other mindless topic conceivable with my besties, one thing is pleasurably clear—my youthful spirit has not deserted me with the cessation of my thirties, and there is not a damn thing wrong with that.

August

I'm devoting the afternoon to cleaning my apartment. This involves scrubbing my bathroom and kitchen counters, using the Swiffer WetJet on my living room, bedroom, and bathroom floors, dusting all of my bookshelves, shredding all of the junk mail I've allowed to pile up, and vacuuming the dust balls which have collected on my area rug. Emptying the contents of the shredder machine into several plastic bags had the side effect of disbursing tiny flecks of paper all over my apartment, and I attempt to vacuum those up as well. I turn off the Dyson and wipe some sweat from my brow as my phone rings. I freeze in place when I see who the call is from.

I stare at the phone as it rings, once and then a second time, wondering why Philip would be calling me on a Saturday afternoon, or at all for that matter. We stopped working together over two months ago, and a winter, a spring, and much of a summer has passed since we dated. Considering he ended our relationship to reconcile with his wife, I would hope he'd call someone else if he craved a little afternoon delight. But what if it's an emergency—like the death of a partner? Maybe someone died, and he is calling on me to find a creative way to spin it. I'm aware this is a preposterous idea and, no doubt, not the reason for his call. And then I worry something might have happened to Melanie, and I quickly pick up the phone before letting it go to voicemail. "Hello?"

"Maggie."

I'm tempted to respond, "That's my name, don't wear it out," but refrain. Wanting to skip the small talk, I ask, "What happened?" while my heart beats rapidly under my t-shirt.

"Nothing happened. Calm down."

"Melanie's okay?"

"Melanie is fine." After a pause, Philip adds, "As far as I know. Haven't seen her since yesterday."

I clear my throat and try to calm the tremors running through my body at his unexpected call. In an attempt to display some semblance of coolness, I respond, "Oh."

Yeah. Real cool.

"Are you home by any chance?"

"Yeah. I'm cleaning. Why?"

"I was wondering if I could come by. I'd like to talk to you."

I wonder if he's going to try to convince me to come back to the firm again. "Sure. What time can you be here?" I glance down at my dust-stained Mickey Mouse t-shirt and gray drawstring sweatpants which should have been thrown out a decade ago and mentally inventory my closet for a change of clothing.

"I'm downstairs."

"Um, okay." I race to the bathroom and scrutinize my reflection in the mirror. *Crap.* "I'll ring you in." I kick off the sweatpants and pull a pair of black yoga pants from the top shelf of my closet, bringing down most of the remaining contents with them. I close the closet door and slide on the yoga pants. When the doorman rings, I tell him to let Philip up and I pray for the elevator to stop at every floor between the lobby and mine. Maybe it will even stall on the third floor by someone lugging in several heavy baskets of laundry. With my remaining time, I slick my hair back into a ponytail and apply a layer of mascara and a dab of lip gloss. I keep the Mickey Mouse shirt on. It might be dirty, but it's cute.

I jump when the bell rings, even though I was expecting it. Taking a deep breath, I remind myself it's Philip calling on me—not the other way around—and I have nothing to fear. I open the door and flash him a smile. Gesturing for him to come inside, I say, "Well, this is a surprise."

Stepping into my apartment, Philip says, "I hope I didn't catch you at a bad time. I was in the neighborhood."

I follow him into the living room. "Excuse the appearance of my humble abode." The vacuum cleaner is in the center of my rug because I didn't have time to move it. The Swifter WetJet is leaning against one wall with a dirty cloth still attached to it, and bags of shredded paper line another wall. "I was in the middle of cleaning and didn't quite finish."

Philip looks around the room and grins. "No worries. It's not like I gave you any notice."

No, you didn't. "Have a seat. Are you thirsty?"

Sitting on my couch, Philip waves me away. "I'm fine. Please sit."

I join Philip on the opposite side of the couch but angle my body so I'm facing him. We sit in silence for somewhere between five seconds and eternity. I fight the urge to initiate conversation because I want him to lead the discussion. I raise my eyebrows, hoping he'll take the hint and say something.

Finally, he says, "How's the new job?"

"It's great. Challenging, but I'm enjoying the work so far." I take a deep breath. "So if you're here to persuade me to come back, you can skip the hard sell."

Philip shakes his head. "I wouldn't dare. I asked once, and you said no. I can take a hint."

Since I've eliminated Melanie and my former job as the reasons for Philip's visit, my impatience rises. "Why are you here, then?"

Philip throws his head back and laughs. "Oh, Magpie. I've missed you."

His use of my nickname doesn't sit right, and I clench my jaw. With a slight nod in Philip's direction, I say, "Well?"

Running a hand through his dark locks, Philip sighs. "Here's the thing—"

This is the same expression Philip used when he told me he was getting back together with his wife, and I interrupt, "I think I've heard that before."

Philip stares at me, a crease forming in his forehead. "I don't follow you."

I raise my hand in dismissal. "Forget it. You were saying?"

"Sheila and I have decided to continue with the divorce proceedings after all."

My eyes open wide. "Oh, wow." I swallow hard. "I'm sorry."

Philip pushes out his lower lip, which makes him look like a teenage boy instead of a forty-something man. "Thanks. We agreed a permanent split is for the best. And since we sought therapy and attempted reconciliation first, we won't have to wonder if we gave up without a fight."

Trying to come up with something supportive to say, I smooth out my ponytail with my palm and offer, "A mutual and well-thought-out decision is good, I guess. Right?"

Philip nods. "Right."

If I wait for Philip to mention the white elephant in the room, I'm afraid we'll be here until my forty-first birthday. "Is there a reason you're telling me this, Philip?"

Chuckling, Philip says, "You're not a patient woman, are you?"

"Excuse me, but you did show up at my door unannounced." The edge in my voice is unmistakable.

With a crooked smile, Philip says, "Technically, I announced myself before I arrived at your door. I was across the street when I called."

My lips curl up against my will. "Semantics."

"The reason I'm here..." Philip pauses and locks his eyes on mine. "The reason I'm here is because I've missed you. And I'm hoping maybe you've missed me too."

I am stunned to silence and stare at Philip with wide eyes. "Wow." I gulp, wishing I had a glass of water nearby.

Philip gives me a sheepish grin. "I wanted to ease into the conversation, but Ms. Spitfire wanted an explanation post haste."

The "thump thump thump" of my heart pounds in frantic speed. "I, uh, wasn't expecting this at all."

"You know I never meant to hurt you, right?" Philip stares into my eyes like they're the pathway to my soul.

Nodding, I say, "I know," in a soft voice.

"I wanted to do the right thing by my family, and didn't think quitting a twenty-year marriage for a woman I had only been dating a couple of months was it."

A bit stung by his words, I reply, "I thought your marriage was over before we started dating. If I had any inclination it was a temporary separation, I wouldn't have gotten involved with you."

Philip sighs and scratches his beard. "I apologize. That came out wrong."

"It's okay. I know what you meant."

Smiling hopefully, he continues, "Since we don't work together anymore, we won't have to deal with all of those complications like ethics and sexual harassment. We can be a regular couple."

I jerk my head back. "You never seriously thought I would file sexual harassment charges, did you?"

Philip reaches an arm across the couch and gently pats my shoulder. "No. Of course not. But as a partner, I had to consider it, and it's something the management committee would certainly be leery of."

I study Philip as he repeatedly taps his leg against the floor. He's nervous, and it's rare to see him without the upper hand. "What do you say? Assuming you're not already dating someone else." He scans the room as if expecting another man to come out and stake his claim on me, but there is no other man hiding behind a piece of furniture, and I'm not dating anyone else.

It would be so easy to give in and say yes—yes to giving my relationship with Philip another chance, and yes to being part of a couple again. Philip wants me, and I'd be lying if I said I wasn't scared, lonely, and very sex deprived. Succumbing to Philip could take the edge off all of those feelings. And the sex was great. He was a bit on the rough side, and I am tempted by the knowledge that if I said the word, he would kick the bags of shredded paper to the side, throw me against the wall, and take me.

I shake myself out of my sexual fantasy and return to reality, and the reality is that Philip is not the right guy for me, and jumping into the sack with him won't change anything. Despite the lingering physical attraction, my fascination with him ended as fast as it started.

And so, for the second time in just a few months, I thank Philip for the opportunity but tell him the answer is no.

*   *   *

After Philip leaves, I play the "Fierce Female Artists" playlist I created on my iPod. First song is Katy Perry's "Roar," and I turn the volume all the way up and continue cleaning. Then I grab a large box of Hefty bags from my kitchen cabinet. Removing one, I pluck the drawstring sweatpants from my closet floor and throw them inside. It's time to clean house.

Several hours later, I have gone through the entire contents of my closet and a few of my dresser drawers, but I've only managed to get rid of a few items. I can't bring myself to throw away the numerous oversized t-shirts Doug left behind. The only reason I haven't worn them is because I didn't know they were there. They would be perfect as night shirts. I also can't part with the black leather pants I purchased at the Gap in my mid-twenties. They still cling perfectly to my tush like they were painted on, and even though they are not currently in style, tight leather pants always make a comeback.

My underwear drawer is next, and I dump the contents on the floor in one fell swoop. Among my favorite thongs and boy shorts are the Hanes briefs I never wear but keep around in case of underwear emergencies; bras in almost every style in existence, mostly in neutral colors but a few red, pink, and even polka dot varieties add pops of color to the collection; gym socks, argyle socks, hunter socks, linen socks, and socks missing their other half but never thrown out because I was certain I would find the complete pair eventually; and an embarrassingly large collection of black tights.

I take a deep exhale and remove another Hefty bag from the box. Any sock not part of a pair is tossed aside. Being a singleton myself, I feel a twinge of guilt, but I remind myself that socks are not people, and I am not discriminating against the romantically unattached by throwing them out, especially the ones with holes in the toes.

I intend to sort through the tights next, but when I remove a pair from the top of the pile, I spot a white paper envelope underneath. My name is written on the back in bright pink marker. At first, I have no clue what the envelope holds, but as I slip my hand inside and remove the contents, I remember and gasp out loud. Inside the envelope is my thirty-ninth birthday present from Cheryl—two open-ended tickets to Six Flags Great Adventure.

I walk over to my bedroom window and pull up the shades. Looking out onto 27th Street, I see the sun is shining brightly, and I wonder what Doug is doing today. Maybe he and Lindsay went to Central Park for the afternoon. Perhaps they rented a pair of city bikes and took a ride up the West Side Highway. Do they live together now? Are they engaged? I shouldn't be thinking about him anymore. It's been a year. He's moved on, and according to his new girlfriend, I didn't share his dreams anyway.

But my heart insists we have unfinished business and won't allow me to let go—not only in my waking moments, but in my sleep. Doug makes appearances in my dreams almost nightly, as if my subconscious won't give up on the possibility of reconciliation. I allow my memory to revisit the fateful day in January when I asked him to take me back. He shot me down because I couldn't pinpoint the source of my apprehension. He said if I didn't know why I had doubts in the first place, how could I be sure the uncertainty wouldn't rear its ugly ahead at a later date? I didn't have an answer for him, so he walked out of the bar and out of my life. He also said something else—something I forced myself to forget because it didn't make a difference at the time. But now I remember—he said he still had feelings for me.

My heart begins to beat faster, and the blood rushes to my face as I realize something—I have an answer for Doug now. But do I deserve a second chance?

There is only one person I trust to give it to me straight. I scan the recent contacts on my phone until I locate Cheryl's number and hit call before planting myself on the couch and extending my legs across the coffee table.

"Hey," Cheryl answers.

"Was I a shitty girlfriend to Doug?"

"Um...what?"

I bite on my knuckle and flex my leg muscles to keep from shaking. "Besides the obvious faux pas—asking for a break—did I treat him poorly when we were together?" I brace myself for her answer since I know she won't blow smoke up my ass.

She doesn't say anything.

"Cheryl?" I say in a soft voice.

"You weren't a *bad* girlfriend. You didn't cheat on Doug or physically or verbally abuse the guy, and you definitely made him happy..." Her voice trails off.

"But..."

I hear her exhale into the phone. "You sure you want to hear this? You might not like it."

"I'm aware."

"Let me put it this way. I can name off the top of my head at least ten single women who wish they were dating Doug, and probably just as many married women who wish their husbands were more like him, but you..."

I swallow hard. "What about me?"

"You almost held his good qualities against him. As if he'd somehow be worth more if he wasn't so wonderful."

I open my mouth to argue, but clamp my lips together before any sound comes out because she's right.

"Remember how he'd always be the most sober guy at the party in case there was an emergency, and someone needed to take action?" I ask.

"I recall you telling me that. You teased him for being 'soft.'"

My stomach churns at my cluelessness. "Did you know he has a portion of his salary automatically donated to various charities?"

"I didn't know that."

"Do you think I could make it up to him? I mean, if he took me back, am I capable of being a worthy partner to him?"

Without hesitating, Cheryl says, "I think you've learned a lot this year, Mags. If you ask me, things would be different if you were with Doug now."

I agree with her assessment of my growth over the past twelve months, and as always, Cheryl's validation is reassuring. "One last thing—do you think he's too good for me? I don't want to be one of those couples folks look at and question, 'why is he with *her*?'"

Cheryl laughs. "No. He's a wonderful guy, but you're an amazing woman, Maggie. You're just a late bloomer when it comes to this love stuff."

"That's my story, and I'm sticking with it. Thanks, Cheryl."

After we hang up, I remain unmoving for a few seconds, lost in thought.

Maybe it's too little too late for Doug and me, but what if it's not?

*   *   *

While waiting in line at a coffee cart outside the Time-Life Building, I keep an eye out for someone I recognize from CBS Radio, where Doug works as a copy writer. I hope to spot one of his colleagues walking into the building, but I'm terrified Doug will see me first. Personally handing the letter to Doug would be the most surefire way to confirm he received it, but having someone else give it to him is the chicken-shit way and, make no mistake, I am chicken-shit. The Time-Life Building is only a few blocks away from HBO headquarters, and so with any luck, one of his co-workers will walk by soon, agree to play messenger, and I will get to work on time.

After I exchange my two dollars for a small coffee and throw a five-dollar bill in the tip jar for good karma, I drop my oversized sunglasses over my eyes and hope it's a good enough disguise. Then I hide behind the giant blue cube-shaped statue outside the building and try to be inconspicuous. I'm glad I never considered a career in undercover anything. I clearly suck at it.

I sip my coffee and, as I check the face of each person who walks by hoping to spot a familiar one, I think about my plan and marvel at how easily it all came together—*in theory*. Doug is the key to making it work in practice. My coffee cup almost empty, I glance down at my watch. Almost ten minutes have gone by, and I release a frustrated sigh, afraid I'm going to fail my mission, but then I see her—Heidi—one of the broadcasting assistants. We did multiple shots together at the last Christmas party I attended with Doug. Hoping to reach her before she gets into the building—since I won't get very far without identification—I speed walk over to her, suppressing the desire to shout her name. The wedges I'm wearing allow for more speed than the high-heeled pumps she sports, and once I am arm-distance away, I lightly tap her on the shoulder.

"Can I help you?" she asks after turning to face me. There is zero recognition on her twenty-something face, but her eyes look patient, and I hope this means she'll agree to help me.

"Heidi. It's Maggie. Doug's ex-girlfriend?" I remove my sunglasses in case my disguise is working too well.

Recognition lights up her face. "Maggie. How are you?"

I breathe a sigh of relief. "I'm good. This is gonna sound weird, but can I ask you to do me a very small favor?"

Worry lines appearing on her forehead, she says, "Sure. Is everything all right?"

"Everything's fine, but I don't want Doug to see me. Do you have a minute?" Afraid Doug will show up at any moment, I motion my head toward the statue.

When we are hidden from sight, I remove the Betsy Clark stationary from my purse and extend it towards her. "Can you please give this to Doug for me?"

Heidi removes the card from my hand and cocks her head of blond curls to the side. "That's it?"

I nod. "Pretty much, yes. But if you can give it to him personally instead of leaving it on his desk or somewhere else it could get misplaced, I would appreciate it. I need to make sure he gets it." I hand her my business card. "If there's any problem, please call and let me know."

"Sure, but you can give it to him yourself. I can let you—"

"No." My cheeks burning in shame, I say, "I can't face him." I bite my lip and avert eye contact, but then she pats my shoulder, and I meet her gaze.

Smiling at me with kind eyes, she says, "I'll take care of it. No worries."

"Thank you." I glance at my watch again. "Crap. I'm late for work."

"You'd better go, then." Raising and lifting the envelope, she says, "I promise this is in good hands."

I thank her one more time and walk away. Second guessing myself, I turn around just in time to see Heidi disappear into the building. Knowing it's too late to turn back now, I sprint to my office.

*   *   *

"Do you want us to wait with you?" Melanie asks, completely ignoring her sons, Jessup and Lloyd, who are running around her in circles.

Melanie's face is ripe with worry, and I'm terrified it's because she knows I'm being stood up. I fake a confident smile. "No thanks. I should be alone when he shows up." *If he shows up.* I glance at my phone. It's only eleven thirty. I wanted to get a head start in case we hit traffic, so I took a nine-thirty train to the Summit, New Jersey station, where Melanie, Barry, and the kids picked me up in their SUV Station Wagon. After a quick stop at McDonalds, we got on the road, making good time, especially for a Saturday in the summer.

Pursing her lips, Melanie says, "Gotcha. Please keep your phone close by. I'll be checking in. And don't forget to reapply sunscreen. It's hotter than Hades today."

She's right about the sweltering heat. It's a sunny August day, with temperatures expected to reach 90 degrees. My hair is up in a long ponytail, and I'm wearing a royal blue ribbed tank top and white denim shorts.

Doug always liked me in white and said blue brought out the color of my eyes. Assuming he shows up, I hope he'll be distracted enough by my outfit not to notice the perspiration dripping down my neck and between my breasts. On second thought, I would love Doug to take notice of my breasts, with or without sweat. "Hopefully, he'll get here early." I wouldn't have taken such an early train if I knew the traffic would be so light.

Melanie crosses her fingers. "Hopefully."

"Do you think he'll come?" Please say yes.

Biting her lip, Melanie says, "I *hope* he does."

"That's not what I asked," I mumble.

"I wish I knew, Maggie. I know he loved you once. But it's been a year. Whatever happens, you should be really proud of yourself for taking the risk." She gives me a thumbs up sign.

I nod absently.

Melanie laughs and bumps her shoulder against mine. "For realz."

Tugging on Melanie's leg, Jessup moans, "C'mon, Mom." From behind him, her older son Lloyd says, "Yeah, I'm ready to go on the Drop of Doom."

I cast my eyes upward, where tall rollercoaster tracks in yellow, blue, and green line the sky. It's been two years since my last trip to Six Flags, and I'm guessing the rides have gotten much scarier. I hope my forty-year-old heart can take it. "Yikes. I've never heard of the Drop of Doom. What is it?"

"The world's tallest drop," Barry says unenthusiastically.

His face is devoid of color, and I can't help but chuckle. "I take it you're not a fan of rides?"

"I can handle rides just fine, but not the tallest drop tower ride in the world which only opened this year. It's not been tested enough for my liking." In a lower voice, he adds, "Kind of hoping the boys are too short."

"Good luck with that," I say with a giggle.

After momentarily forgetting the real reason I begged Melanie and Barry to drive me to Jackson, New Jersey that morning—suggesting they combine it with a fun family outing—the churning of the nervous knots in my stomach serves as a reminder, and I take a quick scan of the people heading in our direction. I see lots of families with young children, and groups of teenagers, but not Doug.

Wrapping her arms around her two boys, Melanie says, "Okay, little men. Time for us to go. We'll check back in with Maggie later." She smiles at me. "Maybe all of us can ride the Drop of Doom together."

"I'm terrified I'm going to experience my own drop of doom in a couple of hours," I say, blinking back the tears threatening to escape. What was I thinking? He has a new girlfriend, a new life. What kind of evil person concocts a grand gesture to steal another woman's boyfriend?

"For what it's worth, I think what you're doing is beyond cool," Barry says, readjusting his aviator-style sunglasses over the bridge of his nose.

"You don't think I'm nuts?" I ask. Why did I think meeting at Great Adventure was such a brilliant idea when it would have been much simpler to suggest a drink at a local watering hole? And a much closer commute to the comfort of my bed if I'm stood up.

Shaking his head, Barry says, "I think you're the coolest chick I know. If a girl did something like this for me, I'd ask her to marry me."

Melanie rolls her eyes. "And all I had to do was swallow."

"Swallow what?" Jessup asks.

"Never mind," Melanie and Barry say in unison while I laugh quietly into my hand.

Giving me a hug, Melanie says, "Good luck, Mags. We love you."

"I love you too," I say. "Have fun. And thanks for doing this for me."

Melanie says, "Anything for you," and with a kiss on the cheek and a wave, I watch her and Barry walk away holding hands while their sons skip alongside them.

*   *   *

I take a sip from my water bottle and wipe the corners of my eyes. Even though I stored the bottle in the freezer overnight, the solid piece of ice has already melted, and the water is now room temperature at best. Bored, I pull my phone out of my bag to check Facebook. It's approaching one p.m., which means I've been waiting for almost an hour and a half. In between searching the crowd for Doug, I've answered numerous texts from Melanie, Jodie, Amanda, and Cheryl, all asking for a status update. I replied with more than a little embarrassment that Doug hasn't shown up yet. My mission has failed, which makes me a failure. I know they say "nothing ventured, nothing gained," but if you don't hit the ground running, you can't fall flat. I wonder which is worse—living with the what ifs, or being full-on rejected without any room for hope or delusions.

I close my eyes and summon to memory a mental picture of the letter I wrote to Doug:

Dear Doug,

I told you I would find a use for this vintage 1970s stationery someday.

The first thing you need to know is I love you. I'm in love with you, and of this, I am one hundred percent positive.

When I tried to get back together in January, you wanted to know why I wasn't certain about us before. I understand why you needed to know, but unfortunately, I didn't quite know myself. I do now, and I'd very much like to tell you, assuming you still want an answer.

I'm enclosing a pre-paid entrance ticket to Six Flags Great Adventure. If there is any part of you that still loves me, or even if you're just itching to ride El Toro, please meet me at the entrance any time between noon and 2:00 p.m. next Saturday, August 13th. I will be waiting.

Maybe it's too late. I want you to be happy. If you don't show up, I will assume you are where you want to be, and a future with me is permanently off the table. I will leave you alone for good if it's what you want. But what I want, Doug, is you.

Maggie

What went through Doug's mind when he read it? I like to think it touched a part of him that still hasn't given up on me. I want to believe after reading it, he closed his eyes and was flooded with memories of the good times we shared together as a couple. I hope his curiosity about what I have to say overpowers the stubborn doubts he has about my feelings for him. But of course, I'm thinking like Maggie and not like Doug. If Doug has truly moved on, a note from an ex-girlfriend might elicit anger, not stir up buried feelings of love. When he thinks about the times we went to amusement parks together, he might choose to recall the way I whined during the long lines and hogged all of the water as opposed to the fits of laughter we shared at the end of each ride—our hair tousled and our faces flushed with happiness.

Glancing at my watch again, I note the time with despair—it's almost 1:35. I should text Melanie for their location so I can meet them at their next attraction. I'll paint on a temporary happy face for the sake of the boys until Melanie insists on leaving them with Barry so she can tend to me at the closest bar. I confirmed ahead of time that alcohol is available for purchase in the park—partly in case Doug and I wanted to celebrate our reunion with a toast, but mostly in case I was stood up and needed to drown my sorrows. I sadly suspect it will be the latter.

I am torn between complete devastation that Doug has truly moved on and anger he would put me through this—that he would let me come all the way out here and wait in the blistering heat if he wasn't going to show up. One of Doug's most admirable qualities, in my opinion, is how sensitive he is to the feelings of others. He would never intentionally kick someone who's down. The Doug I know would have called me or, at the very least, sent an email letting me down easy, instead of causing needless suffering or humiliation. And since he is the one who insisted I get a full examination by a dermatologist every year because of my fair complexion and abundance of freckles, the Doug I know would *definitely* not want me to sit outside in the sun for longer than necessary. With this thought, I remove the container of sunscreen from my bag, cover my eyes with my other hand, and spray it along the length of my body—something I've done at least five times since arriving at the park. Even if the love Doug felt for me once is gone forever, there is not a cruel bone in his body.

And this is why, when I open my eyes and see him walking toward me, my eyes well up—not only with tears of joy over not being stood up, but with tears of relief that Doug is still "the Doug I know."

I take him in as he approaches. He's wearing brown cargo shorts and a graphic t-shirt, and he's looking directly at me. He doesn't appear nervous or excited, happy or sad, and I can't gauge his emotions at all. When he stands before me, I choke out, "You came," in barely a whisper. I swallow hard. "I'm so glad." I study his face—his gorgeous, honest, and completely smoochable face which I took for granted for close to three years—and try to read his mind.

Doug nods. "I would have been here earlier, but there was an accident on I-95."

"I hope it wasn't serious."

"No Jaws of Life, so it could be worse." He smiles.

I adore his smile, especially the pronounced dimple in his left cheek. "It certainly could." The one year I spent Thanksgiving with Doug's relatives, we passed the Jaws of Life three times on our way to Long Island. We measured the intensity of car accidents by the absence or presence of them ever since.

"In any event, I'm here now." He holds his ticket out to me. "Should we go inside?"

I let out an involuntary gasp of surprise. "You don't want to talk first?"

Narrowing his teal eyes at me, Doug says, "I haven't decided if I'm here because I want to see you or because I want to ride rollercoasters. I figure we can talk while waiting in line. That way, if I don't like what you have to say, at least there will be a ride at the end of it."

I gape at him, not knowing how to respond.

Doug offers a bemused smile and gently pushes me toward the entrance. "After you."

There is no line to get into the park, not surprising at this late hour of the afternoon. My stomach rumbles, but I'm not sure if it's because I'm hungry for the sugar-laden delights offered at many of the stores inside the park or if it's nervous energy. In any event, I hope Doug can't hear it. I rehearse my speech to myself while occasionally taking sidelong glances at him. His focus is straight ahead, and he seems to know where he's going. He's walking briskly in the direction of Adventure Alley, and I have to double my steps to keep up.

Stopping in front of a ride called the SkyScreamer, he says, "We're here," and looks up.

I follow his gaze toward the rotating gondola ride. "Is this new?"

Still staring at the ride, he says, "It's a couple of years old. They got rid of the old swing ride, and I know you like to ease your stomach into these things. And your nerves."

He heads to the end of the line, and I follow him. "Thanks. I need to get used to the motion on all of these rides. Can't go directly to a crazy rollercoaster."

Smirking at me, Doug says, "I know. I've accompanied you to amusement parks before." But then he showcases his dimples again, and I know he's teasing. Leaning his back against the metal fence encasing the line for the ride, he crosses his arms against his chest. "You have something to say to me?"

"I do," I say, as my heart begins to pound against my chest. I take a deep breath and swallow hard. Motioning to the bottle of water peeking out of the backpack Doug never leaves home without, I timidly ask, "Can I have a sip of your water, please?"

Handing it to me, Doug says, "Where's your water? You need it on a day like today."

I take a long gulp, hoping it's enough to keep my throat from drying up while I say my piece. "I drank it while waiting for you."

"I didn't mean to be so late. I'm sorry."

I pat him playfully on his upper arm. "Just admit you were trying to punish me by waiting until the last possible minute to show up."

His mouth a firm line, Doug says, "That's not the way I roll, Mags."

I feel the blood rush to my face. Perhaps this is not the time for me to initiate playful teasing banter. "Of course it's not." When Doug doesn't respond, I take it as my cue to continue. "You asked me what our problem was, and I said I didn't know. I know now."

Doug nods, urging me to continue. The ride has ended and, as a new set of people get on, we move closer to the front of the line.

I try to remember my speech, but my memory has escaped me like a soap opera character suffering from amnesia, so I wing it. "There was no problem with us, and there was no problem with you. There was a problem with *me*. Let's face it. I didn't grow up with good role models for relationships. My father behaved more like a distant uncle, and my Aunt Helen and Uncle Walter's idea of a conversation was him asking for a second helping of roasted potatoes, and her saying he'd have no one to blame but himself if he dropped dead of a heart attack. Which he did. It's not a great excuse, but I learned everything I know about falling in love from books, television shows, and movies, where everything is drenched with conflict and angst. The couple always experiences so many highs and lows before they ultimately have their happily ever after." I pause to take a breath, and I eye Doug's water bottle longingly.

He hands it to me without a word.

I take a few sips and then continue. "I know how ridiculous

this sounds, Doug, and I'm mortified." I give the water bottle back. "The thing is, I never felt those crazy highs and lows with you. I was never nervous or anxious around you, and you never made me feel like I had to work hard to get your attention. I never worried you wouldn't call me again, or that you'd leave me for another girl. You never made me cry. I didn't have sleepless nights freaking out over you. There was no drama." Ashamed by my confession, I drop my eyes to the ground for a moment before forcing myself to face Doug head-on. "I thought somehow the absence of this anxiety meant I didn't feel enough for you. But now I know what we had is the definition of a healthy relationship."

I study Doug's face. I'm not sure he's convinced, so I press on. "But please don't mistake the safety for lack of passion. I love kissing you. I love sleeping in your arms. I love your hands. You have great fingers. I love your control and how unselfish you are in bed. Not surprising, since you are unselfish in life." I look at him pleadingly. "Doug, I love you. I'm *in* love with you, and it's not because I'm lonely and it's not because I'm forty." I withhold a giggle, thinking about Harry Burns' speech at the end of *When Harry Met Sally*. "It's because you're the absolute best person for me, and I think I'm the absolute best person for you. Who besides the two of us would rather postpone a trip to Cape Cod than miss out on hearing J.J. Abrams speak at the 92nd Street Y?" I pause momentarily, remembering the time we delayed a vacation for just that reason. "I asked for a break, and you didn't want to give it to me, but I don't regret taking it. Without that break, I don't know if I would have learned what love is, and love, Doug, is you and me. My greatest mistake was not comprehending what I had until I lost it, but I promise to never take you or us for granted for the rest of my life if you'll take me back." I stop talking, satisfied I said what needed to be said. The rest is up to him.

As Doug opens his mouth to respond, the conductor of the ride (who's probably a college student on summer break) yells, "All aboard!" I was so singularly focused on bearing my soul to Doug, I didn't notice us moving up the line, and now we're at the front.

Doug and I make our way over to a vacant two-person swing-like chair and sit down. Without saying anything, Doug straps us in, pulls the safety bar across our chests, and we sit side by side with our feet dangling.

After the conductor checks to make sure everyone's swings are secure, we start to slowly swirl and revolve around the tower in the center of the ride. We begin to climb, and the higher we go, the faster we spin, my ponytail slamming against my neck as it blows in the wind.

Doug has yet to utter a word, and I can't resist the urge to turn my head so I can see him. Noting the red in the whites of his eyes, I gasp and reflexively look straight ahead. Either he got dirt in his eyes, or he's shedding silent tears. Another covert glance at him confirms he's choked up, and I hope beyond hope it's because he still loves me, and not because he's despondent over having to reject me again.

As if reading my mind, Doug answers my question with one move. His right hand covers my left one, and his fingers entwine with mine in an all too familiar display of affection decidedly missing from my life for the last year. I cock my head in his direction, and he winks at me. Unable to hold back, I beam at him. We smile goofily at each other until the swing slows down, and we descend to the ground.

While the other passengers jump off of their swings and rush to the exit and to the next thrill ride on their agendas, we remain sitting. Leaning over me, Doug releases my strap and slowly brings his face closer to mine until we are forehead to forehead. Unmoving, he whispers, "I love you," and plants a butterfly kiss on my nose.

I close my eyes and murmur, "I love you too," as his lips touch mine. As the kiss, gentle at first, deepens, Doug holds my face in his hands. I reach up and run my fingertips along his earlobes, one of his erogenous zones.

Alarms ring around us, and even with my eyes closed, I see flashes of light. I wonder if these are the fireworks you're supposed to see when you kiss your soul mate. I reluctantly break away to catch my breath, and that's when I see them. Everyone in line—from small children and their young parents, to pimple-faced teenagers, to grandparents—is watching us while the conductor waves his foghorn and flashlight in our faces. "Now that you've come up for air, do you mind getting a room so we can start the next ride?" he asks with a smirk on his face.

I bite my cheek, suppressing a giggle. Doug jumps from the swing first and extends his hand to me. I accept it and climb off the swing. Not letting go of each other, we offer mumbled apologies and hightail it to the exit against a backdrop of applause.

*   *   *

"I'm positive this is the best burger I've ever had," I say to Doug fifteen minutes later. Famished, we made our way directly from the SkyScreamer to the Great Character Café in the Fantasy Forest section of the park for a late lunch.

Doug plucks a fry from the plate we are sharing and dips it into a paper cup of ketchup before biting into it. Looking at me doubtfully, he swallows before saying, "You sure about that? I can name at least ten places in the city with better burgers than these. I think the reason you like it so much is because we're essentially eating inside a giant ice cream sundae."

I follow Doug's eyes as he muses appreciatively at the fiberglass moldings in the shape of ice cream and candies. "You might be right," I say, nibbling on a fry. I scoot my chair closer to him and place my free hand on his thigh. "But there's another reason."

Twirling a piece of hair that had escaped my ponytail during the swing ride around his finger, Doug says, "What's the other reason?"

"I'm just really happy, and food always tastes better when I'm happy," I say assuredly.

Doug reaches into his backpack and pulls out a map of the

park. Reading it, he says, "New England Hotdogs is in Loony Tunes Seaport. We can test your theory on relish."

I make a sour face. "I'll pass." I hate relish, and Doug knows this.

Doug laughs for a second, and then his face turns serious. "I've missed you so much, Mags."

I swipe my hand lightly along his cheek. "I've missed you too. So much." My gaze rests on his chest. "Have you been working out?"

A film of pink painting his cheeks, Doug says, "Sort of. Lindsay was addicted to the gym, so I started going and got into it."

My face drops at his mention of the *L* word. "About that."

"Yeah?"

"I'm so unbelievably thrilled and relieved and stoked and a gazillion other positive emotions that we're back together..." Scrunching my forehead, I say, "We *are* back together, right?"

Doug plants a soft kiss on my lips in answer.

I take a deep exhale. "Good."

Doug smiles.

"But I don't want to be the reason you don't have children. I'm not saying I definitely don't want children, but I'm not in a rush, and I should be at my age. I don't want you giving up your dreams for me."

His head cocked to the side, Doug says, "Where did that come from?"

"Where did what come from?" I repeat, confused.

Doug shakes his head. "Where did you get the idea my dreams included having children? We never really discussed it."

I bite my lip. "I know we didn't, and I'm so sorry you didn't feel comfortable admitting it to me."

His brow creased, Doug says, "There was nothing to admit. My relationship with you is—and always was—more important to me than having a family with anyone else. If it happens, it happens. All I want is you."

"That's not what Lindsay said—"

His eyes wide, Doug interrupts me. "When did you talk to Lindsay?"

I recall the day I ran into her in Sephora. "I think it was April. She was shopping with some friends and said you were out with Connor."

Jerking his head back, Doug says, "Are you sure it was April?"

"Maybe it was March. Or May. It was this spring." Shrugging, I say, "Why does it matter?"

"Because I broke up with Lindsay in February," he says matter-of-factly.

My mouth falls open. "I had no idea. I assumed you were still together." I momentarily think back to the nights I cried myself to sleep, imagining them blissfully happy and in love. Returning to the here and now, I say, "In any event, it was definitely after February. I remember because it was finally warm enough to leave my hat and scarf at home, and I was wearing my funky black and purple Vans, not boots, when I ran to the subway, crying." My voice trails off at the end of the sentence.

His eyes protruding, Doug says, "She made you cry? What did she say to you?"

Not wanting to revisit the day in detail, I give Doug an abbreviated version of my conversation with Lindsay. I conclude with, "She said you realized we weren't compatible, and then she thanked me for making you available to her."

Doug gapes at me incredulously. "And you believed her?"

"Why wouldn't I? I had no reason to doubt her. Although I was surprised to learn how much you wanted to have a baby."

Doug's eyes well up again—which oddly has the effect of completely turning me on. There is something about a sensitive man, especially a gorgeous one who adores me.

"I broke up with her about two weeks after we ran into you at the ice skating rink." Doug pauses. "When you fell on your ass."

"You had to mention that part, didn't you?" I say, shaking my head at him.

"I knew I would never feel for her what I felt for you," Doug says. "Even though I wasn't ready to get back together with you, I'd rather be single than jerk an innocent girl around."

"Only she wasn't so innocent," we say in unison.

Doug rolls his eyes. "Jesus. What a psycho."

"You're gonna have to curtail the 'Jesus' talk in front of my mom and Aunt Helen," I tease.

"I'll be a nice agnostic boy in front of your family, I promise."

"*You're* my family," I say.

"And you're mine," Doug says.

"And you'd be okay if we were a family of two?" I hate to be so one-note, but I have to make sure.

Doug gazes at me earnestly. "Kids are too short to get on rollercoasters. We'd have to take turns watching them."

Nodding, I say, "And the unsubs on *Criminal Minds* would give them nightmares."

"And we'd need a lock on our bedroom door for when we...you know." Doug winks.

"Oh, I know," I say. "What did the conductor guy say about getting a room? Do they rent by the hour here?"

Giving me a sheepish grin, Doug says, "I want you so badly, I'll probably last three minutes the first time."

"That's okay. You're a young stud. I'm sure you'll be ready to go again in no time."

Glancing at his watch, Doug says, "I'm not getting any younger, and we need to do one more thing before I take you home—to *our* home—and screw you senseless."

It's been so long since I've been screwed senseless by Doug and I can't wait. "What's the one thing?"

Without answering me, Doug stacks our containers of food and tosses them in the closest garbage can. When he returns to our table, he takes my hand in his. "You ready?"

Feeling like I can take on the world, I nod eagerly.

*   *   *

I stop feeling like I can take on the world the second I step in line to ride the Kingda Ka rollercoaster and the newly constructed Zumanjaro: Drop of Doom. Before the addition of the Drop of Doom, the Kingda Ka was the fastest rollercoaster in the world. Now it's also the tallest. I dig my fingernails into Doug's palm and try to breathe easily.

Leaning into me, Doug whispers, "You all right there, kid? You look like you might be sick."

I swallow hard and wipe the film of sweat from my brow. "I'm fine," I lie. "Just dandy."

"Okay," Doug says with a smile before prying his hands out of my death grip.

From behind us, I hear Jessup and Lloyd chant, "Drop of Doom! Drop of Doom!" and I turn around in time to witness them pumping their fists in the air. They've spent the past twenty minutes bragging to anyone within earshot that they've already ridden twice.

"You'll love it," Melanie assures me.

"How would you know, Mom? You chickened out the last two times," Jessup mocks.

"I didn't want all the salt water taffy to go to waste," Melanie says.

The boys chortle. "Whatever you say."

Barry pulls his wife into a hug. "Leave your mother alone." As Melanie rests her head against his chest, he points his finger to her back and mouths, "Chicken."

I reclaim Doug's hand. "I'm scared."

Doug looks at me thoughtfully. "Think of something else that scared you."

"Asking you to meet me here," I say without hesitation.

"And how did that turn out?" Doug asks with a crooked smile.

"Pretty well," I concede.

"Risking your heart is a hell of a lot scarier than any theme park ride, and you did it." He pauses. "You did it for me, Mags, and I love you for it. Among other things."

"Are you saying I'm brave?"

Doug nods. "The bravest woman I know."

It's not the first time I've been called brave, but it's the first time I agree with the description. The line moves along, and as we follow the thrill-seekers in front of us and lead those in back, it occurs to me that every decision I made over the past year took courage—from confronting Doug about my doubts, to throwing myself into a fling with Philip, to trying rock climbing, to asking Doug's forgiveness the first time, to taking a chance on Ben, to ultimately admitting Ben wasn't the right guy for me, to saying no to a second chance with Philip.

And all of my choices led me exactly where I needed to be— holding Doug's hand as we sit side by side, harnessed in by over-the-shoulder restraints, embarking on the adventure of a lifetime.

In Memory of Alan Blum

You were always a fan and you stood your ground even when I didn't feel worthy. Whenever I'm down, I recall your words of encouragement and your unflagging faith in me, and I'm lifted up. You may be gone, but you'll always remain in my heart and memories.

Friendship never dies, especially one like ours. Merrybeth and Alan's "rappaport" was second to none and will never be duplicated. With all my love. Forever and always.

Meredith Schorr

A born-and-bred New Yorker, Meredith Schorr discovered her passion for writing when she began to enjoy drafting work-related emails way more than she was probably supposed to. After trying her hand penning children's stories and blogging her personal experiences, Meredith found her calling writing chick lit and humorous women's fiction. She secures much inspiration from her day job as a hardworking trademark paralegal and her still-single (but looking) status. Meredith is a loyal New York Yankees fan, an avid runner, and an unashamed television addict. To learn more, visit her at www.meredithschorr.com.

Books by Meredith Schorr

JUST FRIENDS WITH BENEFITS

A STATE OF JANE

HOW DO YOU KNOW?

The Blogger Girl Series

BLOGGER GIRL (#1)

NOVELISTA GIRL (#2)

Henery Press Books

And finally, before you go...
Here are a few other books
you might enjoy:

BLOGGER GIRL

Meredith Schorr

The Blogger Girl Series (#1)

(From the Henery Press Chick Lit Collection)

What happens when your high school nemesis becomes the shining star in a universe you pretty much saved? Book blogger Kimberly Long is about to find out.

A chick lit enthusiast since the first time she read *Bridget Jones's Diary*, Kim, with her blog, *Pastel is the New Black*, has worked tirelessly by night to keep the genre alive, and help squash the claim that "chick lit is dead" once and for all. Not bad for a woman who by day ekes out a meager living as a pretty, and pretty-much-nameless, legal secretary in a Manhattan law firm. While Kim's day job holds no passion for her, the handsome (and shaving challenged) associate down the hall is another story. Yet another story is that Hannah Marshak, one of her most hated high school classmates, has now popped onto the chick lit scene with a hot new book that's turning heads—and pages—across the land. It's also popped into Kim's inbox—for review.

With their ten-year reunion drawing near, Kim's coming close to combustion over the hype about Hannah's book. And as everyone around her seems to be moving on and up, she begins to question whether being a "blogger girl" makes the grade in her offline life.

Available at booksellers nationwide and online

Visit www.henerypress.com for details

THE BREAKUP DOCTOR

Phoebe Fox

The Breakup Doctor Series (#1)

(From the Henery Press Chick Lit Collection)

Call Brook Ogden a matchmaker-in-reverse. Let others bring people together; Brook, licensed mental health counselor, picks up the pieces after things come apart. When her own therapy practice collapses, she maintains perfect control: landing on her feet with a weekly advice-to-the-lovelorn column and a successful consulting service as the Breakup Doctor: on call to help you shape up after you breakup.

Then her relationship suddenly crumbles and Brook finds herself engaging in almost every bad-breakup behavior she preaches against. And worse, she starts a rebound relationship with the most inappropriate of men: a dangerously sexy bartender with anger-management issues—who also happens to be a former patient.

As her increasingly out-of-control behavior lands her at rock-bottom, Brook realizes you can't always handle a messy breakup neatly—and that sometimes you can't pull yourself together until you let yourself fall apart.

Available at booksellers nationwide and online

Visit www.henerypress.com for details

WAKE-UP CALL

Amy Avanzino

The Wake-Up Series (#1)

(From the Henery Press Chick Lit Collection)

Sarah Winslow wakes up with a terrible hangover... and a kid in her boyfriend's bed. She makes the horrifying discovery that, due to a head injury, it's not a hangover. She's got memory loss. Overnight, five years have disappeared, and she's no longer the hard-living, fast-track, ad executive party girl she thinks she is. Now, she's the unemployed, pudgy, married, stay-at-home-mom of three kids under five, including twins.

As she slowly pieces together the mystery of how her dreams and aspirations could have disintegrated so completely in five short years, she finds herself utterly failing to manage this life she can't imagine choosing. When Sarah meets the man of her dreams, she realizes she's got to make a choice: Does she follow her bliss and "do-over" her life? Or does the Sarah she's forgotten hold the answers to how she got here... and how she can stay?

Available at booksellers nationwide and online

Visit www.henerypress.com for details